DUTY DEMANDS

A PRIDE AND PREJUDICE VARIATION

ELAINE OWEN

Dedication and Acknowledgements

To my ever-patient husband and family: I love you.

To my friends, both online and in real life- thank you for being my support and sounding board. You mean more to me than you'll ever know.

My unending gratitude also goes to Jane Austen herself, for creating such memorable characters.

Finally, Darcy's line in chapter one, "I shall make you happy, Elizabeth. I swear it--and the oath shall be kept," is a direct quote from the masterful novel _Jane Eyre_. I hope my readers appreciate its use in several parts of this story.

Table of Contents

CHAPTER ONE

Elizabeth Bennet Darcy jumped at the knock that sounded on the communicating door between her room and that of her husband, who had been her husband for all of twelve hours. The sound was expected, but still sudden and startling. Without further warning, Darcy entered the room.

"Leave us," he said tersely to the maid, although the instruction was unnecessary. She had already abruptly put down the brush she was using on Elizabeth's long, loose curls. She made a swift curtsey and addressed Elizabeth. "If that's all you'll be needing me for, ma'am?"

Elizabeth did not answer. Indeed, she could not have answered if her life depended on it. The maid left, with a smile of encouragement for her mistress, and Elizabeth was alone for the first time with her husband.

She watched in the mirror as he slowly approached her from behind, noting that he was in a wine colored housecoat that made him more handsome than ever. She herself was clad in the new white nightgown and housedress purchased for the occasion, and lovingly packed for her by Jane just this morning, a lifetime ago. Darcy halted directly behind her and laid a hand gently on her shoulder. "You are beautiful, Elizabeth."

"Thank you, sir." Elizabeth could not get any more words out. Her throat had gone suddenly dry.

"No matter how lovely you looked in your wedding finery this morning, you are even lovelier to me now."

"You are very kind."

Darcy's other hand descended upon her other shoulder, and he bent to kiss the curve of her neck. "I shall make you happy, Elizabeth. I swear it--and the oath shall be kept."

"I shall do my best to please you," she answered unsteadily, feeling the warmth of him on her skin and against her back. What other remarkable sensations awaited her, she wondered. Hill had given her rapid instructions this morning on what was to come, but she had been too nervous to ask many questions, and had instead turned away with dread in her heart. But the moment was now approaching quickly.

Darcy's hands had traveled caressingly down the length of her arms, and he now took one of her hands in his, lifting her to her feet. "Then-- shall we?" he asked, motioning towards her bed with his free hand. She nodded dumbly and followed him as he guided her to it. The coverlet was already turned down, and he indicated that she should get in and pull the blanket up around herself. She did so and waited as he joined her, casting aside his robe.

She understood her duty well, and was determined to fulfill it as soon as possible. She was to produce a son, in accordance with the marriage contract signed by her uncle, the heir needed by Pemberley for the continuation of the family line. To produce that heir she must take Fitzwilliam Darcy into her life, her heart, and her bed. This was the price of her family's security. For her family's sake, she would pay any cost, suffer any indignation, and willingly take on every task asked of her.

Darcy's arms gently enclosed her, and her eyes drifted shut as he began to fulfill his husbandly duties. She was now Mrs. Fitzwilliam Darcy, and her life would never again be the same.

CHAPTER TWO

Elizabeth Bennet had never imagined that she might one day be the wife of Fitzwilliam Darcy, the man she roundly denounced to others as the proudest and most unpleasant man she had ever met. Had anyone told her this fate awaited her, she would have laughed and advised them to look to children for more amusing fairy tales.

She had encountered Darcy and his remarkably charming friend, Charles Bingley, at an assembly the previous autumn in Meryton. Darcy had disdained everything and nearly everyone at the country ball. The rooms were too small, the dancing too rustic, the company falling far short of deserving his attentions. He appreciated the presence of Bingley's family, a Miss Caroline Bingley, a Mrs. Louisa Hurst, a Mr. Hurst, and of course Bingley himself. The rest of the party he found insupportable. He described Elizabeth as tolerable, but not handsome enough to tempt him, and he did not hesitate to say that Jane, Elizabeth's oldest sister, smiled too much.

Great wealth will normally atone for a great lack of manners, but in this case, Darcy's superior, condescending air ruled the day, and confirmed everyone's worst opinion of him.

By contrast, Bingley contained more appeal in his smallest finger than Darcy could have held in his entire person. He could not praise the countryside enough; the music was to his taste and all the women were uncommonly beautiful. He had confirmed his good nature and superior manners by singling out Elizabeth's sister, Jane, for his unmistakable attentions, and the two were soon the subject of neighborhood gossip that supposed the couple well on the way to matrimony.

Six months later, circumstances had changed so much as to be almost unrecognizable. Charles Bingley had left Jane behind while he traveled to London, making his desertion of her clear; and exposing Elizabeth's dearest sister to the pity and scorn of half the county. He had certainly felt affection for Jane, but that affection was not enough to overcome the disadvantages of an uncle in trade and an immediate family with no fortune at all, and with a noticeable lack of decorum. In the end, he had allowed his sisters and friend to talk him out of the match, and Jane had suffered low spirits for several months as a result.

Elizabeth had meanwhile traveled to Kent to visit her dearest and closest friend, Charlotte Lucas, now Charlotte Collins, who had married Elizabeth's pretentious fop of a cousin. Mr. Collins would inherit Elizabeth's family home upon her father's death, and now, it seemed, so would Charlotte. However, Elizabeth did not blame Charlotte for accepting such an advantageous offer of marriage. She had in fact been somewhat relieved, since Mr. Collins had proposed to her first, and she had incurred her mother's anger by turning him down emphatically.

While in Kent, Elizabeth had again encountered Fitzwilliam Darcy, who was visiting his aunt, the noble and imperious Lady Catherine de Bourgh. After meeting his aunt, Elizabeth understood where the family pride originated, and was amazed that Darcy could be at all civil to her while in his aunt's presence. Lady Catherine's smug superiority made Darcy seem almost congenial at times.

She met Darcy several more times as she took her customary solitary walk each morning in the environs around the parsonage where the Collins family lived. Fitzwilliam--at that time, Mr. Darcy to her--had asked odd, unconnected questions of her, inquiring after her thoughts about her cousin's household and her enjoyment of Kent. She had thought nothing of it, and certainly did not think he had developed an interest in her at all.

Abruptly, in the middle of the night, she had received an urgent missive from home. Her father had collapsed from a weakness of the heart, and was thought to be near death. She had traveled home with all possible speed, but was not in time to see her father take his last breath on this earth. Mr. Bennet had slipped quietly from this world only an hour before she arrived, leaving behind a widow, five unmarried daughters, an entailed estate, and a fair amount of debt. Elizabeth's world was now a very different place than it had been only a day earlier.

The household would have to be broken up. Neither Mrs. Bennet's sister, Mrs. Sophia Phillips, nor her brother, Mr. Edward Gardiner, had enough room in their home to take in six more people. The three youngest members of the family would stay in Meryton with Mrs. Phillips and her husband. The three eldest would need to remove to town, to live with the Gardiner family in Cheapside. All their belongings not immediately necessary for daily living would have to be sold to cover the cost of the unpaid debts and to assist with the family's support in their new homes. Their estate, Longbourn, would shortly devolve to Mr. Collins and Charlotte. With breathtaking speed, immediately following Mr. Bennet's funeral, arrangements began to be made.

They came to an equally rapid halt when Darcy suddenly appeared on the front steps of Longbourn, mere weeks after Mr. Bennet's death, and requested an immediate interview with Edward Gardiner. Two hours later, Elizabeth was summoned to her father's former study and informed by her uncle of the new arrangements to save her family's home and their place in society. Her cooperation was needed, of course, but she knew very well that she had no choice in the matter. Too much advantage to her family rested on it. She assured her uncle that she would, indeed, marry Mr. Darcy in return for Darcy leasing Longbourn from Mr. Collins. Her sisters would have dowries and her mother would receive a small yearly allowance from him. This, together with support from Mr. Gardiner, would ensure her mother and sisters of their continued presence and position in the only home and neighborhood they had ever known. She accepted Darcy's gloved hand reluctantly as he took hold of hers, but she faced the future bravely.

Now she slept in her new bed in her new home, at Darcy House, in town. She had married Darcy yesterday, and he had entered her room and made her his wife last night. He had not left afterwards, to her surprise. As she began to stir she felt him also move, and she opened her eyes to see that he was leaning up on one elbow, looking down at her with concern. He smiled slightly when their eyes met. "Are you well?" he asked.

"Am I in a dream, or is this real?" she asked him sleepily.

"Dreams this sweet never come true for me," he answered. "It must be real." He began to kiss her again, and Elizabeth allowed her mind to drift effortlessly away.

∞

She looked at her husband carefully over breakfast sometime later, served in the small dining room by a discreet staff that exited the room after his brief nod in their direction. What would life be like now with Fitzwilliam Darcy, she wondered, when she would be subject to his will in everything? She belonged to him in every way, down to the very name by which she would now be called. His word was law in this household, and his wishes would prevail utterly.

She began to discover his wishes immediately. Darcy spoke brusquely as they began to eat, laying out plans for the day.

"I have matters to attend to at my club this afternoon. You shall use that time to speak with Mrs. Moffat and begin to learn the management of the household accounts. I suggest that you start with the kitchen accounts and plan our meals for the next week or two. That should keep you occupied for some time."

"I need no assignments in order to keep me occupied. I am well able to order my own activities."

He continued as though he had not heard her. "If you have time, visit a modiste today to have new dresses made. Mrs. Moffat will give your driver the directions to the proper locations. Everything will be placed on the Darcy account, and I expect the new clothing to be completed and delivered here for you within a week, unless there is something that requires more specialized work. They already know to expect you, and what will be required." He had not looked up from his plate as he delivered these instructions in a crisp, businesslike tone.

"Are my present clothes inadequate for your purposes?' Elizabeth asked, stung by the implied criticism.

Darcy must have heard the edge in her voice. He looked up at her for the first time. "Your current wardrobe was adequate for the station in which you were raised, but you are much greater than that now. You are no longer Elizabeth Bennet of Hertfordshire, but Elizabeth Darcy of Pemberley. Your clothing should reflect your new status. And besides, I cannot have you act as hostess or accompany me to events in town in your mourning clothes."

"I intend to mourn my father for a full six months," Elizabeth said, with her chin raised defiantly.

Darcy nodded approvingly. "And so you should. You have my permission to wear your mourning clothes inside Darcy House as much as you desire, unless you have callers. Then you must change into something appropriate for the occasion. Outside the house, of course, you will dress in normal attire. I want no gossip about our union. Nobody is to know the circumstances of our marriage."

"You are all consideration, sir," she said aloud. "And all condescension besides," she added privately to herself, her mouth curling down.

Darcy finished eating in silence, and then took his leave of her for the day. "You need not plan any meal here for this evening," he told her. "My aunt and uncle have invited us to dine with them. You should be ready to leave at eight o'clock. My uncle does not favor tardiness. I will see you then."

Elizabeth waited until he had kissed her on the cheek and gone out of the house before rising from her seat. Facing the direction in which he had gone, she made the deep curtsey she imagined appropriate for a member of the royal household--perhaps even the prince regent himself. Then she returned to her room, determined to find the very blackest mourning attire she had. Perhaps Mrs. Moffat would be able to add black ribbons or combs for her hair. *Prince* Darcy, she decided, had little idea of the woman he had married.

CHAPTER THREE

"Why does he want to marry me?" Elizabeth had asked her uncle on the fateful day when Darcy came calling, while she and Mr. Gardiner were alone in the study at Longbourn. The shelves of books had been removed in preparation for packing and the desk was mostly bare; the room had a general feeling of upheaval.

"He wants an heir," her uncle answered. "He needs one, in fact, as all great men do."

Elizabeth nearly snorted in disbelief. "Of course he does, but it does not follow that I am the only one who can provide him with one."

"Perhaps he finds you attractive."

Now Elizabeth really did snort. "No. On that point, he made his opinion quite clear last autumn. He finds me tolerable, nothing more."

"Does it really matter why he picked you, Lizzy?" her uncle asked. "This offer he makes will save your family, and add to their security in no small measure. What more really matters? Accept his proposal; it is a godsend."

"Not until I understand more of what he wants, and why." Elizabeth looked at her uncle defiantly.

Mr. Gardiner rose and walked across the room to the window, already denuded of its curtains, which overlooked the lawn. "My dear, there are certain things that do not need to be spelled out between gentlemen who understand one another."

"I wish you would not be so obscure, uncle."

"I may offend your feminine sensibilities by speaking plainly."

"You will offend me more by not so speaking. Please say what you are thinking."

"Very well; I will be explicit." Her uncle turned to face her. "Darcy thinks that he can get what he wants from you, and that you will make no further demands on him."

Elizabeth was truly puzzled. "I cannot imagine what you mean."

"How many carriages do you suppose a man like Darcy owns? How many servants are under his command? What family jewels are his?"

"I have no idea."

"Of course not, because you are not of his sphere. His manner of living is so high above yours that you can scarcely imagine it. Therefore, you will not ask him for the luxuries that a woman from a higher social standing might expect."

Elizabeth let one corner of her mouth tip up. "Then he does not know my mother. There is no end to her imagination."

"Nonsense. Even your mother has only a vague idea of the resources that will be at your disposal as Mrs. Darcy." He paused. "Darcy also thinks that you will be biddable, that you will make no complaint when he takes his mistress to his bed instead of you."

Now Elizabeth was truly shocked, not by her uncle's words but by the fact that he was speaking of such things to her. "Does he have a mistress?"

Mr. Gardiner shook his head. "Again, there are certain things understood between gentlemen. One does not ask another about his paramours, but a man of Darcy's standing has probably had at least one, perhaps several."

"I had not considered such a thing," Elizabeth answered, beginning to have an idea of just how different her world was from Darcy's.

"The marriage contract says that you will provide Darcy with an heir. It does not say what will happen to your relationship after that happens. The common understanding among men of his standing is that after you have given him a male heir, your life will be your own to live, with an appropriate level of discretion."

Elizabeth was speechless for a moment. "I would never agree to such an arrangement."

"Elizabeth, he will not be faithful to you. You must not expect it, or you will be crushed. Also, it is very likely that, after you have performed your duty, he will allow you the same freedom. It is the way of the world, and especially the way of the society in which he moves."

Elizabeth sat silent, struggling to comprehend such a different mindset.

"Of course, if you choose not to complicate your life with your own love affairs, he will not be concerned. Regardless, you will still act as the hostess at all social functions which he chooses to hold, and it is expected that you will act in your children's best interests by furthering the interests of the Darcy family. You are intelligent and well-spoken. It could be that he sees you as a potential asset to the family in this way."

Elizabeth shook her head emphatically no. "I wish to marry for love, uncle."

"You are not alone in this. You wish for love, Jane wishes for love, and all your sisters wish for love. Is there a person on earth who does not? Probably even Darcy himself would choose to marry for love if he could. But he has picked you to marry, knowing that the difference in your stations means you will be grateful to receive anything at all from him. You will be utterly without resources, save what he can give to you. He can have his children with you, and have you serve as a suitable hostess at social functions besides; while his own life carries on much as it has until now, with no further demands or expectations of him."

"But why wouldn't he pick a bride who brings him a dowry? He could have anyone he wants."

"I think he prefers that you come to him penniless, as you are. A woman of wealth or standing might feel capable of standing up to him, and perhaps work against his interests in favor of her own family. With you, he knows what he is getting. Elizabeth, why are you laughing?"

"I was just thinking of poor Caroline Bingley, who has been trying to attract his attentions for as long as I have known her. Perhaps I should tell her to have her brother cast her out on the streets, and see if Mr. Darcy will notice her then."

Mr. Gardiner pursed his lips. "Are you ready to accept him? If so, then I will bring him in."

Elizabeth hesitated only briefly. "Yes. Please tell Mr. Darcy that I will be pleased to receive him."

CHAPTER FOUR

Dearest Jane,

I am writing to you at the earliest opportunity that I have been given, considering the rather constant schedule of activities which Mr. Darcy has laid out for me, full of visits to his family and friends, along with various shopping expeditions. I hope that you, Mama, and my sisters are all well.

We dined with Mr. Darcy's uncle and aunt, the earl and countess of Matlock, Friday last. Mr. Darcy, who would probably appreciate being addressed as my lord, has decreed that I not wear black mourning clothes to social occasions, for what reason I do not know. Can you imagine such nerve? I did not wish to flatter his vanity by actually obeying such an absurd directive. I was completely determined to defy him at first, but then I remembered that he is my husband and it would be better not to incur the wrath of such an ill-tempered man, so instead I wore a new dark blue bombazine which is so dark it looks practically black. If he noticed my small act of rebellion, he said nothing of it.

The countess is a very fine woman with a lively sense of humor and an excellent sense of style. I counted sixteen pearls sewn into the lace on her sleeves alone. If I had that many pearls on any of my dresses, I would spend the evening in a perpetual state of terror lest I damage or lose any of them, but she paid them no attention at all. The countess has a very congenial air about her, and she laughed aloud when I described the absurdities of our cousin Collins to her. I did not tell her of Mr. Collins' ridiculous proposal to me, for my husband would surely have disapproved. He did not join in our hilarity. He just sat and looked at me with a face so serious I was tempted to make fun of him, but that would never do.

The countess has asked me to call on her soon and she and her husband are coming here for dinner next week. I predict that we shall be fast friends in no time. The earl of Matlock, on the other hand, is very like his nephew. Need I say more?

I have not met the famous Miss Georgiana Darcy yet. Mr. Darcy says I shall meet her when we travel to Pemberley a week from tomorrow. He said that he does not care for the season very much and that he does not plan to spend much time here in town for it next year, or any year at all.

He did not ask my opinion, of course. I am holding my tongue for now, remembering your advice, but I am afraid that one day he will receive my opinion whether he wants it or not. You may not say that I did not warn you!

I am including a small sum of money for you and Mama to spend on some little luxury for all of you. You need not worry that it will be missed. This is my own pin money and I am free to do as I like with it. Mr. Darcy had his steward explain to me the amount of pin money that I will have to spend each month and stated quite particularly that I am to let him know if it is not adequate for my needs. I suppose my husband's pride would be offended to think that his wife might actually be in want of anything. I will never avail myself of this option unless it becomes absolutely necessary. I have my pride as well.

Please write soon. I live for your letters.

I am, as always, your loving sister,

Elizabeth Darcy

Darcy entered the room just as she was signing and closing the letter, coming to stand next to her. "Elizabeth, are you ready to go yet?"

"Yes, I am at your disposal as soon as I seal and post this letter."

"Seal it, but leave it with Mrs. Moffat to be posted. She knows your family's direction. I do not like to be late to the theater, and this is a recital I have been looking forward to for some time." He frowned as he looked at her more closely. "Is that a black comb in your hair? I thought we agreed you would not wear mourning in public."

"You made your wishes clear. This is not mourning clothing; it is only a black comb, which may or may not be considered as an indication of my bereavement. I purchased it three days ago."

Darcy's frown did not change. "I noticed the dress you wore to my uncle's last week. It was very nearly black, despite our agreement."

"It fulfilled your requirements in every way," she answered, wondering what he would say. "It was, in fact, blue, if you looked at it closely enough. It is not my fault if your eyes perceived it as black."

She braced for a protest, but nothing came. Instead, she saw a pensive look settle on his face as she looked up to reach for the sealing wax.

"You must still grieve your father," he said, in a much more gentle tone than what she had expected.

"Of course. It has only been seven weeks since he passed." She did not look at him as she poured the wax onto the envelope and pressed the heavy seal with the ornate letter D into it.

"I have never seen you weep," he commented, more a question than a statement.

She would not allow herself to grieve in front of this stranger. "My grief is expressed in private."

"I understand. My father passed only five years ago."

"How did it happen?"

"It was much like your father's. His heart suddenly weakened. There was very little time to say goodbye, and afterwards I had to be strong, for my sister and for the household staff at Pemberley. I did not allow myself to grieve in front of anyone."

He seemed determined to talk. She looked at him warily. "It must have been very hard on Miss Georgiana, to lose both parents at such a young age. When did you lose your mother?"

"Our mother passed shortly after Georgiana's birth." Darcy's face had settled into a mask and he looked straight ahead, unfocused; she could not read his expression. "In some ways, it still feels as though it happened yesterday. A song I hear, or a phrase I read in a book, may suddenly bring home memories and a new sense of loss to me when I least expect it."

Elizabeth could not imagine why he was speaking to her so intimately. "Has Miss Georgiana fully recovered from her father's loss?"

"It is not something from which one can make a recovery. One simply accommodates oneself to a new way of living, as you are now doing. It becomes easier over time."

The wax on the letter had cooled. Elizabeth stood and looked at Fitzwilliam, letter in hand, waiting for him to wave her ahead of him so that they could proceed to the carriage together. Instead, he said, "I have purposely kept you involved with a variety of activities each day, so that you would not be focused on your loss, but we need not be out every night. If you would prefer to stay quietly at home this evening, then I will stay home with you."

Good heavens, she thought, an entire evening spent at home with Fitzwilliam Darcy, with maudlin tales of sorrow and woe for entertainment. An evening in company was much to be preferred. "I think being active outside the house helps me not to brood," she answered, smiling politely but with no real warmth. So saying, she took the initiative and preceded her husband to the front door, dropping her letter in the silver salver reserved for outgoing mail as she went. As she reached the front door, Darcy's hand on her elbow stopped her, slowly turning her to face him.

"Elizabeth, did you wear the dark blue on purpose, knowing how close it was to black? Did you mean to disobey me? "

Should she tell him a polite untruth and let him reach his own conclusions, or did she dare to speak honestly? She answered carefully, "Many of your friends and family are aware of my recent loss. It would look odd not to acknowledge my status in some way."

"And you wear the black combs in your hair for the same reason?"

She nodded, and he pressed his lips together in a flat line.

"I wanted you not to wear black in public, Elizabeth, in order to avoid gossip. It is unusual for a bride to be in mourning. But if you do not mind receiving strange looks and comments, I will say nothing further on the subject. You may wear black as much as you wish."

"I thank you, sir," she replied, not certain if she had actually won a victory or not. He was giving her the right to mourn if she wanted, but he was still dictating her choices to her. Perhaps this was all the consideration she could expect in this strange farce of a marriage.

Darcy offered her his arm, and they proceeded to the carriage together, Elizabeth still unsure of exactly what to expect from her new husband.

CHAPTER FIVE

"Elizabeth, my man tells me your things are not yet packed."

Elizabeth looked up in surprise as Darcy entered the parlor, where she was carefully arranging a bouquet of flowers. "We are not traveling to Pemberley until the day after tomorrow, so I have not yet asked my maid to prepare. There is little for me to have put in my trunks in any case."

Darcy's brows knit together. "We leave for Pemberley tomorrow, not the day after tomorrow."

Elizabeth stopped what she was doing to face her husband. "That is not possible. We are hosting your aunt and uncle for dinner, here, tomorrow night."

"*That* is not possible, since we shall be well on our way to Pemberley by that time," her husband retorted.

"If you wish for me to be your hostess, I will have to be here to do so. You have known about this dinner for a week."

"I have known no such thing. I told you quite clearly, last week, that we were leaving for Pemberley the end of this week."

"And I told you, quite clearly, that I wished to invite the earl and countess of Matlock, your uncle and aunt, to dine with us on Wednesday next. You agreed. You said that you appreciated my willingness to take on social obligations so quickly."

Darcy glowered. "I do not recall any such conversation."

"And yet you took an active part in it." Elizabeth stood waiting, with her arms crossed, ready to do battle.

Darcy brushed a frustrated hand through his thick hair. "I still do not recall. You will have to cancel the invitation."

"I will do no such thing." Elizabeth had staked her claim, and was ready to fight for what she wanted. "To cancel a dinner invitation the day before the event, especially to an earl and countess, would be abominably rude. I have already prepared the menu, ordered the food to be delivered, and am now making cuttings of all our fresh flowers to use on the table. If I was not going to be allowed to *have* a dinner for your aunt and uncle," she paused dramatically, "then why was I allowed to *plan* one?"

Her husband took a step or two past her, and then turned to face her again. "What did you think I meant when I said we would leave at the end of the week?"

"I believed Thursday or Friday to be the accustomed days to start a two day's travel to points as far north as Derbyshire! Neither day would interfere with a Wednesday night dinner with your aunt and uncle."

"You could have confirmed it with me before sending the invitation."

"I had no reason to confirm it! You had just thanked me for suggesting the idea."

Darcy stared at her for a moment, then turned on one heel and exited the room without another word.

Elizabeth resumed arranging her flowers, angrily tearing out a small bud that had dared to raise its head in the wrong spot. The blame was entirely on her husband. She was trying her best to fulfill her duties as a cooperative wife and willing hostess, was she not? It was not her fault if Darcy could not remember what he had heard and said from one day to the next. She really did not care if he became angry when faced with his own mistake.

Her husband, she knew, could be dreadfully ill-tempered when the mood struck him. He had been unusually civil to her since their marriage, but she remembered his past silences and disapproving airs when he was in Hertfordshire, at the beginning of their acquaintance, long before he made an offer for her. She recalled only too well hearing about the petty vengeance he had worked on his childhood friend, George Wickham, denying him a living as reprisal for the favor the former Mr. Darcy had showed to the son of his steward. No doubt the old gentleman had had his reasons, especially when faced with such a temperamental son of his own. She would have to guard her words more carefully the next time she saw Fitzwilliam, to avoid provoking any more displays of temper.

She avoided her husband's notice the rest of the day and took supper in her own rooms that night, hoping Darcy would not wish to join her in her bed that evening. If he did not come, it would be the first time they had spent a night apart since their marriage, for his attentions had continued without fail. She did not know whether to dread his appearance or welcome it, for how could she conceive a child if he did not come to her? But she had no desire to spend intimate time with an angry man.

As she finished her bath, lost in thought, it was not Darcy's knock that startled her, but her maid's, coming on the front door of her bedroom.

"If you'll pardon me, missus, my master has asked that you join him in his chamber tonight."

So he had decided to humiliate her by summoning her like any common servant. It was to be expected, she supposed. She sighed with resignation. "Very well. You may tell him I'll be with him shortly."

Minutes later, she knocked lightly on the connecting bedroom door and received permission to enter. When she went in, closing the door carefully behind her, Darcy was reclining on his bed, reading a book. He acknowledged her with a brief nod, shutting the book carelessly. "I hope you do not mind my calling you here. I find that I would prefer to have you in my bed tonight, rather than going to yours."

"It is no difference to me," she answered, bracing herself to receive his attentions once again.

"I believe you have been angry with me regarding the dinner party," he added, setting the book aside and looking at her seriously. When she did not answer, he went on, "I am forced to admit that you were correct about inviting my uncle and aunt for dinner. After thinking about it for some time, I recalled that you and I did, in fact, speak of inviting them. I was distracted with other matters at the time, and was not attending properly. We will hold the dinner as planned."

"Thank you," she answered, trying to be gracious in her small victory. "Cancelling would have been awkward, at best."

"I agree, and I thank you for reminding me of it. It would not do to insult my family, even family members with whom we are on intimate terms." He paused and smiled briefly at her. "If this was our first disagreement as a married couple, I am glad it was so easy to resolve. No doubt it will not be our last." Elizabeth heartily agreed with him on that point, though she said nothing aloud.

"Are you ready to go to bed?" he asked then, and Elizabeth nodded. She moved to what she assumed to be her side of the bed, shedding her housecoat as she went. She was wearing her customary white nightdress underneath, one that fit closely and made her feel attractive, although it was not the one she had worn on her wedding night. Darcy stood to shake off his housecoat before joining her. He was wearing nothing more than a loose fitting overshirt, but even in such a plain garment, she had to admit that he was still one of the most handsome men she had ever seen.

Both climbed into the bed and settled themselves in among the sheets and blankets. Darcy turned to blow out the lamp that stood on the table next to him, and as the room sank into darkness Elizabeth felt him move closer and reach out for her. He took her face in his hands, kissing her gently. "I am greatly fatigued and feel in need of rest. Good night, Elizabeth." He pulled away again.

"Good night," she answered automatically, but her mouth dropped open. Had he really summoned her to his bed simply to tell her that her dinner party would take place as planned? Did he think to take revenge on her for her fault of being in the right, by refusing to carry out his husbandly duties? If so, it would be a petty form of vengeance indeed.

Darcy turned over, his back to her. After a few moments she heard his steady breathing.

Elizabeth remained wide awake, staring up at the dark ceiling, trying to decide what to do next. If married relations were not to take place that night, she might as well return to her own room. She would sleep more easily away from this proud, condescending man. But did she dare to leave? What if he awoke, having changed his mind, and became angry that she was not immediately available to him?

She would take the chance. Anything was better than lying awake next to him, wondering what was to come next. She carefully turned back the covers and started to swing her legs out, but Darcy roused at once.

"Where are you going, Elizabeth?"

"Back to my own room."

"Why?"

"As you said, you are fatigued."

"Come," he commanded. "I would have you stay, if you would."

Elizabeth lay back down reluctantly. If Darcy wanted her to stay, then she would have to obey, but she moved as far away as possible, settling down on the far side of the bed. It was too late. Her husband reached out for her again, pulling her close against his body, wrapping his arms around her. She remained awake for some time, but eventually, lulled by his warmth and the feeling of security it brought, she fell asleep.

CHAPTER SIX

What a strikingly peculiar man, she thought the next morning as she ate breakfast with her husband and then began to prepare for the activities of the day, which would culminate in the dinner with the earl and countess that night. As was his custom, Darcy said little at the table beyond telling her his schedule for the day. He kissed her on the cheek and then left the dining room, allowing her time to ponder his strange behavior.

She had never met with such an odd mixture of distant coolness and determined courtesy in one person. Pride he certainly had, in abundance, as shown by his determination to avoid gossip and his disapproval of her wardrobe. His condescension knew no bounds. Elizabeth could scarcely believe the easy way with which he made free with her schedule and activities, and how he did so without even asking her opinion of his choices. But then his solicitude had demonstrated itself as well, by asking after her wellbeing and admitting his error in the matter of the dinner party. His conversation about his parents' deaths had proven that he had a more vulnerable side than she would have guessed.

His most perplexing act so far had been in summoning her to his bed the night before and then not availing himself of his rights as a husband. He had been content, seemingly, to have her close but nothing more. The experience left her bewildered.

She remembered her uncle's words of warning about Darcy's expectations from her. If Darcy had a mistress, Elizabeth had seen no evidence of her to date, so early in their marriage. Who could the woman be?

Considering Darcy's pride, Elizabeth felt certain she would be someone who was well off and highly educated, able to dress with style and hold a witty conversation with ease. Of course she would be sophisticated, to have such a worldly understanding with Fitzwilliam; probably a member of the Ton. She must be relatively free to make her own choices in life. Perhaps she was a widow, or, worse yet, someone else's wife, under a similar arrangement with her own husband. Perhaps she was out of town just then, or beyond Darcy's reach in some way, and so he was making do with Elizabeth in her stead. But that would be absurd--she and Darcy were newlyweds, and without doubt he wanted an heir as soon as possible. It was not surprising that he was choosing to spend so much time with her.

Darcy had looked at her at breakfast several times this morning with a faintly puzzled expression, though he had said nothing of whatever was on his mind. She needed to remember that, regardless of any other relationships he might have, she and her husband were still strangers thrust into a marriage together, and somehow they must find a way to make the arrangement work. Perhaps he found her as confusing as she found him.

She was practicing a piece of music on the pianoforte that afternoon, preparing to perform it that evening if requested, when she heard a loud banging on the front door of the house. A delivery would be made to the kitchen door, just below street level, or else to the back door altogether. No one Elizabeth knew would rap on the front door in such an insistent way. Curious, she moved to the nearest window and peered out onto the street. The carriage outside was turned in such a way that she could not see if there were any markings on its side, but the footman standing at rigid attention beside the open carriage door wore livery that looked oddly familiar. While Elizabeth stood trying to remember where she had seen such a uniform before, the front door opened and the visitor's voice assailed her ears.

"I insist upon seeing my nephew at once! Darcy, where are you? Somebody show me to him immediately!"

Elizabeth sighed heavily, recognizing Lady Catherine's strident tone immediately. This would not be a polite social call. Lady Catherine could not be happy to hear that Darcy was no longer available to marry her own daughter, Anne.

The butler standing in the entry way shifted uncomfortably, but did not move. He glanced sidelong at Elizabeth, his expression neutral, but still managing to communicate extreme discomfort with their visitor. Perhaps she was a frequent guest in her nephew's home. Elizabeth approached quietly, her steps unnoticed by her ladyship until Elizabeth was almost at her side, and curtsied briefly. "Lady Catherine, perhaps I may be of assistance."

"You!" cried Lady Catherine, turning her head and seeing her for the first time. "How do you dare to show me your face, Miss Bennet?"

"Perhaps you have not heard of my recent marriage. I am not Miss Bennet. I am Mrs. Darcy, your ladyship," Elizabeth replied with as much dignity as she could muster.

"That is exactly why I am here! Colonel Fitzwilliam told me of my nephew's marriage, but I refuse to believe it. This must be a scandalous falsehood! I insist on seeing Darcy myself."

"I am afraid you will be disappointed," Elizabeth answered coolly. "He is out."

"Is he out, or is he afraid to see me?" Lady Catherine answered, looking at her through narrowed eyes.

"Mr. Darcy has no reason to avoid you. If your ladyship had sent us word of your visit, I am sure he would have made every effort to be here to receive you," Elizabeth said, raising her chin proudly. This was her husband's aunt, and although her manners had often been objectionable to Elizabeth, Darcy would not appreciate angry words spoken to his mother's sister.

"You are mistaken, Miss Bennet. He would have fled in fear, if he knew how much he has angered me. Indeed, he probably *has* received word of my anger, and chosen to flee rather than face me himself! To ally himself with such a disgraceful family, he must have been quite out of his mind. What did you do, to make him take leave of his senses in such a way?"

Elizabeth felt her anger rising, but she took a deep breath before answering. "If you wish to speak with me, Lady Catherine, I will insist upon being addressed by my proper title. Mr. Darcy and I married just over a fortnight ago. My title now is Mrs. Darcy. I will not answer to any other name. May I offer you the opportunity to sit and wait for your nephew?"

Lady Catherine took a moment to survey Elizabeth, her eyes sweeping over her from head to foot. "Upon my word, you speak your mind quite freely, for one of your age and status."

"This is, I think, a trait of mine with which you have already been acquainted," Elizabeth responded archly. "As for status, I now share the status enjoyed by your nephew."

"I think not, Miss Bennet." She rapped her cane emphatically against the floor for emphasis. "I think you will be surprised at how little advantage you will gain from this marriage, when it is better known. Oh, I know Matlock and his wife will welcome you with open arms, as they do to anyone, showing their lack of discernment and taste. But the rest of the family will know better. They have no reason to receive you at all, and you may be sure they will learn never to speak your name, no matter whether it is Darcy or Bennet!"

"You have insulted me in every way possible, Lady Catherine," Elizabeth said, resentfully. "I must beg your pardon for taking my leave of you." She made as if to walk away, but Lady Catherine stopped her.

"Not so fast, if you please! Do you know why my nephew married you, girl?" she asked with a sneer. "He may have been taken in by your impertinent manners, your wit, or your appearance. You may have temporarily entrapped him with your arts and allurements. But when he comes to his senses, he will remember his obligations. He will recall his duty to marry for the best interests of the family, and he will find a way out of this marriage which he has contracted with you."

"You know not of what you speak, madam, and I must ask you to importune me no more."

Lady Catherine continued without interruption. "When Darcy comes to his senses, I will find a way to get him out of this entanglement. There is always some error in a marriage contract."

Elizabeth stared at her in disbelief. "You cannot be in earnest, madam."

"I *am* in earnest, and you shall discover it soon enough. But enough of this talk. If Darcy is not here, I shall take *my* leave. Pray tell him that I will return again and again, until he has the courage to speak with me himself. I leave no compliments, Miss Bennet. I am seriously displeased with you both." She turned and left as quickly as she came, but took the time to wipe her feet off carefully before stepping into the carriage.

Elizabeth waited until she was certain Lady Catherine was gone, then made her way to the parlor and asked for tea to be served, feeling a need to fortify herself before her husband returned to the house. She would have to speak to Fitzwilliam, obviously, and tell him of his aunt's forceful disapproval of his marriage. Should she tell him everything Lady Catherine had said?

Lady Catherine's threat to find a way to dissolve the marriage contract ran through Elizabeth's mind again. Knowing her nature, Elizabeth had surmised that she would oppose her nephew's marriage, but she had not anticipated such a forceful reaction. The threat of ending the marriage had certainly never crossed her mind. Was it possible that a signed marriage contract could be set aside, that it could even be broken, through some means she had never heard of? Did Lady Catherine have that much influence over her nephew?

No. Her uncle Gardiner, who had overseen her marriage to Darcy, was a businessman. He understood the nature of legal agreements. He would never have agreed to any arrangement that could be easily set aside, leaving Elizabeth disgraced and putting her family in peril again. Besides this, Darcy himself, whatever his other faults, was a gentleman. No gentleman would knowingly enter into a contract, especially one as serious as marriage, with an eye towards dissolving it later under dubious circumstances. Her husband wished to avoid scandal, not to court it. Lady Catherine's threat was no more than wishful thinking on her part, a reflection of her own feelings of self-importance.

But then, hadn't Darcy disregarded the terms of his own father's will, in order to deprive George Wickham of his living? How had he accomplished that? There were more forces at work here than what she understood.

In very short order the sound of the front door opening broke into her thoughts, and then she heard Darcy's deep voice as he gave his outer things to the servants. On an impulse, she rang the bell to have a maid ask her husband to join her, and to have his own setting brought for tea.

Darcy strode into the drawing room a few minutes later, looking as impeccable as though he had just come from his tailor, and wearing an expression of surprised anticipation. Elizabeth realized that this was the first time since their marriage that she had deliberately sought out his company. He had to wonder at the occasion, but he did not seem averse to joining her. His words of greeting confirmed her impression.

"Mrs. Darcy, this is an unexpected pleasure," he said formally, sitting across from her and looking at her in that enigmatic way that never told her what he was thinking. She thought she saw a pleased look in his eyes.

"I was serving myself tea, and thought perhaps you might enjoy some as well," she answered, beginning to pour him a cup. "You have been out most of the day, after all."

"There were several business matters to conclude before leaving for Pemberley," he answered, smiling slightly as he saw her add the scant cream and generous sugar which he preferred. She stirred it and then handed him the teacup and saucer together. He accepted it with a nod of approval and she let him take several sips before speaking again.

"I also wanted to tell you that you missed your aunt, Lady Catherine. She called here a short time ago."

Darcy's face took on a wry expression, his mouth twisted up on one side. "I suppose she came to extend her congratulations on our marriage?"

Elizabeth noted that he took his aunt's disapproval for granted. "She certainly had strong feelings on the subject, which she did not hesitate to make known. I cannot say that I was surprised."

Darcy grimaced. "I am sorry I was not here to receive her myself. You should not have had to bear her visit alone."

"It is no matter. I accepted her sentiments on behalf of us both."

"I am certain that you did. I have always admired your ability to deal with difficult relations." Elizabeth wondered if he was referring to his relatives, or to her own, but in either case, he was extending her a compliment.

"I suppose she had nothing in particular to say besides giving us her blessing?" he asked. The mocking half-smile on his face told her that he knew how ironic his statement was.

"She said to tell you that she will return as often as necessary until she can see you herself."

Her husband did not seem troubled by this statement. "I will send her a card with my regrets in the morning. By then we shall be safely off to Pemberley, and there will be no opportunity for her to call again. She must have come from Rosings only today."

Elizabeth took a deep breath. "She also refused to address me as Mrs. Darcy, calling me instead Miss Bennet at every opportunity."

"Good God, Elizabeth!" Darcy set down his tea abruptly. "Was she truly so forward?"

"She spoke in her usual manner, only more so. She did not hesitate to speak her opinion of me."

Darcy stared at her, his shock obvious. "Tell me everything she said. I need to know the particulars."

"It was not a lengthy discussion." Elizabeth repeated the conversation as best she could, including his aunt's words about the marriage contract, and watched her husband's reaction closely. With every word she spoke, his anger became more obvious, and by the time she finished her short recital, his expression had taken on the haughty look she remembered from before their marriage.

"This will have to be answered. My aunt, as you know, has her own notions of nobility and the privileges it affords. She does not hesitate to make me know them." He stood and walked to the window, looking out of it with his hands clasped behind his back.

"Mr. Darcy," Elizabeth said, hesitating, wondering how to ask the next question, "Do the privileges of nobility include setting aside a marriage contract when it no longer suits?"

Darcy turned and looked at her, his face unreadable. "What do you mean, Elizabeth?"

She had no wish to incur her husband's wrath, but the question was too important to ignore. "Is it possible for a gentleman to do as your aunt said, to find an error in a marriage contract and use that to free himself of the relationship?"

"I have heard of it being done," he answered grimly, "but no gentleman worthy of the name would behave in such a way."

"Forgive me for the question, sir, but your aunt seemed rather certain of herself."

"You wish to know if I would avail myself of the option?" He smiled, seeming to find the question humorous; then crossed the room to place one hand on her shoulder, looking down at her reassuringly. "You need not fear; so far I have found married life pleasing enough."

Since he made light of it, so would she. "I am glad to hear it. It would be a shame to lose a husband so quickly after gaining one! I, too, have found marriage to be tolerable so far."

He looked at her again with the odd, quizzical expression she had seen at breakfast, then dropped his hand and moved back towards the front entry. "We shall speak more of this later."

"Where are you going?" she asked.

"My aunt has overstepped her bounds, and I shall have to deal with her. She will not be permitted to simply come to my home, insult my wife, and then leave again without being held accountable for her behavior. I am going now to see if she is at her house here in town and call on her there. I intend to pay her my *respects*," he said the word disdainfully, "and return before the earl and countess arrive tonight."

"I shall see you at dinner then."

"Indeed, you shall." He hesitated before leaving, looking at her one more time. "There is no need to worry, Elizabeth. I will not allow anyone, not even my aunt, to treat my wife in such a way." With a quick turn and confident step, he left the house.

CHAPTER SEVEN

Darcy did return in time for dinner, but he was in a black mood, the likes of which Elizabeth had not seen from him before. He did not arrive until after the earl and countess had made their appearance, and he apologized for his slight tardiness with only the barest of civility. When they went in to dinner together it was up to Elizabeth to carry the bulk of the conversation at dinner with Lord Robert and Lady Eleanor, while Darcy stared moodily ahead of himself and added little to the discussion around the table. Elizabeth looked at him questioningly several times, but he continued to observe without comment. Elizabeth grew increasingly uncomfortable as the evening progressed, which cut deeply into the growing feeling of companionship she was enjoying with Lady Eleanor.

When dinner was over and she and Lady Eleanor removed to the drawing room, the gentlemen did not join them for much longer than was expected; and when they finally did appear, Lord Robert began to make his farewell at once. Darcy made no objection, his face showing nothing but ill humor. Lady Eleanor, of course, had to follow her husband's lead, although the look on her face showed her own surprise and displeasure. At length, however, with many apologetic looks from Lady Eleanor to Elizabeth, they did leave. Darcy at once offered Elizabeth his arm to escort her upstairs, still barely speaking or even looking at her. He seemed to feel that extending his arm and asking, "Are you ready to retire now? We have a long day's travel tomorrow," was enough conversation for the evening.

"I am not ready," Elizabeth answered, hurt and disappointed by the dinner's outcome. Little of the lively conversation or discourse she had anticipated had taken place, and she had no idea when she might see the earl and countess again. "I wish you would tell me what happened when you went to see your aunt. It seems to have preyed on your mind all evening."

"Happened? Nothing happened," Darcy answered, letting his arm drop. "The encounter ended successfully."

Elizabeth aimed for a tone that would demonstrate her concern, conscious that there must be something serious weighing on her husband's mind. "Can you not tell me more about it? Your manner does not match your words."

"My aunt does not approve of my marriage, as I had known she would not," he answered without looking at her, "and I could not refute her arguments, though I did my best. The experience was not pleasant."

"But you said the encounter ended successfully? What arguments did she make against your marriage?"

"I do not see the need to repeat them. We are both tired, and tomorrow will be a long day."

"I am not the least bit tired, and surely your aunt could say nothing worse about me than what I heard already."

Darcy looked directly at her. "She spoke at length of the inferiority of your connections, your want of fortune, and the lack of decorum often demonstrated by your family, as related to her by Mr. Collins. I could not answer those charges, since they were all true."

Elizabeth stared at him, unwilling to believe her husband would repeat such a thing to her. "Did you not defend your wife at all, sir?"

"I told her that she must address you as Mrs. Darcy in the future if she wishes to be a guest at Pemberley again. She reluctantly agreed."

"And that was all?"

"We spoke of other matters as well, none of which need concern you."

Elizabeth looked at him for a second more, and then walked away angrily before turning around and facing him again. "I think this does concern me, Mr. Darcy. I would like to know everything that was said, please."

Darcy's face clouded over and his expression became stern. "They were personal matters. I am not obligated to share them with you."

Elizabeth's temper finally flared. "Of course you are not, since I am from such a low-bred family. But perhaps before you criticize my family's manners, sir, you might look to those of your own family first!" She gathered her skirts and began to go up the stairs, intending to pass him and retreat to her own room, but Darcy shot out a hand and took her wrist as she went by.

"What would you have me say, Elizabeth?" he asked, holding her back. "Did you expect me to rejoice in the inferiority of your family? Did you think I would be glad to be the nephew of a man in trade, even if only by marriage? My family's standing in society is so far above yours, it is no wonder if some of my relatives can hardly believe I made you an offer. I can scarcely believe it myself at times. It certainly went against my better judgment."

"Being insulted by you is far worse than being insulted by your aunt," she answered angrily. "And my aunt and uncle are superior to your Lady Catherine in every way. Let me go!"

This time when she pulled away, he made no resistance, and she swept up the stairs and into her room without looking back at him. There, she sank onto the edge of her bed and held her hands to her flaming cheeks as she fought down the urge to weep. She was not entirely successful; a few tears rolled down her face, and she wiped them fiercely away.

How could an evening that should have been so enjoyable have taken such an ugly turn? She had so looked forward to the countess' lively companionship, despite the fact that Lady Eleanor was so much older than her. Lord Robert had been his taciturn self, polite when addressed directly but not volunteering conversation. But even his reluctant participation was better than her husband's silent brooding. If her husband had at least tried to participate, it might have been one of her most enjoyable evenings of married life yet.

Then, to have her husband insult her own family so casually! Everything he had said was true, but to point it out in such a callous way was not what she had expected. She had thought he was going to defend her to his aunt, but instead he seemed determined to agree with her. At least he had insisted that Lady Catherine use her correct title; what he had said to gain that point, she could not imagine.

She clasped her hands tightly together in front of her, forcing herself to take deep breaths and exert her will over her traitorous emotions.

If she had wondered before about her husband's view of their marriage, she need wonder no more. Everything her uncle had told her was true.

Yet even so, from Darcy's standpoint, he had more than fulfilled his obligations to her. The marriage contract he had signed so willingly had saved her family from ruin; she needed to remember that, and to be grateful. He had defended her, at least, to his aunt, though he could not defend her family. She really had no right to ask anything more of him, and it was incautious of her to speak to him with such anger. She would have to apologize at her first opportunity.

The bedroom door opened, but Elizabeth, caught between anger and humiliation, did not look up. Her surprise knew no bounds when the door closed again and she felt Darcy sit down next to her on the edge of the bed. "Elizabeth, we must talk."

She continued to hold her hands together, making no response.

"If I was harsh in my words to you just now, I apologize. I can understand that being reminded of your family's shortcomings might make you angry."

Elizabeth took a steadying breath. "I should not have spoken to you the way I did. You have been more than generous to my family, and I am grateful."

"It is only appropriate for me to provide for my wife's family, no matter the difference in our stations. But perhaps it is not gentlemanly of me to remind you of that difference. You cannot help the family you were born into, and I certainly do not hold it against you."

"It is kind of you, sir," she answered, swallowing the bitterness in her words. Her wounded pride was urging her to protest his air of superiority, but she had no standing in this household. She was defenseless against him when he only spoke the truth. Still, his words hurt, and she could not help saying, "They are my family, and I do love them."

"Of course you do," Darcy answered at once in a gentle voice, putting a companionable arm around her shoulder. "They are a part of you, and I would not have you deny them."

The sudden touch was her undoing. The frustrations of the evening, combined with the tumult brought on by Lady Catherine's visit, made the tears she had been denying suddenly overflow. She covered her face with her hands, but instead of pulling away as she expected, Darcy pulled her closer to him and let her weep on his shoulder. For several minutes, her muted sobs were the only sound in the room.

"I know these past weeks have been difficult for you," he said at length, when her tears had begun to slow. Elizabeth found that she was leaning completely against her husband, with both of his arms around her. One of his hands smoothed her hair while the other caressed her shoulder. "You lost your father in an unexpected way, and then our marriage occurred so quickly after that. You left everything familiar to you when you married me. Please do not think that I am unaware of the enormity of the changes you have experienced."

She reminded herself of the need to show her gratitude. He was being remarkably tolerant of her outburst. "Some of those changes have not been entirely unpleasant."

"I would like to think not." She sensed a smile in his voice. Was her head nestled under his chin? Was Fitzwilliam Darcy really holding her and consoling her the way a parent might comfort a child? It was a far kinder response than she had expected after her angry words. She let herself relax against him.

"We had so little time to speak before our wedding day," Darcy continued after a few moments, his voice soothing. "I hope you do not mind the speed with which the engagement took place. I had no other choice, if I was to protect your family before you were forced to leave your home. And of course I wanted the wedding to take place quickly for my own sake as well."

"I understand." She did not, really, but it made no difference. She already knew he was a determined man, apt to act swiftly in a matter of importance. He had saved her family, and that was all that mattered.

She had recovered enough, now, to sit up and wipe away the evidence of her tears. Darcy watched her closely. "Do you feel better now?"

"Yes. And I thank you for explaining your actions so fully."

"Your family can not be invited to Pemberley, of course, but you must not think that I will not care for them," he continued.

She had expected this. "Not even my aunt and uncle?"

"Especially not your aunt and uncle. He is in trade, after all."

"And I would do well to remember that your family is the superior of mine?" she suggested, wondering how he would respond.

"I do not think we need to dwell on that," he answered, smiling faintly.

"Then I will not mention it again if you do not." She allowed her voice to take on the teasing tone that he seemed to enjoy, and his smile broadened.

"And, Elizabeth," he added, "You need not worry about Lady Catherine calling on us at Pemberley any time soon. There were certain things said between her and me today that make that unlikely. If I seemed to be preoccupied tonight, it is because of those things, not because of you."

"Do you not care to share what was said, sir? I believe it might lighten your burden, if you were to do so."

"It is my responsibility, and no one else's," he said shortly. "You need not concern yourself."

The look on his face would brook no argument. Elizabeth felt as if a door had been opened, briefly, in front of her; and then emphatically closed in her face. She had tried, at least. She could do no more. "Then I suppose we should prepare for bed and for traveling tomorrow. Good night, sir."

"It is not quite good night yet," he answered. "I will see you in my chamber in an hour or so, unless you need more time to prepare."

"An hour will be adequate."

He still wanted her in his bed, despite her heated words and his view of her inferior standing. She had survived another disagreement with her husband, but she realized that she was no closer now to understanding him than she had been when they first married.

∞

Darcy held his wife in his arms late that night, long after she had fallen asleep, replaying the events of the past two months.

It was still difficult, in some ways, to believe that Elizabeth was truly his wife. For months she had been an elusive, intangible ideal in his eyes, the very picture of everything a lady should be, and yet completely beyond his grasp. She was handsome, intelligent, possessed of a mind the equal of anyone he had ever met, and given to a certain arch humor that he adored. She was perfect for him in every way; yet her lower social standing and lack of connections made her completely unsuitable to be his wife. Proposing to her had been his one defiant act of rebellion in a life comprised entirely of duty and responsibility. At times he could scarcely believe he had withstood his family's expectations so dramatically. Elizabeth herself had been the prize he sought, and for her he would have, in the end, dared much more.

He was vaguely worried about her now. After losing her father so unexpectedly and then swept into marriage so quickly, and with her sudden dramatic change in circumstances, even Elizabeth's high spirits were in danger of being overwhelmed. Her conversation at times lacked the sparkle and spontaneity he had come to enjoy so much. She smiled for him, but he noticed that her smiles frequently did not reach her eyes, and she sometimes looked at him with a distant, serious air that was utterly unlike her previous self.

He would do whatever he could to help her in her time of adjustment. At Pemberley, away from the pressures of town society and the danger of confrontation by his aunt, she would find the comfort and solace she needed. Her natural high spirits would do the rest. With the outdoor walks that she relished, the companionship of her new sister, and the fullest attention of her devoted husband, Elizabeth would once again be fully the woman with whom he had fallen in love.

CHAPTER EIGHT

"We will be at Pemberley by late afternoon," Darcy informed her near noon of the second day of their travels. The note of possessive pride in his voice was unmistakable.

They had left Darcy House early the day before and made good time on the dry, clear road. The luxurious Darcy carriage, along with its coachmen and outriders, made Elizabeth recall once again how much her situation in life had changed since marrying Fitzwilliam; and she wondered what changes might still be to come. With the greatest of curiosity she wondered how Pemberley would appear to her for the first time--this new estate where she would live and whose home would be under her care.

"We will eat in the carriage rather than stopping along the way, so as to save time," her husband announced. "I want you and Georgiana to have as much time as possible today to become acquainted. You may unpack the hamper now, if you like."

"I am not hungry yet," Elizabeth dared to contradict him. The hamper had been filled and loaded into the Darcy carriage by the staff at the inn where they had stayed the night before. If their breakfast that morning had been any indication of what had been packed, she would be missing out on something truly delicious. But it would all be like sawdust in her mouth. Her anxious anticipation had stolen her appetite.

"Are you well?" her husband asked, glancing away from the window to look at her.

"Perhaps the motion of the coach has upset my stomach," she suggested, and he nodded.

"That is understandable. You may fare better if you face forward in the carriage, as I do. Come, sit beside me."

He offered her his hand to help her move across the swaying coach and did not let go when she had taken her seat next to him. "We are passing now through countryside more familiar to me," he told her. "We used to visit friends in this area when I was young. Over there is the tree that I favored as being mine, when my father would allow me the freedom to play on my own. I fell out of it more than once."

She had noticed that he was beginning to speak more freely as they came closer to his home. "Did you not learn your lesson the first time? Why would you return to climb the same tree, after falling out of it previously?"

"My father said challenges are made to be overcome, not to shrink away from. They are the measure of a man."

"That is a more appropriate lesson to assign to a grown man than to a young boy."

"The choice to persevere was mine, not his. One learns little from an obstacle that is avoided."

Elizabeth nodded, adding this to her mental inventory of her husband's personality. What he said of himself matched her observations so far. Such resolve had no doubt helped him greatly when his father had died and he was suddenly the master of a considerable estate. By all accounts he had done well in his new role, and Elizabeth silently admitted a reluctant admiration for his decisive character. Not only had he taken on the management of the estate, but also the considerable care of raising his younger sister. Suddenly she wanted to know more about Georgiana.

"Please tell me more about Miss Darcy."

"What would you like to know?"

"Whatever you can tell me. I am curious, having heard so little of her." Wickham and Miss Bingley had given their own descriptions of Georgiana Darcy; she wondered how much her brother's account would vary.

"Georgiana is shy with strangers, but she has a warm, caring nature. I believe she will respond well to your natural ease of manner. I hope that you will be just as much a sister to her as you are to Miss Bennet and the others in your family."

"I recall that Miss Bingley described Miss Darcy as highly accomplished."

"She practices and sings constantly." Darcy's voice took on a tender quality she had not heard in him before. "You will enjoy playing together."

"I am sure her skill will outstrip mine. I practice but little and play quite ill at times."

"You are mistaken. Your playing has a pleasing air, entirely without pretense, and is attractive to all who are privileged to listen. I have never heard you play without the greatest of pleasure." Elizabeth was too embarrassed to say a word. After a moment her husband continued speaking.

"Your devotion to your sister, Elizabeth, is one of the first things that drew you to my attention."

"In what way, sir?" asked Elizabeth, curious. This was the first time he had mentioned anything to her about why he had chosen her for his wife.

"When Jane lay ill at Netherfield I was much affected by the bond the two of you shared. I know of no one else who would walk three miles through muddy fields in order to be with her sister, and the diligent and compassionate care you had for her spoke well of your character. I thought then how pleasing it would be for Georgiana to be the recipient of such affection."

So he had not married her solely to produce an heir. "Then you succeeded admirably in your design. If there is one thing I learned while living at Longbourn, it was how to support younger sisters."

"Indeed, I am sure you will be an excellent influence on Georgiana. I know that she is looking forward to meeting you."

The carriage went over a bridge then, putting an end to any more conversation for the moment, and Elizabeth instead gave her attention to the countryside of Derbyshire passing by. The open, rolling farmland of the south was giving way in places to rising ground, with steeper slopes and faster running streams than she was used to seeing. Darcy continued to occasionally point out areas of interest as they continued their travel, going ever northward, further into Derbyshire.

After several hours they entered the village of Lambton, where her aunt Gardiner had lived for a time; and Elizabeth knew that the journey was almost over. When the carriage turned between two tall, black, wrought iron gates surrounded by verdant trees displaying the heights of summer, Darcy informed her that they had entered the park around Pemberley. The house itself was only a mile or so further on. He assured her that Georgiana would be waiting at the door, alerted to their arrival by their outriders.

As the carriage rounded a small curve in the road it suddenly left the woods, and the house rose abruptly before her. Elizabeth caught her breath in wonder. She had formed no mental image of Pemberley; but if she had, it could not have equaled the quiet elegance and gentle warmth on display in front of her. The house, made of gray brick, lay at the foot of a gradually sloping wood with a stream of some importance rising just in front of it. The banks of the stream were well maintained but had no false air to them; the lines and overall aspect of the house were pleasing and without pretension. Many balconies and windows adorned the house but did not overwhelm it, and the whole effect of the house, stream, and surrounding woods together was an inviting welcome.

"It is beautiful," Elizabeth said softly aloud, without meaning to, and her husband looked immensely pleased by her reaction.

"Welcome to Pemberley, Mrs. Darcy," he said, his eyes glowing.

When the carriage stopped in the driveway in front of the house, Elizabeth looked out the window and saw a score of liveried servants and maids assembled on the steps, together with a somewhat elderly woman and a fair-haired young lady standing side by side. These last, she thought, must be Miss Darcy and the housekeeper, Mrs. Reynolds, whom Darcy had mentioned previously. Her face grew red at the thought of receiving so much attention from everyone present but she lifted her chin proudly; she would not be intimidated.

The young woman she assumed to be Georgiana stepped forward as Darcy handed Elizabeth out of the carriage. She embraced her brother warmly, then faced Elizabeth and dropped a cautious curtsey, which Elizabeth returned. Darcy made the introductions.

Georgiana Darcy was taller than most young women her age, with a well formed figure and fair hair that contrasted sharply with her brother's dark looks. She had an air of reserve that Elizabeth thought could easily be mistaken for pride by those who did not know better; but Elizabeth, seeing the nervous way Georgiana sometimes bit her lower lip, and the way her hands clutched at her skirt, could only pity her. She spoke kindly to the girl and smiled warmly, and was rewarded with a shy smile in return. Darcy made the necessary presentations to the numerous staff, especially to Mrs. Reynolds, and then they all proceeded into the house together.

Elizabeth quickly saw that Darcy was making every effort to forward conversation between her and Georgiana as they walked through the house, though he was not entirely successful. At times Georgiana looked at Elizabeth with real interest, and she listened attentively while Darcy told her of their trip from town; but she asked only one or two brief questions of her own, and seemed embarrassed when Elizabeth spoke directly to her. Eventually, after several awkward pauses, she found that Georgiana was asking if she would like an opportunity to refresh herself, and Elizabeth responded gratefully. Darcy and Georgiana lingered behind, speaking quietly together, as Mrs. Reynolds led her away, promising to bring her back to the drawing room in an hour.

They had not gone far, however, when Darcy overtook them. "If you please, Mrs. Reynolds, I would like to be the one to show Mrs. Darcy her new home." Mrs. Reynolds smiled broadly and curtsied, and Darcy extended his arm to Elizabeth, who took it with an unaccustomed shyness.

Every step she took through Pemberley impressed her more than the previous one, and she gazed at all she saw in disbelieving wonder. The rooms were of a generous scale, furnished with items that displayed as much wealth as Rosings, Lady Catherine's home, but with far superior taste. The dining rooms, drawing rooms, and other areas that they passed by, along with the moldings, the curtains, and the portraits on display--all spoke of a restrained elegance and genuine good breeding. Darcy guided her through a handful of passages and up one flight of stairs, and at last showed her to the suite of rooms which he said had belonged to his mother in the past. "Your maid will draw you a bath, if you wish," he told her. "My own rooms are next to yours, through that connecting door." He motioned towards a small door in the far corner. "I will call for you in an hour, so that I may take you to the drawing room myself."

"Are you afraid that I will lose my way between here and there?" she asked him, allowing herself to smile mischievously, covering her nervousness.

"It has been known to happen," he answered. "It is often overwhelming for people who have not visited before. I would not like to lose my wife, so soon after finding her."

Elizabeth smiled brightly. "I shall be ready in an hour, and you will not need to send out a search party until I have had a little more time to explore on my own. I have no desire to be lost so soon after being discovered." Darcy's face brightened at her playful tone.

Elizabeth's first afternoon and evening at Pemberley went by in a series of activities and conversations that she would later have difficulty recalling in any detail. She and Georgiana passed some pleasant time together along with Mrs. Annesley, Georgiana's companion, while they waited for dinner; though it was evident that conversation even in familiar surroundings was a struggle for the girl. Darcy was also there, but he sat quietly and said little, seeming to relish the opportunity to relax in familiar surroundings. There were many affectionate glances between him and Georgiana, and Elizabeth saw that Georgiana exerted herself to converse more when she was aware that Darcy was watching and silently encouraging her.

After dinner Georgiana agreed, after much patient coaxing, to play on the pianoforte for her brother and Elizabeth while they sat together on the settee to listen. Elizabeth allowed herself to relax as the gentle music filled the room, recognizing that her own haphazard education was no match for the younger girl's determined mastery. Darcy took advantage of his sister's distraction to ask Elizabeth, "How do you find Pemberley so far?"

"It is as beautiful and harmonious a home as I ever expected to see," she answered honestly, looking appreciatively at the room around her. "My imagination could not have invented anyplace so lovely."

"And how do you like your new sister?"

"I like her very much indeed. She reminds me of Jane somewhat, with her quiet air. "

Darcy's expression was more open, and less proud, than she had ever seen it before. "I am delighted that you are pleased with her. My sister's reserved and timid nature sometimes makes it difficult for her to make friends; I believe that at times people think she is proud. Her true emotions are not easy for a casual observer to discern. "

"How very like Jane she is, then. Jane is often misunderstood; she feels more deeply than she displays, and sometimes leaves the people around her in doubt of her sentiments."

Darcy frowned slightly. "Is it possible, then, that she could form an attachment without anyone being aware of it? Does she conceal her feelings to that extent?"

"Jane does not expose her deepest feelings even to me, at least not often; but I do not think she could hide such an attachment from me, since we are so close. It is only people she does not know well who are misled by her calm demeanor. Between her and me there can be few secrets." Elizabeth tried, but did not succeed, in keeping a wistful tone out of her voice. With the limited contact she would now have with her family, she and Jane would lose some of the closeness they had enjoyed all their lives. Jane had lost so much already this year, from Bingley's desertion to her father's death; now she would also have to become accustomed to the loss of the intimate friendship of her favorite sister.

"And has your sister ever formed such an attachment? Do you believe she has ever been inclined to marry?"

"I am sure I could not say." Elizabeth looked away uncomfortably. She did not want to invade Jane's privacy, especially with the very man who, she suspected, may have had a hand in separating Jane from the man she loved. She would not ask Darcy about it, of course. Such a conversation, once started, could not have a happy ending; and she was determined to make the best of the situation in which she now found herself.

She was spared any further response just then when Georgiana reached the end of her piece and looked uncertainly towards her brother. Darcy turned to Elizabeth with a warm smile.

"Perhaps you will favor us with a performance tonight, since you had no opportunity to play our last night in town?"

"I will play with Miss Darcy, if you wish."

"And will you sing for us? I do not believe you have done so since we have been married."

"I have no wish to frighten you away, sir," she answered lightly. "I have never been properly trained in the art; you may regret your request."

"There are some people whose natural talents are so pronounced that they please others with no conscious effort on their part," he answered gravely. "For them, formal training would merely add luster to a chain of gold."

Bemused, she arched one eyebrow as she looked back at him. "Well spoken, sir. I wonder how long you studied ahead of time, to devise such a compliment. Do you make a habit of flattering your sister in a similar fashion?"

"My brother never flatters," Georgiana said unexpectedly from her seat at the pianoforte, with a certain amount of alarm. "He always speaks the absolute truth."

"Then he is guilty of an even greater fault, which is that of leading his sister to believe in his own infallible taste." Georgiana looked amazed at her impertinent response, and even more amazed by the smile she saw on her brother's face.

"You will find, Georgiana, that unlike most fashionable young women, my wife speaks her mind freely. She will criticize me to you for hours if you permit it." Darcy's voice held only amusement, not reproof.

"But unlike certain gentlemen of my acquaintance," Elizabeth retorted, "I will only criticize where I see a real defect of character. I will say nothing of you to your sister that you do not deserve."

"Then I pray you speak not at all," he answered gallantly, "for my faults are too numerous to mention, and I would not make my sister acquainted with more of my defects than she already knows."

"In that case, sir," she answered, "you ought to have married someone who truly was a fashionable young woman, and not likely to speak her mind."

"I do not regret my choice," he responded, looking directly at her, "for your criticism is always tempered with charity." Elizabeth returned his look for a moment before speaking to his sister again.

"I will sing, if you wish, but only if you play, please, Miss Darcy. And then you must tell me honestly if your brother's truthfulness or his tastefulness is more in question." She crossed the room to stand next to the instrument, looking at the music and preparing to do her part while Georgiana played. When she glanced up again, she saw that her husband's eyes still rested on her, and his expression was one of the warmest possible approval.

CHAPTER NINE

Darcy's look of approval stayed in Elizabeth's mind the next few days as she began to settle into her role as lady of the house, beginning to learn the household accounts and becoming familiar with the servants and their duties. Many times in the past she had seen a more reserved look on Darcy's face as he gazed at her, an expression she had taken to indicate disapproval or even simply the workings of a distracted mind. Yet in that interaction with her husband, as she stood by the piano and prepared to sing, his neutral features had rapidly changed into a look of open pleasure. She might even have thought that he admired her, based on that one expression. That could not be, of course--but he had chosen her as his wife. It was gratifying to realize that his opinion of her must have been better all along than she had thought.

In the late afternoon each day, when she had finished her work with Mrs. Reynolds, Darcy sought her out and took her on a tour of various areas around the estate. The first time they went together the tour was conducted in a carriage, but after that time they walked together to whichever destination her husband had selected for the day. As they walked, Darcy pointed out items of interest, explaining how they fit into the history and holdings of the vast property, and sometimes asked her opinion of them. He seemed to want her to become familiar with everything about her new home.

These excursions, to her surprise, were pleasant. She discovered that Darcy could be an excellent conversationalist when he wished to be, and he had a wealth of information that he shared freely with her. His pride was on display, but it was no more than any man would have while showing a visitor the details of his estate. No question Elizabeth posed was too trifling to answer, and he provided every possible opportunity to increase her enjoyment of her new home. This was proven one day when Darcy guided her through the formal gardens, which ringed either side of the main house.

"Your gardens are charmingly laid out," Elizabeth told him, as they strolled along a pretty path with rose bushes on one side and Spanish chestnuts on the other. "There is such a natural air to everything in them, and in how they are arranged. You must tell me who deserves the praise for the easy, open design."

"They have been the work of many generations," he answered. "The credit for their layout could not possibly go to any one person; there have been too many involved along the way. Do not forget, they are now your gardens as well. You may make any improvements you see fit."

"I do not know how they could possibly be improved; they are already perfection itself. This path, for example, is shaded very cleverly by those trees, and with the view of the stream just beyond it is delightful in every way. Surely there could be no place anywhere else nearly as peaceful, or so soothing to troubled spirits."

"Are you experiencing troubled spirits, Mrs. Darcy?" he asked courteously, and she laughed at him.

"You must not take everything I say quite so seriously, Mr. Darcy! I speak in generalities only. It is difficult to believe that anyone could have troubled spirits at Pemberley for very long, but if they did, this place would certainly cure them. What is the name of that purple flower over there? We have nothing like it in Hertfordshire."

Darcy did not know, and said so. Walking away from her briefly, he returned with one of the gardeners, a Mr. Witherby, who was happy to see Elizabeth's interest in the grounds. He answered her questions about the plant, its habits and manner of growth, quite thoroughly.

"I wish Jane could see this flower," Elizabeth said, wistfully, holding a specimen in her hand. "She is much more of a gardener than I am, and I know she would be delighted to have such a lovely thing in her own care, at Longbourn."

"You surprise me," Darcy commented, looking at her with pleased interest. "Considering how much you enjoy the out of doors, I would have thought you to have the greater interest in gardening."

"It is true that I love to walk outside, while Jane tends to enjoy more sedentary pursuits. But nurturing plants and watching them grow takes patience, which Jane has in abundance and I sorely lack. I merely enjoy the fruit of her labors and then express my gratitude for her superior virtues."

"If you think your sister would enjoy adding this plant to her collection, it can be arranged easily enough. Witherby, when you feel that the time is right, when a new planting would be most likely to be successful, please take a cutting or a stem or root or whatever else is needed, and have it sent to the direction which Mrs. Darcy will supply."

Elizabeth, flattered and happy, smiled as she expressed her gratitude, and received an easy and open smile in return. Her opinion of her husband was improved by such generosity; despite her own misgivings, she was beginning to feel more and more comfortable in his presence.

She had not married for love, as her dream had always been; but she was beginning to find more pleasure in her new life than she would have thought possible previously. The challenges of running a house of Pemberley's size aroused her interest and stimulated her mind, and Georgiana was close at hand whenever she missed her sisters. In her free time she also made use of the extensive Pemberley library, and discovered to her delight many volumes which she had long desired to possess but had never been able to purchase on her limited budget. On numerous afternoons, especially if the weather was foul, she curled up in a window seat and lost herself in the pages of her favorite novel.

She did not forget her obligations as a wife. She made herself available to her husband whenever he wished, taking care that he should know he was welcome when he knocked lightly on the connecting door between their bedrooms several times a week. With the initial embarrassment past, she did not find this obligation completely distasteful, and invariably Darcy would remain in her bed for the entire night before rising to take breakfast with her. Elizabeth did not object. She found, to her surprise, that she rested easier when he was nearby, his warmth and steady breathing a soothing presence that lulled her peacefully to sleep. Pemberley was still a strange new home and it was comforting to have something familiar at hand, even if that something was her enigmatic husband. After breakfasting together, he would depart for his duties on the estate and she would not see him again until late in the afternoon.

Being a sister to Georgiana was neither chore nor duty. Rather, it was the natural result of being in her new sister's company every day. Underneath Georgiana's shy façade, Elizabeth found Mary's intelligence and Jane's quiet pleasure in everything, along with a deep desire to please those around her. Little incidents here and there showed how much she admired Elizabeth. She complimented Elizabeth at once when Elizabeth's maid changed her hairstyle to increase the number of soft curls around her face; and she silently gazed at her new satin dress soon after it arrived from an order placed in town, looking at it with admiring eyes. When she saw the pattern of stitches Elizabeth was using around the border of a kerchief, she immediately began to incorporate the same pattern into her own needlework. Elizabeth commented on it while she sat with Georgiana and Mrs. Annesley in the parlor, sewing.

"Your pattern looked so pretty, so delicate and yet so functional, that I wanted to try it for myself," Georgiana said timidly in answer to Elizabeth's question. "I hope this is not wrong of me."

"Wrong! No indeed. What could be wrong with imitating a pattern you have seen another woman put to use? I am flattered it pleased you so well that you wanted to copy it for yourself. What is it that you are making?"

"It is a gown for an infant due to be born next month, to a family that is one of my brother's tenants. Fitzwilliam asked me to supply them with whatever assistance I could, as they are not prosperous."

"Doubtless they will be grateful for your kindness."

"They have expressed their gratitude many times."

"I am surprised that Mr. Darcy would be aware of such a need among his tenants," Elizabeth commented idly, concentrating on her stitching. "Most gentlemen would let that duty would fall to their steward."

"Not my brother!" Georgiana answered quickly, showing an eagerness to defend him. "Fitzwilliam knows and cares for all of his tenants, especially those who are not well off."

"He knows all of them?" Elizabeth repeated, trying not to sound doubtful. "That is a heavy burden. There must be scores of families at Pemberley, at least."

"Mr. Darcy is known as a fair and generous landlord, and takes great care of the poor," Mrs. Annesley said in her amiable way. "I have been told many times that he is like his father in this regard."

Mrs. Annesley had impressed Elizabeth already as a quiet, well-bred woman who appeared to be genuinely fond of her young charge. She was a widow a few years older than Elizabeth, impoverished by the sudden death of her husband; and she had been Georgiana's companion for a year or so. With Elizabeth's arrival in the household, her presence was no longer needed; but Georgiana had asked Darcy to keep her on until she found a new position. Darcy, ever indulgent, had agreed.

"I have never heard any complaints against my brother as a

landlord," Georgiana said solemnly. "Many families wish they could live on Pemberley lands, but we do not have room for them all."

Elizabeth smiled at her. "I am sure there is no greater pleasure for a sister than to hear her brother praised." And no one dependent on the brother's good will would dare to criticize him to the sister, she thought wryly.

Georgiana looked at the material in Elizabeth's hands. "The handkerchief you are stitching--is it for you, or is it a gift for Fitzwilliam?" she asked.

"Has your brother expressed a preference for handkerchiefs with bright purple flowers?" Elizabeth looked at the stitching skeptically, imagining her reserved husband with such an obviously feminine accoutrement.

"I saw your initials on it, and thought perhaps he had asked for a token."

She shook her head. "Mr. Darcy has made no such request. This is going to my sister Jane when it is finished, if I can ever manage the more difficult parts. Needlework is not my forte."

"Fitzwilliam would treasure anything you might give him," Georgiana assured her seriously, making Elizabeth cringe inwardly. But she looked at the younger girl with genuine fondness.

No, she had not managed to marry for love. In the end she had made much the same choice as Charlotte--to provide for her family by marriage to a man whom she found disagreeable. But she had made the better bargain. Whereas Charlotte had to tolerate the humiliations of a fool and an overbearing patroness, Elizabeth had merely to abide the attentions of a distant and proud near-stranger; and to balance this she had the soothing balm of a warm-hearted sister and the delights of Pemberley itself. Though her life was not the fulfillment of all her wishes, in her more reflective moments she had to admit that her choice might have ended in a manner much less agreeable to her personally. Overall, she had no cause to repine.

CHAPTER TEN

The first month at Pemberley had gone by quickly, and they were in the heat of a mid-summer's day when Darcy entered the parlor with a look of pleased satisfaction on his face. Georgiana was concentrating on a watercolor she had recently started while Elizabeth sat admiringly by. In Elizabeth's lap was a basket of stitching for the poor, and she was making steady progress on a sturdy work shirt while Georgiana's skillful touch brought out a depiction of the stream which rose in front of Pemberley. They both startled when Darcy's quick step came down the hall.

"Elizabeth, Georgiana, I have had a letter from someone you both know," he said without preamble. "Mr. Bingley sends his greetings."

It was the first time Bingley's name had come up between Darcy and Elizabeth since their marriage, and her mind instantly flew to her sister. "How does Mr. Bingley?" she asked politely.

"He is well. He asks to be remembered to you particularly, and extends his congratulations to both of us."

"Is he still in London? I suppose he must be; he has no real reason to return to Hertfordshire."

"Yes, he is still in town. He is not likely to return to Hertfordshire. He says that he has decided to give up the lease on Netherfield entirely, and he may begin looking for an estate closer to Derbyshire soon."

Elizabeth felt bitter disappointment rise in her. The only reason Bingley might have had to return to Netherfield was Jane, but he had made his intentions clear. There was a good chance Jane would never see him again, since Darcy was not likely ever to allow Jane to visit Pemberley; though they might, she supposed, encounter each other in town. She broke off a thread in her mouth, wincing as her teeth came together. "It is a pity Meryton could not get a settled, stable family in the house. A more involved land owner might do much good in the neighborhood."

"Bingley is at a time in life when friends and amusements are constantly increasing, and to be confined to such a small town as Meryton is not his pleasure. I am surprised he kept the lease as long as he did. There is little in the neighborhood for diversion."

"He was diverted enough, I am sure," Elizabeth said tartly. "I hope he is able to find another home soon."

Darcy looked at her for a moment with his eyebrows drawn together, as if considering her response. "Bingley asks if he might beg permission to trespass on our hospitality when he arrives here in a few weeks. He is traveling to Scarborough to see his aunt and uncle, but he would like to stop here first."

Elizabeth pretended to be distracted by threading her needle. Somehow she had forgotten that her marriage to Darcy would necessarily put her into Bingley's company from time to time. Given a choice, she would rather never see the man again, but there was nothing to do for it now. "I will be glad to renew his acquaintance," she finally said, keeping her voice as neutral as possible.

"Excellent." Darcy looked relieved. "I would like for you to organize a gathering here at Pemberley while he is visiting, if it is not too much trouble. It ought to be a small dinner."

"A small dinner?" she echoed, wondering what he had in mind.

"Yes. I would have preferred that you had more time to learn your new duties first, but I am sure you are equal to the challenge. Nevertheless, feel free to decline if you think it will be too much."

Elizabeth paused in her needlework for a moment as she looked at her husband. "I can assure you, Mr. Darcy, that I am more than equal to any entertaining you might wish to carry out at Pemberley."

"Of course," Darcy acknowledged. "Mrs. Reynolds can give you a list of the families in the neighborhood. Not everyone will be able to attend, of course, but propriety dictates that all of them should be invited. It should be a very basic menu. As this will be your first social event to hostess since our marriage, nothing elaborate is to be attempted."

"As I said before, I am equal to any task you ask me to take on."

"I have no doubt of it, but simplicity will make your arrangements easier to plan and carry out, and will be appropriate for one who is newly arrived at an elevated station in life. This will be your first chance to make an impression on the neighborhood, and it will serve also to introduce Bingley, possibly to his future neighbors. I want it to go well."

Darcy's voice had taken on the condescending air that Elizabeth remembered from the first few days of their marriage. In response, she stabbed her needle through the material in her hand with such force that she accidentally stabbed her own finger. "I will keep your guidelines in mind, sir."

Satisfied for the moment, Darcy turned to his sister. "And what do you think of this news, Georgiana? Would you like to see Mr. Bingley again?"

"Of course, if that is what you want." Georgiana did not look away from the canvas as she moved her hand lightly over the image.

"And would you be pleased if he bought an estate close to Pemberley?"

"Mr. Bingley is your friend. I am glad if you will be able to see him more." Georgiana spoke quietly, but there was a sudden reserve in her words that made Elizabeth look at her closely.

"Yes, of course; but do you want to see him?" Darcy asked, a trace of impatience coming through in his voice.

"If you want me to." Georgiana's voice was very soft; Elizabeth almost had to incline her head to catch the words. She looked at her husband. Darcy's lips tightened; something in her response had not pleased him. He turned back to Elizabeth.

"Bingley will be here for several days, at least, in the middle of August. I look forward to us welcoming him to Pemberley together."

He turned and left the room, leaving a mystified Elizabeth in his wake. It was clear from Georgiana's expression that she did not share her brother's enthusiasm at the prospect of Bingley's visit, but Georgiana looked steadily away from her. She seemed embarrassed by the discussion; and although she and Elizabeth were friends, they were not yet confidantes. Unless the younger girl raised the subject first, Elizabeth did not feel free to ask her about it.

∞

The next afternoon Elizabeth was with Mrs. Reynolds, beginning to gain familiarity with the items in the still room, when a loud noise of delivery caught her attention. Going from the kitchen to the door on the side of the house, most commonly used for large items, she saw draymen handling a rectangular object, chest high and on delicate wooden legs, covered with a protective cloth. Mrs. Reynolds, following her, said, "That will be the new pianoforte the master ordered for Miss Georgiana. He had it special from town, as a surprise."

Elizabeth moved closer and drew back a corner of the cloth to run a hand over the polished surface, admiring the wood's fine grain. The wood was so smooth that it flowed like satin under her fingertips. "A thoughtful gift, from a most attentive brother," she commented to nobody in particular.

Mrs. Reynolds answered with all the confidence of a long-standing servant, "He is the best of brothers, ma'am. Whatever can be done for Miss Darcy's pleasure is sure to be done in an instant. This is always the way with him."

Elizabeth looked at Mrs. Reynolds carefully. "You have served the family for many years, if I recall correctly."

"Yes ma'am. The previous Mrs. Darcy hired me when the young master was but four years old."

"Can you tell me what Mr. Darcy was like when he was young?"

"He was the sweetest child that ever lived," Mrs. Reynolds answered, smiling gently at the memory. "There was never a boy as good-natured as he. And he has not changed at all, from that day until this. I have never had a cross word from him in all my life, nor have any of the servants here, I am sure."

Mrs. Reynold's expression was so earnest and free from guile that Elizabeth could not doubt her sincerity, but to hear her husband described as universally good-natured was remarkably far from her own rather mixed experience. "A very paragon of virtue, it seems," she said, keeping her tone light. She did not want to be taken too seriously.

Mrs. Reynolds nodded. "He is as good a man as ever lived, though I expect that you know that already."

"I was hoping that you could tell me a fault or two of his, so that I might have something to reprimand him with later!" Elizabeth answered, half-teasingly, wondering how Mrs. Reynolds would respond to such an inquiry.

"I am sure that he does have his faults, but I have never had occasion to see them. You will find hardly a servant here who has any kind of criticism to make."

There must be something in the air of Pemberley, Elizabeth thought, which made even the servants sing the praises of Fitzwilliam Darcy. "You will not oblige me by describing even one secret failing?"

The housekeeper smiled even more broadly. "He is altogether too serious at times, ma'am, or at least he was until he married. Since then he has been much more at ease."

Clearly, inquiries in this department were useless. "His faults are safe in your hands, I see! Never mind--please see that Miss Georgiana's gift is placed wherever it should go. She is out walking with Mrs. Annesley, so this is as good a time as any for the delivery to take place. I will go tell Mr. Darcy that his gift has arrived." Despite her resentment towards her husband, Elizabeth was glad of the excuse to break away from the musty smells of the still room. She would find Darcy, tell him of the arrival of his sister's gift, and then take a brief walk along the stream before returning to her duties.

Darcy was in the small orchard on the side of the house, speaking earnestly with his steward, who bowed and moved courteously away when he saw Elizabeth. Darcy greeted her and nodded approvingly when she told him why she had sought him out. "Mrs. Reynolds can manage the delivery. I saw Georgiana and Mrs. Annesley taking their constitutional a little earlier, going over the stream in that direction, so I suppose there is no danger of her arriving home too soon. But perhaps you could walk with me and help divert her if she returns before her gift is quite ready."

"If you would like," Elizabeth assented, and took his proffered arm. They walked together through the orchard in a silence that seemed, at least to Elizabeth, stiff and awkward. As often occurred, Darcy seemed content to be in her presence without the need for conversation. Elizabeth herself was lost in thought, mulling over the strange and contradictory behaviors her husband had demonstrated since coming to Pemberley. Great men could often be capricious in their likes and dislikes, she had heard her uncle say; and for proof of it, she had the man walking next to her, with all his changeable moods. She would have to write to her aunt soon and give her a full report of her married life.

"You are very quiet today, Mrs. Darcy," her husband suddenly broke into her thoughts, and Elizabeth roused herself. "What are you thinking about?"

She could not share her most recent thoughts with him, of course, so she quickly deflected the question, lest he press her for an answer. "Oh, it is nothing worth telling, merely the wanderings of a distracted mind."

"I would be pleased to hear your thoughts on any subject, if you would care to share them." His hand resting on hers, as it lay on his arm, pressed a little more warmly.

How charming he could be, when the mood took him! Their path had taken them alongside the stream, and she seized on the opening it presented. "Very well, if you insist on knowing, I am comparing the vagaries of life, with all its unexpected twists and turns, to the water in the stream in front of us. One never knows what unexpected path one might be forced to follow."

"A rather serious topic for today."

"Indeed; but you did ask."

"Very true." His mouth quirked up for a moment. "It is true that none of us knows exactly what path our life is going to take. The most obvious course is not always the one taken, and unexpected twists and turns often sweep us away to a different destination than the one we had planned."

Elizabeth thought of the circumstances that had brought her to live at Pemberley. "I suppose you have had few such unexpected turns in your life, Mr. Darcy. Other than losing your father at a comparatively young age, your life appears to have gone very much as planned to date."

"And losing my mother as well," he reminded her.

She acknowledged the omission with a slight inclination of her head. "I beg your pardon; you are correct. To lose both parents, and then to have to take on the responsibilities of your estate and raising your sister at such an early age, could not have been what you expected in your future. Nevertheless, the outcome did not change. Your father's passing meant that you took on those responsibilities earlier than you had planned, but your final destination remained the same."

Her husband agreed. "You are perfectly correct, of course. Save one exception," he pressed her hand again, "my course has proceeded exactly as planned to date."

Was he speaking of his marriage to her? He must be; his family had expected him to marry Miss de Bourgh, but he had chosen Elizabeth instead. She would not have expected him to mention it. "I am surprised, Mr. Darcy, that you were the one to press me to speak today. Usually it is the other way around."

"Indeed. You are undoubtedly a better conversationalist than me. I have often admired the freedom with which you speak to your familiars and strangers alike."

Elizabeth laughed. "What you call freedom, my mother sometimes calls impertinence. It is very little less at times. I have often been upbraided for speaking my mind, and been encouraged to keep my thoughts more to myself."

"You need not feel that way with me. Your ease of address is a refreshing change from the formality most gentlewomen maintain. I wish I had your facility of words."

"I thank you. But there is little lacking in your conversation, sir, once the conversation has begun. It is only its beginning that you seem to find difficult. Once it is well underway you hold forth as well as anyone I know."

Darcy looked sideways at her, suddenly serious. "That is the first time you have ever complimented me, Elizabeth."

Casting her mind back over the history of their acquaintance, she was forced to admit he was right. "It is something in the air here at Pemberley, I think. Even Mrs. Reynolds gave you what my aunt would call a flaming character, when we spoke of you just now."

Darcy looked amused, and smiled when she repeated the housekeeper's words. Daringly, she went on. "You are altogether a different person here in Derbyshire than when I first knew you."

"How did my character first impress you, Mrs. Darcy? What did you think of me when we first met?" he asked, looking down at her as they continued to walk together.

Why had she opened such a dangerous topic? The relaxed air at Pemberley was loosening her tongue. "When we were in Hertfordshire you were somewhat reserved and silent, sir; quite the opposite of how you are now. I hardly recognize you."

"And while in Kent? I hope my company improved upon you somewhat during that time."

Elizabeth recalled their brief walks in the park and one or two evenings in company at Rosings. "You spoke a little more, I suppose."

His hand pressed hers again. "I regret that you found my conversation less than adequate during our courtship. I hope it did not distress you."

Elizabeth gave him a startled look. "Our courtship, sir?"

"Yes, before I proposed." He said this in such a matter of fact tone that Elizabeth stopped walking to stare at him.

"Sir, my father's sudden passing may have removed certain events from my mind, but I must admit that I do not recall a courtship occurring between us when you made your offer to my uncle."

He gave a slight smile. "Of course I did not court you while you were in mourning; I am speaking of the time when you were visiting your friend. Do you not remember our walks together in the morning, and when I called on you at the parsonage?"

"There were only three walks, and your cousin accompanied you to the parsonage!"

"So you do recall. I regret that you had to wait so many weeks to receive my offer. I would have made it to you before you left your friend's house if other events had not intervened."

Elizabeth, amazed by his presumption, looked away. At length she said, uncomfortably, "I was not waiting for your proposal, sir."

"You were not?"

"No. An offer from you was the furthest thing from my mind, I assure you."

"Indeed." Darcy frowned slightly. "You had no idea of my interest in you at all?"

"None whatsoever. Charlotte--" she paused, embarrassed. "Charlotte told me that she suspected you of an interest in me, but I did not believe her."

He smiled, bemused. "Perhaps it is fortunate that I approached your uncle first instead of you, so that you were not startled into rejecting me by mistake. That would have been a sorry surprise for me."

She had a difficult time comprehending his lighthearted comment. Clearly, it had never occurred to Darcy that she might not respond favorably to him. Resentment swelled at his easy assurance. "Indeed, had you asked at a different time, I might have been tempted to give you a different answer," she said archly, hoping her husband would not examine her words too closely. "Look, I believe I see Georgiana and Mrs. Annesley returning through that grove of trees. We must move to intercept them before they reach the house."

Elizabeth's strategy worked; Darcy, apparently believing she spoke in jest, smiled at her in a rather distracted fashion, and together they made their way to Georgiana. The conversation with her husband was dropped, and the topic was not raised again that day.

CHAPTER ELEVEN

The pianoforte had been a grand success. Georgiana, delighted and overwhelmed, could not thank her brother enough, and once the instrument had been set up she would hardly step away from it. Even now, as Elizabeth prepared to retire, she could hear the sounds of a light, airy sonatina floating up from the music room. No doubt it was past time for her to think of bed, but on this evening Darcy would indulge his sister for a little while longer.

Elizabeth herself was sitting in front of her looking glass while her maid brushed her hair, thinking again about Georgiana's reaction to the news of Bingley's visit.

Elizabeth had always suspected that Darcy hoped for Georgiana to make a match with Mr. Bingley, and she further suspected that this desire had played a role in his helping to separate Bingley from Jane. But she had not anticipated such an open forwarding of the scheme on his part. The more she thought about it, the more certain she was that Georgiana understood exactly what her brother's goal was.

When she forced herself to be objective, she could admit to herself all the reasons why Darcy might want to promote such a union. A marriage between Bingley and Georgiana would be advantageous to both families. While Bingley could not afford completely to disregard fortune, Elizabeth did not believe him to be mercenary. Georgiana would gain a respectable, kind, and loyal husband; and one who (she thought wryly) could easily be guided by his new brother. Bingley, of course, would benefit from the increased connection to superior society, and Caroline Bingley might make a more advantageous match as a result. As Bingley's station in life was elevated through his connection to the Darcys, the Bingley family's position in society would benefit as well. No, there was no fault to find in the arrangement.

Georgiana's feelings about it, however, were ambiguous. Elizabeth did not yet know her well enough to judge if her reaction to her brother's news was due to embarrassment, awkward interest, shyness, or perhaps some other unnamed emotion.

A knock came from the door connecting to her husband's room, breaking into her thoughts; and Elizabeth motioned to her maid, who curtsied and left the room swiftly. In another moment Darcy stood in the doorway. He had not yet changed from his dinner clothes, and Elizabeth instinctively pulled her housecoat closer around her. Darcy said nothing at first, merely looking at Elizabeth with the steady gaze which she had come to realize did not indicate disapproval. Instead of moving into her room, however, he held out his hand to her. "Come."

"Sir?"

"Elizabeth, please come. There is something I wish to show you."

She rose and went to her husband, who took her hand and led her through his bedroom and through the door leading to the balcony off his suite, sweeping the door open as he did so. Elizabeth felt the summer air, warm and humid, hit her face as they stepped onto the balcony together. The sky was dark, but the light of a thousand stars shone around her and Darcy, giving just enough illumination for her to make out the railing of the balcony; there was no moon visible. All was quiet except for the muffled sound of the nearby stream. Nothing seemed out of the ordinary.

"Mr. Darcy, I fail to see why--"

"Elizabeth, you may address me as Fitzwilliam when there is nobody else present."

"Very well, but such familiarity does not explain what you have brought me here to see."

"Look up there." Darcy pointed his right arm towards the horizon.

Elizabeth strained her eyes, but saw nothing unusual. "I am afraid I do not see whatever it may be."

"Can you not see it, just above the horizon in that direction?"

"I think the tree branches might be in my way."

"Here. Move towards me." Darcy put a hand on her waist and guided her to stand in front of him, reaching around her with his other hand to point. "It is a comet, a star with a tail stretching out for miles behind it. Do you see it now?"

Elizabeth caught her breath in surprise and pleasure. "I believe I do. I have never seen such a thing before! How long has it been there?"

"Several weeks, at least. I heard it mentioned while we were in London, but being in the city, it was difficult to see then, with the height of the surrounding buildings."

"I can see the comet but not the moon," she said after a moment, searching the sky.

"Indeed, we are fortunate that the moon is obscured with clouds tonight. If the moon's light were visible, the comet would not be."

"How long will this marvelous thing be visible? Do comets last very long?"

"Not usually. Yet this one has been observed for some months so far, and astronomers believe it may go on being visible for quite some time. It was first seen in April, I am told."

"I wish my father could have seen this!" Elizabeth exclaimed without thinking. "How he would have marveled at it."

Darcy's hand had left her waist, but he still stood directly behind her, close enough that she could feel his warmth. "Some people, blessed with fanciful imaginations, might say that the comet is a sign from your father to you."

"A sign! Do they suppose it to be a message?"

"Perhaps. They might say that its appearance indicates that your father is watching over you now, guiding and protecting you."

"And what do you think, sir?" Elizabeth asked, her eyes still on the sky. "Do you put any faith in such charming fancies, or is this heavenly phenomenon nothing more than a celestial mixture of gas and dust?"

"I am a practical man. A comet is, of course, in a physical sense, exactly as you have described it; yet I would like to believe it is more than just that."

Elizabeth turned to look at him. "Whatever do you mean?"

Darcy looked down at her, his eyes nearly as dark as the night itself. "I believe we were all put here for a purpose, Elizabeth. We all have our appointed tasks which we must complete before our time on earth is through, and if our lives are cut off prematurely, who is to say whether our Maker does not grant us a little while longer to look down on those we love, and perhaps have a second chance to complete our assigned tasks?"

"That is a whimsical notion, sir."

"Whimsical it may be, but life thrives on such fancies and wishes; they nurture the soul and give it hope."

"I confess I did not expect to hear such a statement from you," Elizabeth said, her head still tilted at an angle to look up at him. It occurred to her that this was an odd conversation for a man to have with a woman he had married only for convenience and to fulfill the demands of society; a woman he found beneath him in every way. She waited for him to respond but he made no answer, and after a moment she turned back to gazing at the comet. The silence stretched out for several minutes.

"I have heard," Elizabeth finally said, "that the ancients used to believe in making wishes on stars as they fell to the earth, thinking that wishes made at such times would be granted. Never having observed a falling star in person, I have never had the opportunity to try it for myself."

"And what would you wish for, if you could?" Darcy's voice was deep and warm in her ear.

"Why would I need to wish for anything?" she answered lightly. "You and Georgiana are very kind, and my family is safe and happy. I want for nothing."

"There must be something," her husband protested. "Everyone has at least one thing that they desire, some wish that has not yet been fulfilled. I wish you would tell me what yours might be."

Once she had wished to marry for love, but that chance was now gone forever. "You are very gallant, Mr. Darcy. If you insist on knowing, then my desire would be to see a falling star for myself. But now, since you have discovered my wish, I must know yours. What would you ask for, if you could?"

"To know the hearts of the people closest to me." Darcy's voice was suddenly grave. "To understand their thoughts--to know their desires completely, and to bring them nothing but the greatest of happiness."

"You are speaking of Georgiana, of course," Elizabeth said, serious in her turn.

"Georgiana--" Darcy's voice suddenly seemed choked. "Yes, of course. My sister."

"I saw her reaction when you announced Mr. Bingley's visit. She seemed strangely agitated when you asked her if she would like to see him again. Has she always shown such discomfort at the prospect of guests?"

Darcy seemed to weigh his words before speaking. "Georgiana is uncomfortable around anyone who is not a member of the family."

"Even Mr. Bingley? As long as she has known him?"

"Though she has known Mr. Bingley through me for many years, lately her acquaintance with him has taken a different direction. It is difficult to say if her reticence is due to this fact, or if there are other circumstances influencing her at this time."

Elizabeth frowned. "I wish you would not speak so obliquely. If I am to be of assistance to Georgiana, it would help if I were to know everything that might be affecting her peace of mind."

"They are private matters which do not directly involve you. You need not concern yourself." Again, Elizabeth felt as if a door was being shut in her face. She bit her lip in disappointment.

"I think I would like to go in now. It feels like rain."

Darcy obligingly let her precede him back towards the balcony door, but as she began to move across the threshold, he reached out and held her back with a hand on her elbow. She turned to face him, and his other hand moved up to lightly caress her cheek, his eyes warm and intense. "You are very beautiful tonight, Elizabeth."

He had never done that before. Not once since their wedding night had he expressed any appreciation of her physical form, and their contact until now had always taken place completely within the confines of their chambers. Elizabeth closed her eyes as Darcy leaned down to kiss her gently, then opened them again when he pulled away and let his forehead rest against hers. "Stay in my bed tonight, Elizabeth."

As a dutiful wife she was willing to accommodate his request. It was not unusual; she had been summoned there before. "As you wish, Mr. Darcy," she replied, and moved inside his room. Darcy did not move from his spot as she walked obediently to the bed, pulled back the counterpane and climbed in; but she caught a glimpse of his face just as she put out the lamp. She could have sworn his expression was one of disappointment.

CHAPTER TWELVE

Something had changed overnight, something undefinable and yet unmistakable, a comprehension which Elizabeth could not put into words. She felt it in the terse commands Darcy gave to the servants as they arranged breakfast on the sideboard, in the guarded expression in his eyes as he looked at her down the length of the table, in the short, clipped replies he gave in response to her questions about his plans for the day. The silence between them lengthened uncomfortably while she looked down at the food on her plate and wondered what she had done now to provoke her mercurial husband.

Georgiana, too, seemed troubled by her brother's mood, glancing at him uneasily while she ate and leaving the table as soon as courtesy would allow. Elizabeth prepared to follow her, but she was stopped by her husband's voice.

"Elizabeth, I would like you to stay for a minute."

"As you wish." Elizabeth resumed her place in the seat from which she had just arisen. "How may I be of assistance, Mr. Darcy?"

Darcy looked at her with unconcealed irritation. "I have asked you before not to address me as Mr. Darcy, at least not when we are alone."

"I beg your pardon," she said hastily, concealing her own annoyance. When her husband behaved in such a distant, formal manner, how did he expect her to address him? "I will make more of an effort to remember that in the future. Is there something in particular which you wished to discuss with me?"

"Yes." Abruptly Darcy stood and walked to the picture window that overlooked the lawn with its majestic oaks and Spanish chestnuts. His back was ramrod straight, his hands clasped tightly behind his back as he said, "I have been thinking about our conversation yesterday, when we were walking in the garden. Do you remember it?"

"Of course," Elizabeth said, frowning as she tried to recall the details.

"You said that you had not been expecting my addresses at the time that I made an offer for you."

"That is true."

"Might I ask you how your uncle informed you of my proposal?"

Elizabeth could not imagine why her husband was interested in revisiting that particular topic, but she saw no harm in humoring his whim. "My uncle was very straightforward," she replied. "He said that you had requested an audience with him earlier that afternoon, and that you had asked him for the honor of my hand in marriage. He said that if I was agreeable, the wedding would be held right away."

"And what did he say to persuade you to accept my offer?"

"To persuade me? I am not sure what you mean."

"Did he mention the material advantages of marriage to me?"

"I was already aware of your fortune. Mr. Gardiner did not see fit to belabor the point."

"Did he tell you about the arrangements I had made for an allowance for your mother, the dowries for your sisters, and for the permanent lease of Longbourn?" Darcy's voice was terse, clipped.

"Yes, he did inform me of those things," Elizabeth answered, still wondering why her husband insisted on knowing these details. She had, after all, accepted his proposal; what more did he want to know?

"And what was your reaction to this remarkable news?"

"I was surprised, of course. As I mentioned, I had no idea of you regarding me as a possible marriage partner."

"I see." Darcy paused. "And did Mr. Gardiner mention anything else about my proposal?"

Elizabeth thought back to the fateful conversation with her uncle that day. Most of it, of course, she could not repeat to her husband. Certainly she would say nothing of her uncle's shocking view of Darcy's purposes for selecting her as his wife. "He said that it was a generous offer, one that would be advantageous to my whole family."

"And did he say nothing else?"

"Not that I can recall."

Darcy spun on one heel to look at her fully. "Were you forced to accept my offer?"

"No, of course not!" Elizabeth raised one eyebrow as she looked at her husband. "Surely you know by now that I would not take well to being forced into anything."

"You would never be forced, but you might perhaps be convinced against your will," Darcy suggested, one eyebrow rising questioningly.

"Not in this matter. Marrying you was my own decision," Elizabeth answered, raising her chin proudly.

"I see." Darcy turned back to the lawn. Another long pause ensued, broken when he finally asked, "Are you happy here at Pemberley?"

"Sir?"

"I have never noticed before how much distance one small, simple word can put between two people," Darcy said, turning back to face her. He sounded suddenly weary. "I am not "sir" to you, Elizabeth; please address me as Fitzwilliam from now on. I asked you, are you happy here at Pemberley?"

"I believe so. You and Georgiana are very kind, and the staff has been more than accommodating."

"Do you have everything you need? Is your pin money adequate?"

"I have barely spent my pin money." It was true; aside from sending small gifts to her family, she had had no need to purchase anything more than her husband had provided. "It is more than adequate."

"And is there nothing more that you desire? I had thought by now that you might want to have your own rooms, at least, re-done to your taste."

"Not at all. They are lovely just as they are. May I ask, sir--" she caught herself, biting back the forbidden word. "I beg your pardon. Might I ask to what these questions pertain?"

"It is nothing." Darcy's voice had become brusque and businesslike. "I try to see to the comfort of those under my care; that is all. I take my responsibilities seriously, even when they might be somewhat taxing to carry out."

"I can only hope that seeing to my comfort is not too taxing for your sensibilities, then."

One corner of Darcy's mouth pulled down in an expression she had never seen before. "Please let me know if there is anything else I can do for your comfort. Good day, Elizabeth."

The words and look together were plainly a dismissal. Darcy spun on his heel and was gone before she could say anything more.

CHAPTER THIRTEEN

Darcy's attitude towards her had completely changed, seemingly overnight. In the three days since their conversation in the breakfast room, he had been polite but cold, saying only what was necessary at meals and then leaving the table without further word. He had not sought her out in the late afternoon each day, as his habit had been up until now, and he had not knocked lightly on the door of her bedroom even once.

Perhaps, as her uncle had said, Darcy was finding consolation in the company of a mistress somewhere nearby. Yet she was beginning to realize that such behavior would not be in his character.

She began to feel regret that she had not asked her uncle more questions about Darcy at the time she had accepted his proposal; there were still so many parts of him which she did not understand. The more Elizabeth tried to tease out a pattern to her husband's moods, the more confused she became.

"Why bother to seek me out, only to push me away?" she asked herself. "Why ask for my opinion and good will on one hand, and then treat me like a common servant at other times? Aggravating, ill-natured man!"

Yet Darcy was not ill-natured, as she had believed him to be upon their first acquaintance. On the contrary, in the whole of their time at Pemberley, and even before then in town, she had to admit that he had shown a more even temperament than she had first believed. He had been abrupt with her, and some of his words had been insensitive to her feelings, but she could not fairly complain of receiving unkind treatment at his hands. The staff at Pemberley, too, did not dread his presence as she would have expected them to do, and many of them had expressed, by either word or action, their pleasure at being in his service. Nobody from the housekeeper to his own sister had ever said a critical word of him, not even in jest--and Elizabeth was well aware that no serious faults in the master of the house could be kept from the mistress of the house forever.

The new disquiet with her husband did not seem to extend to Georgiana. Towards his sister Darcy was just as he had always been-- solicitous, considerate, spending time with her. In the evenings he spoke freely with her or listened attentively as she played on the new pianoforte. With the staff, too, he seemed his usual courteous self. It was only in Elizabeth's company that he seemed to revert to the man she had first come to know in Hertfordshire.

She caught herself waiting to hear his hand on the latch of her bedroom door at night, watching for his tall form crossing the lawn, or listening for the sound of his voice calling her name as she and Georgiana walked outside. Against her will she had begun to be dependent on him in some strange, inexplicable way which she could not, or did not wish, to examine too closely.

∞

Elizabeth was delighted, the next day, to receive three letters from home. Jane always wrote faithfully, but she rarely heard from her mother and sisters, busy as they were in their normal lives. Elizabeth's absence had been barely noticed except as her marriage had given them more monetary advantages. Still, to receive correspondence from her mother and Kitty as well as Jane was a real pleasure. As much as she was coming to enjoy Pemberley and her new life here, she still longed for contact with her family. They might be embarrassing, vulgar, or unseemly; but still they were familiar and welcome, a part of her that was otherwise gone forever.

She retreated to the solarium with all three letters and decided to set aside Jane's for last as being the one most likely to bring her pleasure. Instead, she opened her mother's letter. The first part of it contained a short account of the small dinner parties they had recently attended, as well as gossip of a light, inconsequential nature. The final paragraphs, however, caught her attention.

How well your new name still sounds--Mrs. Darcy! You may be sure that I say it as often as I can to anyone who calls at Longbourn. We are become quite the envy of all!

I was delighted to receive your recent letter with the little bit of money you were able to include under the seal. I am sure you are very generous, but has not Mr. Darcy allowed you a great deal more pin money than that? You must write again soon, and be sure to include more this time than last.

We heard from Lady Lucas yesterday that Mr. Bingley is giving up

Netherfield. He is such an odious young man! To come to Meryton and make my daughter fall in love, and then leave her just when we thought it was a settled thing! But we will not miss him here at Longbourn at all, since you can put your sisters into the path of many other rich men.

Your aunt Phillips is asking me how many carriages you have and where you go in them. Do you drive around Pemberley and Lambton in a chaise and four, or do you use a barouche for every day? How many families do you dine with? You must write and tell me all about them, so that I may have something to speak of with Lady Lucas when she calls again. Some people, you know, think of nothing but money and consequence when they are visiting their friends.

I am your loving mother
Mrs. Fanny Bennet

Kitty's letter, though much shorter, was of a piece with her mother's.

Dear Lizzy,

Mama says that I am to write to you immediately. Will you send me money to buy a hat that I saw yesterday at Mr. Brown's millinery? It is ten shillings, which Jane says would be an abominable price to pay, but Mama says you can afford to get it for me as well as anyone. Maybe you should ask Mr. Darcy to open an account for me at the milliners. It would be much more convenient than having to settle accounts every quarter. Otherwise, we are all well here. Lydia is going to stay with her friend Mrs. Forster at Brighton next week and we will see no more of her this summer. Mama is sad that she is going but I am not, for she insists on going before me, even though I am older.

Kitty

Neither of the first two letters had disappointed Elizabeth in their absurdities. They were just what she had expected—vain, frivolous, lacking any appreciation for how narrowly they had escaped an irreversible slide into poverty, and certainly not expressing any gratitude for their changed circumstances. As she opened the final letter she could not help hoping her oldest sister would redeem her decision to sacrifice herself for her family, by showing that there was one member, at least, who deserved such consideration.

My dear sister,

I trust that this letter finds you well, and that Pemberley continues to be everything delightful.

Mama may have mentioned that Lydia has been invited by her friend Harriet Forster to visit her in Brighton soon. In fact, by the time you receive this letter she may be already gone. It is a scheme that gives me some uneasiness, since the regiment which was stationed here in Meryton is there now. Since the shock of our father's death and then your marriage, Mama has not been as careful with my sisters as she used to be. Now to allow our youngest sister an entire six-week away from home, in the presence of so many officers--I cannot criticize our mother, of course, but I am not entirely certain that Papa would approve of this plan if he were still with us. However, Mrs. Forster seems a good-hearted, sensible soul, and I am sure that I am worrying needlessly.

Mama and Kitty will probably ask you to send more money. I beg you not to do so, dearest Lizzy. I will be writing to our uncle Gardiner directly after this letter to ask for his assistance in curbing my mother's needless expenditures. Until then, anything you send would be merely good money thrown after bad.

We have received news about Netherfield. In fact, I dare say that you might tell us the news, since you may well have heard it through your husband already. Maria Lucas heard from her maid (who is acquainted with the gardener at Netherfield) that Mr. Bingley is giving up the lease. This past week saw the removal of all his furniture and other belongings and the release of most of the servants. The house will be let again as soon as another family can be found, which may not be for some time. I cannot pretend to be surprised by this news. It was you who always believed more firmly in the strength of Mr. Bingley's attachment to me than I did myself, and therefore, I am not affected by this news in any way whatsoever, except for the disappointment that it has created for our mother.

Please do write again soon. Your letters are my most constant companion and truest comfort.

I remain your loving sister,
Jane Bennet

Elizabeth ran her fingers over Jane's signature at the bottom of the page. A few days earlier this page had been in Jane's hands; her eyes had read the same lines Elizabeth was now perusing. It was the closest she could come to her beloved sister, and a wave of homesickness washed over her, an almost tangible longing for the family she had left behind. A lump rose in her throat.

Behind her came the sound of a footstep. Turning, she saw Georgiana turning hastily away and she wiped her eyes as she called out, "Georgiana, were you looking for me?"

"No!" Georgiana answered, looking embarrassed. She flushed and looked down at the ground, refusing to meet Elizabeth's eyes. "That is, I had thought to speak with you if possible, but I see that you are occupied. I do not wish to disturb you."

"You are not disturbing me. I was just reading a few letters from home, and I can do that at any time. Please, come and sit with me." Georgiana sat down hesitantly on the bench next to her and fixed her attention on the ground, while Elizabeth waited patiently. She had the feeling Georgiana was working up the courage to speak.

"It is a lovely day to sit outside, is it not?" Elizabeth finally said encouragingly, trying to start the conversation. Georgiana agreed that it was, but then looked down again at the ground, seemingly hesitant to say anything more.

"I have been here only a short time, and yet the woods and grounds of Pemberley feel like familiar acquaintances already," Elizabeth persisted. "For someone like you, who has been here their whole life, they must be considered practically members of the family."

Georgiana smiled a little at the fancy, and owned that she was very fond of them as well; but then she said nothing more. After another minute of silence Elizabeth, sighing, decided to take a more direct approach.

"Georgiana, if there is anything on your mind, you may feel free to speak of it without fear of how I may react. I am used to listening to a sister's confidences, and I have often observed that a trouble shared is a trouble halved. Would you care to test the theory?"

Georgiana looked up at her gratefully. "I have been trying to bring myself to speak to you for the past several days. I wonder if I might ask a favor of you."

"Of course you may."

"I was wondering," Georgiana began, and then hesitated, "if it is not too much trouble, if you might speak to Fitzwilliam on my behalf."

"Whatever for?" Elizabeth asked, her curiosity piqued.

Georgiana took a deep breath. "I do not want to marry Mr. Bingley."

"Oh!" Whatever Elizabeth had been expecting, it was not this. She stared at her sister.

Georgiana's words came in a sudden rush of relief, as if she had been holding them back for a long time. "I know it may seem strange to Fitzwilliam, and perhaps to you, that I would not want to marry him; but Mr. Bingley has been like a brother to me. I do not think I could ever see him as a potential suitor, no matter how eligible and amiable he may be. And I don't think he sees me that way either!"

Elizabeth, for once, was at a loss for words. When she could speak again she asked, "What makes you so sure that your brother wants you to marry Mr. Bingley?"

"Has he not spoken of it to you?" Georgiana asked, surprised. When Elizabeth shook her head, she looked relieved. She continued, her voice becoming more strong and certain. "Fitzwilliam has been urging me towards Mr. Bingley ever since last summer, when we first started talking about me coming out. He has done everything in his power to throw us into each other's company, having Mr. Bingley and his sister stay here as often as possible and urging me to write to Caroline."

Elizabeth could make no answer, listening attentively.

"You heard how Fitzwilliam spoke to me about Mr. Bingley coming to Derbyshire. He made a point of asking me if I would like it if he took a home in this area. Fitzwilliam intends for me to come out next season, go through a courtship, and then marry his friend and settle down somewhere nearby. It is all settled in his mind as the best way to see to my future, but it is not what I want to do!"

It was the first time Elizabeth had heard such a passionate declaration from her sister. She finally found her voice. "Surely your brother would not push you into an unwanted marriage. He loves you."

"He still thinks of me as a child, needing his guidance and approval. He probably thinks I will come to have feelings for Mr. Bingley if I spend more time with him. But I will not!"

There was a strange energy in the way Georgiana had said that last phrase. "I have always found Mr. Bingley to be a pleasant sort of gentleman. He was a great favorite in Meryton."

"Yes, he is very pleasant, but he has never shown any romantic interest in me. I enjoy his company, but I have also seen him in love with other women. His attentions never last for long. Miss Bingley says that he fell in love again last winter with someone who was completely unsuitable, but once he realized that the lady did not care for him he gave her up almost at once."

Elizabeth almost stared at her, but Georgiana did not notice.

"And even after that he never showed the slightest interest in me. We are too close for him to think of me in that way. Besides," she added with an unusual show of distaste, "I do not think Caroline and I would suit as sisters."

Elizabeth noticed the unexpected editorial, but she was still too surprised to react to it. "Georgiana, why do you not say all this to your brother yourself? Your reasoning is sound, and you have clearly thought about this a great deal. I'm sure he would listen to you."

"I have tried, but I do not have your confidence, Elizabeth. It is hard for me to think of disappointing Fitzwilliam when he has done so much for me. But you are always able to speak your mind with him. And he likes it! I can tell by the way he looks at you when you are teasing him."

"He might not like it as much as you think," Elizabeth answered shrewdly, remembering the stiff courtesy of the last few days. "And I do not know if he would care for me interfering in his plans."

"But he adores you! He will listen to anything you say."

The poor, romantic child. Her notions of love and marriage were still naïve; clearly she had no idea of the real state of their marriage. "I still think it would be better if your brother were to hear all of this from you," she persisted.

After a moment, Georgiana responded softly, "Fitzwilliam has good reason to question my judgment." She looked appealingly at Elizabeth. "I would rather not say why. Please do not press me for an explanation."

"Of course not, if it is not something you wish to share," Elizabeth answered automatically, though she would sorely have liked to ask more. Curiosity burned within her. There was more on Georgiana's mind than Mr. Bingley, but she realized that Georgiana had said all she was willing to say at this time. There would be no more information forthcoming, at least for now. She patted Georgiana's arm reassuringly.

"If you want me to, I will speak to your brother as soon as opportunity presents. I will make your case as best I can, but you must not think he will be swayed by anything I say." Especially these last few days, she thought but did not say. "He loves you, and he can be counted on to do what he thinks is in your best interest."

"Thank you, Elizabeth." Georgiana clutched her arm gratefully.

"Think nothing of it. This is what sisters are for."

CHAPTER FOURTEEN

Darcy was both surprised and suspicious when Elizabeth knocked on his bedroom door that evening. The last three days he had berated himself endlessly for falling prey to the trap he had always struggled to avoid: the victim of a fortune hunter.

He would have sworn by every sacred oath he knew, before he was married, that Elizabeth Bennet was not like any other woman in his set. Other women fought for his attention, threw themselves in his way, and did their best to attract his notice, but not Elizabeth. She had attracted his interest precisely because she seemed not to care for it. Every step he took towards her she had turned aside, subtly making him aware that his attentions meant nothing to her. She provoked him, teased him and argued with him, always with that intriguing smile; and with every rebuff, his fascination with her grew. Against his better judgment he was in danger of making her an offer before he left Hertfordshire, and he knew it. Retreating to the safe distance of London was as much a reprieve for him as it had been for Bingley, both of them resisting the charms of women they knew were not suitable for marriage.

Then fate, or some perverse mischance, had thrown him and Elizabeth together again in Kent, and he was lost almost before he knew it. Elizabeth's eyes bewitched him; her smile enslaved him. They had shared one or two significant conversations, laden with hidden meanings, which he took to mean that she was waiting for him to declare himself. If Elizabeth had not been called away to her dying father so suddenly, he would have made her an offer before she returned home.

Now here he was, bound in marriage to a woman who did not return his regard, and he had only himself to blame. She had all but admitted that she had married him for material considerations, although those considerations seemed to be more for her family than for her personally. Darcy was aware that she spent almost nothing on her own needs, preferring to send gifts and small sums of money to her spendthrift mother and sisters.

The papers on the small desk in front of him, virtually untouched for some time now, sat silently mocking him. He had accomplished little work due to his preoccupation with his wife. There were tenant accounts to balance, the harvest to organize, and plans to complete for the purchase of needed equipment. Lady Catherine's continued bitter complaints against his marriage, received in a letter from Rosings, lay unanswered in the middle of it all. All of it would have to be addressed, and the sooner the better--but he could not focus on any of it.

Well, he thought bitterly, if he had married a mercenary, at least she was an unselfish mercenary. She had also proven every bit as beneficial to Georgiana as he had hoped. Still, the thought of what might have been rankled sorely against the reality of what he now had: a marriage of duty alone.

∞

Elizabeth knocked cautiously on her husband's bedroom door that evening, wondering if he would be able to hear her rapping over the noise from outside. A heavy downpour, the result of another day of humid warmth, had begun to assault the house. But Darcy heard her well enough. After a moment he responded by opening the door and looking at her warily. "Elizabeth? What brings you here?"

Never had she received such a stern response from her husband, but she responded as evenly as possible, reminding herself not to use the formal titles he objected to so much. "I need to speak to you, please, if I may."

"On what subject?" Darcy's face betrayed no warmth.

"It is about your sister. May I come in?"

Darcy hesitated and then stood aside reluctantly, his expression grim. Taking the gesture as an invitation, Elizabeth entered the room and waited until Darcy had closed the door behind her before beginning her piece. "If I may, I would like to speak to you about Georgiana--and Mr. Bingley."

"Mr. Bingley?" Darcy raised a questioning eyebrow.

Elizabeth took a deep breath. "Georgiana has asked me to speak to you on her behalf. She believes that you are encouraging a match between her and your friend."

Darcy's eyes narrowed as he looked at her.

"I see. What of it?"

He was not making this easy for her. "Is she correct in her belief?"

Darcy frowned and made no answer. With deliberate step he moved across the room to where a bottle of brandy sat on his small writing table.

Elizabeth watched as he carefully poured himself a glass and sat down behind the desk, the dark mahogany gleaming in the candlelight. He sipped from the small glass and set it down before looking at her again. "My hopes for my sister's future are my own. I see no reason to confide them to you."

His manner chilled the air, but she was determined to see this through for Georgiana's sake. She raised her chin and spoke boldly. "After speaking with Georgiana this afternoon, I have reason to believe that such a match would not be congenial to her."

Darcy's frown deepened into a scowl. "How did you come to discuss such a thing with my sister?"

"She told me that she does not have the feelings for Mr. Bingley that she should have in order to consider him as a marriage partner."

"Indeed." Darcy looked at her without blinking.

"And she does not think he will ever have those feelings for her, either."

"I see." Darcy paused, still staring at her with that unsettling gaze. "And why hasn't Georgiana ever mentioned this to me herself?" His tone was heavy, laden with suspicion.

"She would like to, but she fears offending you. She asked me to speak to you on her behalf." The irony of having to speak to Darcy on Georgiana's behalf about Bingley, of all people, was not lost on her. Did Darcy sense it as well? Elizabeth stood unmoving, her chin raised, waiting for his response.

"I see," Darcy said again. Despite his words, Elizabeth felt that he did not see, but she could only wait for his response. Darcy took up his glass and absently swirled the remaining brandy in it while Elizabeth observed in bewilderment. At length he stood and approached her, this time coming close enough to look her directly in the eye when he spoke again.

"Elizabeth, why did you marry me?" As he spoke, a loud clap of thunder outside announced the arrival of the storm that had been threatening all day.

Elizabeth's astonishment knew no bounds. "I beg your pardon--what did you just ask?"

"Do not pretend confusion, madam." His voice was cool, detached. "I have asked an honest question and I am now requesting the favor of an honest answer. Why did you marry me?"

"Mr. Darcy, I fail to see what this question has to do with your sister."

"It has everything to do with her. It is apparent to me now that you came to Pemberley to further your own family's interests by working through me. You wish for Bingley to marry your own sister!" Darcy's tone was accusatory.

Elizabeth gasped. She opened her mouth to protest, but the confusion of thoughts now racing together in her mind robbed her of the ability to speak.

"Bingley has not shown the slightest bit of interest in returning to Hertfordshire in order to court Miss Bennet again, but you hope that if you can turn Georgiana away from him, he will pursue your sister once more!"

"I have done no such thing!" Elizabeth cried, finally angry enough to speak. "Georgiana asked me to speak to you for her, and so I have! Nothing else crossed my mind."

Darcy crossed his arms. "But you do not deny that you wished for Jane to marry Bingley."

"I do not deny it! But I would never try to separate two people who loved each other in order to advance my own family!"

Darcy flinched. "Bingley and your sister--Miss Bennet--would not have made a happy marriage. Separating them was an act of kindness on my part, and I am glad that I was successful in my efforts."

Elizabeth looked at him with a kind of cold triumph. "So you admit what you did."

"Why shouldn't I? Towards him I have been kinder than to myself."

Elizabeth wondered what he meant by that. "You think it kindness to separate two people who care for each other? Your only motive was to unite Bingley with your sister!"

A tinge of pink appeared on Darcy's cheeks. "I do not deny that Bingley cared for your sister, but you cannot say that she had any particular regard for him. Whatever feelings she may have had went no deeper than his purse, I am sure. Better to separate them now, while he can still be easily untangled, than see them later within the misery of a loveless marriage!"

Elizabeth took a deep breath, trying to maintain control. "You mistake the situation entirely. Jane has never been mercenary. She had real feelings for Mr. Bingley; her spirits have never been the same since he left."

"I am sure your mother was just as affected, at the loss of such a suitor," Darcy rejoined, his voice heavy with irony.

Elizabeth drew herself up to her full height. To quarrel with her husband in such a way served no one's interests, and for Georgiana's sake, it would be best to withdraw before saying something she would regret even more. "I am sorry that you are suspicious of my motives; but regardless of what you think of me, I ask you to think of Georgiana. She is not happy at the thought of being pushed towards Mr. Bingley; and you might try, with all your powers of discernment, to determine the reason why! That is the only reason I sought your attention tonight. I will retire now so as not to afflict you with my presence any longer."

She turned and left the room much more quickly than she had entered it, barely refraining from slamming the door behind her. There she stood for a moment, covering her mouth with her hands, willing herself not to cry out against the unjust accusation Darcy had leveled against her. She would not give him the satisfaction of seeing how badly his words had hurt.

It was not to be. Elizabeth was standing transfixed in the middle of the floor, hearing the rain pound against her windows, when Darcy followed her into her bedroom. She barely had time to turn around, let alone protest his intrusion, before he stood directly in front of her again.

"I do not appreciate my wife leaving my presence without as much as a by-your-leave."

Furiously Elizabeth stood facing him. She would not dignify his words with a response. Darcy continued.

"Georgiana is painfully shy, as you know, and Bingley is affable to a fault. He is the least likely man I know of to try to take advantage of her more retiring nature. Besides this, there are advantages of fortune and connections that would make it a most desirable match for both of them. I will not push them into an understanding, but I hope that with time and familiarity, events will take their proper course."

"Oh, they will take their course, so long as it is the course you have chosen for them!" Elizabeth replied spiritedly. She regretted the words as soon as they left her mouth, but it was as though a fount had opened, and she could no more stop what she said now than she could hold back the rising tide. "Do you ever trust your friends to direct their own affairs? I doubt that Mr. Bingley would desire or welcome your interference in his life, if he knew of it!"

Darcy blanched, taking a step toward her. "I have acted only with his best interests in mind!"

"He might not thank you, if you were to tell him what you were doing. And Georgiana certainly does not agree with your present course of action."

Darcy moved away from her until he stood on the other side of the room; then turned to face her, his fists clenched tightly.

"I asked you once before, and I shall ask again now. This time I would be pleased to receive an honest answer. Why did you marry me, Elizabeth?"

Elizabeth looked back without wavering. "If you insist on knowing, my uncle told me that I should accept you in order to help my family."

"So you admit it! You married me for my wealth and connections!" Darcy's disgust was almost palpable.

"I have no wish to deny it! And I am not ashamed of the choice that I made," she answered, looking at her husband with every bit of dignity she could muster. "You made an offer that would preserve my family in their home and provide for my future in a way I could never hope to do otherwise."

"But you had no thoughts or feelings for me as a man? I cannot believe that."

"How could I have feelings for you, when you were the means of unhappiness for my most beloved sister? But I have other reasons; you know I must."

Darcy leaned against the wall, his arms folded, with an air of cynical disbelief. "I would appreciate it if you would enlighten me, madam, on issues of which I am so woefully ignorant."

Elizabeth saw that he meant to be indifferent, and her restraint began to loosen. "Your character was fixed in my mind when I heard the recital of the wrongs you committed, the extreme cruelty you carried out, against Mr. Wickham. You cannot deny ignorance there!"

Darcy changed color immediately. He stood up straight again, away from the wall. "My own wife accuses me of cruelty to Wickham? You take an overly eager interest in his concerns, madam!"

"I know how abominably you used him! How casually you cast off the friend of your youth, how you deprived him of the living destined for him in your own father's will, and how you treat the mention of his hardships with disdain! How do you defend your actions there?"

"His hardships!" Darcy scoffed, taking quick, angry steps across the room. "I suppose he never told you how I paid him for the living at his request, and how he came back to me later and demanded the same living again! No," he continued, turning to look at her, "I see by your face that he did not. But do not blame yourself, madam, for believing his lies. You are not the first woman he has deceived." Darcy's voice was as bitter as she had ever heard. "I would have told you the truth of his tales before, if you had ever asked."

"You have never allowed me to do so!" Elizabeth finally allowed the anger, hurt and confusion from the beginning of her marriage to now to find full expression in her words. "From the first day of our acquaintance until now, you have treated me as an indifferent, sometimes an unwelcome, association! You disdain my family and despise my condition in life as inferior to your own!"

"I deny that!"

"The very first time we ever met, you said I was not handsome enough to tempt you!"

Darcy stood in stunned silence as he looked at her.

"And you yourself told me that you could scarcely believe you made me an offer, considering how low my connections are compared to yours!"

"Is your uncle not in trade? And was your condition in life not decidedly inferior to mine, before we married?"

Elizabeth noted the comments and although she did her best to ignore them, they were not likely to make her any more reconciled to her husband. "Even before then, when I first knew you in Hertfordshire, you impressed me as the most arrogant man of my acquaintance. You despised everyone as beneath you in wealth and importance, and insulted not just me but nearly half the neighborhood."

Darcy stood looking at her with an expression she had never seen before. She continued, "Dpite my best efforts to be a loyal, congenial wife, you have used me without any consideration for my feelings. My uncle warned me that you would see me as your inferior, and he was right. You order me about like a common servant, dictate the terms of my dress, and expect me to make no objection when you make plans or break them on a whim. I am not allowed have my family at Pemberley, I am not permitted to see my aunt and uncle, and you expect me to support your sister more than I am allowed to support my own! Your every manner is one of condescension, arrogance, and a willful indifference to the feelings of others! Your actions have not been those of a gentleman."

Darcy took in a sharp breath. "You cannot mean that."

"I mean all of that and more besides. I have not enough language at my command to express the depth of my resentment towards you. There is no man in the world I would ever have been less likely to want as a husband." She regretted that last statement almost at once, but it was too late to take it back now.

"That is enough, madam! I have heard enough to convince me of what your feelings have been all along, and I can only be ashamed now of what my own have been. I will bid you a good night." With an expression of utmost fury he took the several steps that led to the communicating door to his room.

He had just laid his hand on the doorknob when Elizabeth dared to ask him, from her station across the room, "Mr. Darcy--why did you marry me?"

Darcy turned back to look at her one last time, his eyes as black as night. "It matters not, madam, now that I know your true sentiments. You need not fear that I will ever impose my presence upon you again." He closed the door behind him just as another roll of thunder broke out, and he was gone before Elizabeth could say another word.

CHAPTER FIFTEEN

From sheer shock Elizabeth fairly collapsed into the nearest chair and cried. Her emotions slammed over her in waves; she nearly shook under their assault. She clasped her hands together in her lap and bit her lip until it hurt, determined not to allow the sounds of her weeping be audible over the storm to the occupant of the adjoining room. Not for anything would she give her husband the satisfaction of knowing how much his words had hurt. After many minutes, knowing that she was not equal to her maid Cora's inquiring gaze, she rang for her and then stepped behind her dressing screen. When Cora entered, she informed her that she was not feeling well and did not desire any assistance that night.

"As you wish, madam. Shall I prepare a bath, at least?"

"No, I thank you. You are at liberty until tomorrow, unless I should call for you."

Cora made a polite exit, her voice betraying no curiosity. Elizabeth blew out her lamp and crawled into her bed but could not bring herself to lie down. Instead, she sat in the middle with her arms wrapped around her legs, her head resting on her knees while she listened to the storm rage on outside, unabated; and tried to calm her raging emotions.

She should never have spoken to her husband the way she just had. Why had she allowed her anger such free rein? Darcy wanted a compliant, biddable wife, and he had now discovered in a most unmistakable way what manner of woman he had really married. The look of impassioned outrage in his eyes just before he had turned and left the room haunted her. Although she had sensed that Darcy's attitude towards her had recently hardened, she had not expected the depth of the anger and resentment he had shown.

Darcy, too, was restless. From his bedroom next door she heard the sound of his footsteps moving rapidly back and forth as if the walker were agitated and uneasy; they slowed and stopped for a minute or two before beginning their frantic pace again. His lamp was still lit; the glow of it came in under their shared door, and occasionally she could see from the shadows cast that Darcy was standing, unmoving, outside her room. Was he placing his hand on the knob, preparing to enter her room again? Would he return to continue their argument, despite his parting words?

She prayed not.

Every recollection of their conversation stirred a deep emotion. She would never forget the casual way Darcy had disparaged her family when he called them disdainful, and the easy way in which he referred to her previous condition in life. It was true that her family was not as wealthy as his, but she was still a gentleman's daughter, still her husband's equal in all essentials. If he looked down on her for having relatives in trade, how did he justify wanting his own sister to marry Bingley?

Thinking of Jane made her break out in a fresh bout of weeping. What an arrogant, impossible man, to think that Jane had only been receptive to Bingley because of his money! Everything Elizabeth had suspected was true. Darcy had used his influence with Bingley to separate him from Jane; and he not only admitted it but was undeniably proud of the fact! Darcy and Bingley's sisters had acted together to orchestrate the future of those closest to them, and they had done so with callous disregard for the feelings and desires of others. Given the same circumstances, they would be only too happy to do the same thing again.

She had failed Georgiana. Darcy would never forgive her, nor would he listen to her words about his sister now.

What had Darcy said about Wickham and the circumstances of his living? It was difficult to recall the exact words, which had flown back and forth rapidly in the heat of the moment. Apparently there was more to the story of ill usage and mistreatment than what she had originally thought. She ought not to have said anything about it to her husband until she knew more of the facts.

Worst of all was Darcy's accusation that she had married him for his wealth, for it had the sting of truth to it. She could not deny that she had married him for material considerations. But although his statement was the truth, it was not the whole truth. She had married him in order to protect her family, only after her dream of marrying for love had proven fruitless and when no other option presented itself. Was it really so shameful to marry for protection, if that was the only choice possible? Was it reprehensible to use the only means at one's disposal in order to preserve a dearly loved family? Many marriages were based on less. The bargain was not one-sided; she had done her best to live up to Darcy's every expectation of her.

The final expression on Darcy's face came back to her yet again, the look he gave her when he said that his own reasons for marrying no longer mattered in light of her feelings for him, now that he understood them. What had he meant by that?

Darcy's footsteps on the other side of the wall paused for a moment, and she thought she heard a muffled exclamation. Perhaps he had struck his foot against the leg of his bed or chair, for she heard the sound of something moving as it squeaked on the floor; and the flow of light underneath the door was not broken again. She watched that light as long as she could, hoping and praying that the door would stay shut and that she would not have to face her husband again this evening. This time her prayer was answered; even as she struggled against tears her fatigue overwhelmed her, and she drifted into an uneasy sleep.

CHAPTER SIXTEEN

In the morning Elizabeth woke with a start, surprised to find how much daylight was already in the room. All was still; the storm had passed by overnight. She lay unmoving for a moment, trying to hear something of her husband in the next room, but all was silent. Either Darcy still slept or else he had already risen and gone for the day.

Quietly she rose and dressed without waiting for Cora, then stole down the back stairs and out of the kitchen door. Her head ached from the lack of sleep and the extreme disturbance of the night before. She was not ready to face either her husband or Georgiana over the breakfast table and make polite conversation, not with her emotions still so raw to the touch. Sooner or later she would have to face them both, but she wanted her first conversation with Darcy after their quarrel to be held in private, away from curious eyes.

She struck out on a familiar path, one of her favorites, which led beside the stream for some distance before it rose slightly and doubled back towards the house. She was pleased to note that the storm from the night before had not caused as much damage as might have been feared. The only real evidence left was the swollen water in the stream, which would subside quickly now that the rain had ceased. The accustomed circuit this path took would not return her to the house for at least an hour. Perhaps by the time she returned she would have some idea of what to say to her husband when she saw him again.

She was certain of only one fact: she and Darcy could not go on as they had until now. All pretense of polite accommodation was stripped away, and what was left between them could only be the barest of civility. She must find a way to make amends for her rash words of the night before.

The countryside had changed during her eight weeks in Derbyshire. When she arrived it had been the middle of May, with a damp spring beginning to yield to summer warmth. It was now the height of the warmest part of the year, with green vegetation running riot in all the fields and occasionally intruding into the path where she now walked. Cowslips had given way quickly to purple orchids, to be supplanted in their turn by bluebells on the mossy surfaces of stumps and fallen trees.

In the shade of the thick woods, the heat of the day could not yet be felt; but Elizabeth knew that by early afternoon the warm, humid air would drive humans and beasts alike to the cooler paths next to the water. In the repetitive calm sounds of the moving stream, even the troubles from the evening before seemed to shrink into something less unsettling, until she saw Darcy.

He was standing impatiently on the path just where it took a turn around the fence that separated field from forest, looking straight at her when she came around the bend. He must have had an idea of the path she had taken and been waiting for her to return. It was impossible to avoid him or to pretend she had not seen him. She was nearly on him by the time she realized he was there, and she stopped suddenly in the path when their eyes met. She opened her mouth to speak but he advanced towards her swiftly, his lip curled in disdain.

"I have been waiting for some time to see you," he announced in a haughty tone, and without any attempt at a greeting. "Will you do me the honor of reading this letter?" Before she could reply he offered her a thick brown envelope, which she instinctively accepted. He bowed, then turned and walked quickly back up the path to the house.

All consideration for her aching head disappeared. Without stopping to think, she gazed at the letter in her hands, anxious to see what it contained. It was a thick, heavy letter, with her name written on the outside in Darcy's strong, even script. When she opened the envelope no fewer than seven close-written pages emerged, and the envelope itself was likewise full. She began reading at once.

To my wife, Elizabeth Darcy,

Two charges of a very different nature you laid at my feet not many hours ago. The first was that I separated Bingley from your sister for the sole purpose of uniting him with my own sister, and the second charge, much more serious, was that I willfully and wantonly cast off my father's favorite, George Wickham, in ways which have materially, and perhaps permanently, ruined his prospects. My purpose in writing this letter is to defend myself against both charges as well as I can.

You do not wish to read this, I am sure. I know now beyond a shadow of a doubt your true opinion of me, and although I am afraid that your lack of regard is set in stone, I request and demand as your husband that you read this letter in its entirety. I hope that after you have read it you will at least acquit me of willful indifference to the feelings of others, if not of the arrogance and condescension which you so eagerly pointed out in my character when we spoke together.

The first charge against me was in regards to the abruptly ended relationship between your sister Jane and my friend, my companion and trusted confidante, Charles Bingley; and your belief that it was my intervention that prevented their relationship from reaching its natural conclusion in an engagement. To dispel this belief I shall endeavor to tell you the events of last winter from my perspective, and to explain the logic and reasoning behind the actions I took.

Bingley is five years younger than I, the only son of a prosperous businessman from Scarborough. I was in my last year at Cambridge when we first became acquainted at my club in town; and since then we have been fast, though unlikely, friends.

I have often seen my friend in love before. His is a temperament led often by the whim of the moment, as easily blown in a new direction as a flame in a breeze. Though his attentions to any lady have always been sincere, they have never been of any duration. So when he began to profess his ardent admiration of your sister to me last autumn I thought nothing of it, believing that this infatuation would pass as quickly as many others before. It was not until the night of the ball at Netherfield that I felt any real concern for him, after discerning from Sir William's remarks that an engagement between Bingley and your sister was considered to be a certain thing by the entire neighborhood.

At that time I began to observe your sister more closely, to try to determine if her affection was any more lasting than his. I do not think I deceive myself when I say that I had no reason to believe that it was. Your sister's expression when she was with my friend was open and engaging, but I noticed no particular signs of regard on her part. She spoke with him, she smiled at him, she clearly welcomed his attentions--but she welcomed others in the same way, and with the same marvelous serenity that is, in my mind, her most distinguishing characteristic. In short, there was nothing to make me think her heart was in any danger of being touched. I could not but be alarmed by what I deemed to be a most unfortunate mistaken intention, and to desire to help my friend. I did not want him to be hurt.

You must already surmise what happened next. When Bingley returned to town, expecting to return to Netherfield quickly, his sisters and I quickly discovered that we were of the same mind in this matter. Working together, we spoke to him at length, discovering that he did, indeed, plan to make your sister an offer as soon as he returned to Meryton. His sisters and I did everything in our power to persuade him of the evils of such a choice. We spoke to him earnestly of your family's lack of fortune, your inferior connections and the decided lack of propriety of your mother, your sisters and even--though I hesitate to speak ill of the dead--your father. None of it carried any weight with him, however, until we convinced him that your sister had no particular affection for him.

Bingley is modest to a fault. He believed that your sister returned his regard with a sincere, if not equal, devotion; but upon our assurances that he was mistaken he became despondent, and after that it took no effort at all to convince him to stay in town. The other considerations that I have listed weighed on him, but it was our conviction of the lack of affection in the case which had the strongest effect. He did not know then, and still does not know, of your sister's presence in town in January; as we thought it best not to inform him, lest he succumb to her influence once more.

This was my role in separating Bingley from your sister, and I hope that you can now acknowledge that my actions were carried out with only his best interests in mind. If I have been the means of wounding your sister I apologize, but what is done cannot be well undone. I cannot honestly say that I have any regrets.

You may wonder how I could make so many objections to Bingley marrying your sister and yet have no scruples about making you an offer a scant three months later, ignoring that same lack of fortune and the deplorable connections which were the basis of my concerns for him. I have no answer except to reiterate, as I said last night, that towards Bingley I have been kinder than towards myself.

The idea of Bingley eventually marrying Georgiana did, in fact, cross my mind at the time I spoke to him of your sister's disinterest; but only as a possible source of consolation to him at some point in the uncertain future. I would never allow my own wishes to overrule a prospect for true domestic happiness if I thought my friend had a reasonable chance for it from another quarter. My actions may have been precipitous, perhaps even officious--but they were always entirely disinterested.

The other charge which you laid at my feet relates to my history with George Wickham--that I wantonly and willfully cast off the friend of my youth, that I disregarded the express desires of my father to provide for his godson after his death, and that I have ignored and despised the thoughts of his current comparatively low station in life, with no desire to right the wrongs inflicted upon him. To answer these charges I will lay bare as much as I can of my relationship to that gentleman (whom I call a gentleman out of courtesy, not of merit), and leave you to be the judge between us.

Wickham was the only son of my father's steward, an honest man of fine character who was high in my father's affections; and when Wickham was born my father was honored to be asked to stand as godfather. Although he was not of high birth, my father went to considerable trouble and expense to raise him gently, with the best education and training available. Indeed, Wickham grew up almost as a son of the house itself. He was included in many family gatherings and activities, ate at our table innumerable times, and was afforded every advantage which could be gained from society so superior to that to which he was born. Georgiana, in particular, looked to him almost as another brother; and my father treated him nearly as another son.

I wish I could say that I shared those feelings, but it has been many years since I began to see Wickham in another light. In my father's presence he was clever and winsome, always pleasing to those on whose good opinion he relied for support; but between two young men so closely associated for so long there can be few secrets. I was aware when he began to keep disreputable company in both Derbyshire and town, and I was concerned for his safety and reputation when his debts of honor in both places became more than he could be reasonably expected to ever repay. That was the first of many times when I felt compelled for my father's sake to protect Wickham from public exposure, thus beginning a pattern that continues to this day.

After some years Wickham's father died, and not long after that so did my own father. To the end he had remained innocent of Wickham's true character, and remembered him most generously by leaving him a thousand pounds and a living at Kympton, a family holding, as soon as the living became available. As the will was being settled Wickham approached me, though we had maintained little contact since I went to Cambridge, and told me that he had no interest in a career in the church.

He had instead decided to study law, and asked if I would give him a financial settlement in lieu of the living, considering the heavy debts associated with further study. He made a strong case that the interest from the thousand pounds was wholly inadequate for his support. I was happy to fulfill this request. I knew from his gaming habits and his immoral history with certain women that Wickham ought never to be a cure of souls. We agreed upon a sum of three thousand pounds in lieu of the living; the transaction was made, and all association was then cut off. His society was too dissolute for me to allow him at Pemberley and I believed him to be living in town. I expected, I desired, to see him no more.

Imagine my surprise when three years later he applied to me yet again. This time he had heard of the recent death of the incumbent of the Kympton living, and he wished for me to present the living to him after all, since the study of law had proven very unprofitable for him; and, he reminded me, it was what my father had wished all along. His circumstances, he said, were very bad, and I had no trouble believing it. Further conversation revealed that the entirety of his three thousand pounds was gone, wasted on debauchery, gaming, and undeserving women. You will hardly blame me, I hope, for refusing to go along with this scheme, and for asking him not to disturb my peace or Georgiana's ever again.

After that Wickham disappeared from my life for some time, for which I was thankful, as I had no desire to seek him out or to hear anything more of him.

Unfortunately Wickham has a talent for reappearing where he is least wanted; and last summer I found it necessary to separate him from a young lady, a girl really, who was unaware of his unredeeming qualities, with whom he was attempting to form a most unacceptable connection. It was a fortunate escape for her since he then confessed to being attracted only by her fortune, which was considerable. The lady suffered low spirits for months afterwards and even now occasionally falls into spells of melancholy. Had he succeeded in his scheme the damage to the young lady involved would have been even worse.

Since that time, Wickham and I have not been able to meet publicly without some show of disdain on my side. He deserves much more.

This, then, is the entirety of my history with the man. I could speak more of him, of his moral failings and degenerate tendencies, but out of consideration for your feelings and mine and the privacy of others, I will refrain. If Wickham succeeded in making inroads on your affections before you married me, then his revenge is complete indeed.

I wish I had been master enough of myself last night to explain all this at that time. It is clear to me that you and I entered this marriage with grave misunderstandings about what our life together would be, and what we each hoped to gain from it. I fear that you have long been wishing to escape my ungentlemanly presence, and you shall have your desire: I will not impose myself upon you ever again.

Several crossed out lines blotted the paper after that, but then the closing lines read:

I will only add, God bless you.

Your husband,

Fitzwilliam Darcy

CHAPTER SEVENTEEN

Elizabeth's changes of emotion while reading this letter were extreme. At times she read in humiliated disbelief, her face flushing red in shame, and other parts with wide-eyed horror. Reading a particular paragraph in one place might make her exclaim, "No, this cannot be!" in one tone, and then a section later might make her cry out the same words with a very different inflection. Her feelings could find no way of settling themselves. At length she folded the pages angrily together, shoving them and the envelope inside the pocket of her spencer--but in another moment she had withdrawn the letter again and was eagerly perusing its pages once more. Anger and resentment washed over her in their turn, followed by guilt, suspicion, and a burning shame.

Her husband's anger had not abated since their argument the night before, it seemed. His opening paragraph made it clear that he would not rest until he was satisfied that she had heard his answers to all her criticisms. With a reluctant sense of owing him a fair hearing she determined to read the letter in its entirety, though she seriously doubted that any explanation of his might improve her opinion of him.

Resentfully she read her husband's account of the events in Hertfordshire the past winter--his observations of Jane, his objections to her family; his separation of Jane from Bingley, and how he had taken matters into his own hands when he felt his friend was in danger. How gloriously triumphant she felt, to know that her guesses about Darcy's role in her sister's life were completely correct! How perceptive she was, knowing that she had correctly judged his prejudice and disdain against those lower than him; if anything, she had given him too much credit. He did not have the slightest reservations or misgivings about his actions.

With a sense of complete justification she read the unrepentant words again: I cannot honestly say that I have any regrets. He had not asked her to read his letter; he had demanded it. Her husband was, without a doubt, the most arrogant and condescending man she had ever met. If she had had any doubts before, they were erased now. She could honestly repeat, without a shred of regret, that he was the last man in the world she would ever have married if fate had not forced her hand.

But when she read how Darcy wrote about Jane's manners and

expressions at Netherfield her confidence faltered slightly. Darcy was wrong, of course; Jane's feelings had always been more contained than displayed, and it was presumptuous in the extreme for him to think that he knew her thoughts on any subject at all. Still, although Jane felt deeply and sincerely, Elizabeth knew that, to an unknowing observer, her feelings might be open to misinterpretation. Her temper was not such as to give encouragement to an innocent admirer, let alone convince an outsider of her true sentiments.

However, Darcy's final paragraph relating to Jane, where he defended his partiality to his sister and denied that it had a role in his separation of Jane and Bingley, she completely discounted. Nobody could be so disinterested when the future happiness of a beloved sister was at risk; Darcy was either attempting to deceive her, or had succeeded in deceiving himself. In either case she could not think well of him for it.

Elizabeth's steps had taken her back to the side entrance of Pemberley, and she walked in as unobtrusively as possible, hoping nobody would stop her on her way to her room. She left instructions with the cook that she was not hungry and asked her to inform Mrs. Reynolds that she would appreciate not being disturbed for the rest of the day. Then she took the back stairs to the second floor, where she went into her room and firmly shut the door behind her. A moment later she had removed her spencer, dropping it carelessly on the bed, and sat down at her desk to continue reading.

When she began to read Darcy's words about his history with Wickham Elizabeth knew not what to think. Darcy's words agreed with Wickham's story in many particulars. His letter confirmed what Wickham had said of his parentage, his early education, his relationship with the old Mr. Darcy as a child, and even some of his early adult years. So far the two tales ran the same; it was not until more recent years that the tales took different paths and Elizabeth was forced to choose between the two. As she compared and contrasted Darcy's words with what she could recall of Wickham's words, the differences began to come into sharp relief, and she could not help thinking that there was some great deceit on one side or the other.

To think that Darcy wanted her to believe that Wickham, the man she had so admired, was so utterly depraved! That he was reckless, a liar, a wastrel, and a seducer! Elizabeth could not credit it. Darcy offered no proof. Though Darcy had laid many charges at Wickham's door, Wickham had hardly laid fewer at his, and Elizabeth had no clear way of telling the truth of the matter. On either side it was only accusation and supposition. Her only guide must be her own experiences with both men. She forced herself to set aside the pages of the letter for a minute while she called on those experiences to help her discern the truth of the tale.

When Wickham had first come to Meryton he had quickly become the favorite of the whole neighborhood. His manners had been flawless, his powers of pleasing those around him unending. Mothers eagerly approved of him, girls primped and smiled to gain his attention, and he had unfailingly made love to them all. Nevertheless, was it possible that something very different lay beneath the smiling face, handsome bearing, and charming manners? What actual good had the man done, to make himself so well accepted and approved in so little time? Nothing, she was forced to admit, and with that thought came a sudden chill. No one had known anything of Wickham before his arrival in the militia; and even his arrival there had been recent, so recent that even Denny, his closest friend, could say little about his history. He had had nothing at all to recommend him beyond being young and handsome--but that had been enough to prejudice the entire neighborhood in his favor.

To be sure, no one knew of anything good that Darcy or even Bingley had done, either; but then they had other sources to recommend them. Bingley, affable and pleasing, was known to the neighborhood through his connection to Netherfield; his reputation and background had preceded him. Darcy had Bingley and his sisters to vouch for his character, and by all accounts they had been acquaintances of long standing. It would be hard to imagine how the easygoing Bingley would remain friends with someone as haughty and forbidding, not to mention unprincipled, as Wickham had made Darcy out to be.

Once again Elizabeth forced herself to read the paragraphs describing Wickham's more recent years, his descent into immoral and indifferent behavior, and his application for the presentation of the living promised to him in the old Mr. Darcy's will. She had no way of judging his private behavior, of course--but had not even Caroline Bingley warned Elizabeth that Wickham was not as he presented himself? Had the fault all been on Wickham's side? How she wished she had asked more questions, but at the time she had not been willing to hear anything good about the man she now called husband.

Darcy's description of Wickham as a fortune hunter received a certain amount of confirmation by his treatment of Miss King. Before hearing of that lady's fortune Wickham's attentions had been all for Elizabeth; but once the lady's inheritance was revealed, Wickham had pursued her eagerly, an action which now seemed mercenary in the extreme. If that was true, however, then why had he singled Elizabeth out for so much attention? He must have been deceived as to her father's fortune, or perhaps her sympathy and interest had merely flattered his vanity enough to gain his interest until a woman with better prospects appeared on the scene.

Now Elizabeth could see clearly the folly of listening to the lengthy, intimate sort of communications made by Wickham to her almost every time they had met. How much personal information he had given to someone he knew so little! How quick he had been to attack and tear down a gentleman who had so little to say of him! And how easily Elizabeth had fallen in line with his goal. Wickham had been happy to disparage Darcy at will when he was with Elizabeth, although he claimed that he would never do so publicly; but within a week of Darcy and Bingley leaving Meryton, the whole neighborhood knew as much of the story as Elizabeth ever did. She suddenly remembered Wickham's passionate declaration that he would never avoid Darcy's presence; that Darcy might say as he liked but he, Wickham, would never waver or flee-- and then just a week later he had declined to attend a ball where he knew Darcy would be present.

This was the man to whom she had listened, sympathized with, secretly admired, and half surrendered her heart to! She had favored this man over her own husband! Gratified and flattered by Wickham's attentions, and offended by Darcy's casual dismissal of her person, she had given over any semblance of the sound judgment on which she prided herself. By weighing Wickham in the balance she had found the truth between the two men--and found herself wanting. She bowed her head in shame.

Being now convinced of Darcy's truth in one area made her go back and reconsider the first part of the letter once more. She read his version of the events with Jane again, and this time was forced to give him much more credit than the first time through. Darcy's criticisms of her family were as accurate as they were hurtful. Though he had hesitated to criticize her father, Elizabeth had to admit that her family's behavior in the autumn, even that of her beloved father, had not been above reproach. Elizabeth had lately seen in her mother's and sister's letters that nothing had improved, either. Loud and undisciplined they had always been and likely would remain. Her mother was and would be avaricious and ambitious, and whatever small restraint there had been on her younger sisters' behavior, especially Lydia's, was now gone.

There was some comfort in realizing that they had not been deceived in Bingley. His affection for Jane had been true. But it was only a small comfort, for this knowledge merely highlighted how much Jane had lost-- and most of it had been lost by the actions of her own family.

With these depressing thoughts Elizabeth spent the entire day in her rooms. For the first time in their relationship, from their first meeting until now, she was truly afraid to see Darcy. She feared the look of reproach she would see in his eyes, the stern disapproval that would cross his face. She could not bear to think how he would look at her, now that she knew how utterly she had betrayed him. But when the dinner bell sounded she realized had no choice. She would have to face him sooner or later.

When she entered the dining room, however, her shoulders squared, she was quite alone. Her place was set, along with Georgiana's, but her husband's place was empty. Elizabeth could not help asking Mrs. Reynolds, who stood nearby, "Only two places at the table tonight?"

Mrs. Reynolds looked at her in surprise. "Of course, ma'am. Mr. Darcy left for town this morning."

Elizabeth's hands suddenly clenched the back of her chair. "Did he say how long he would be gone?"

"No, ma'am. He had sudden business, he said, and had to go at once." She looked at Elizabeth with ill-disguised curiosity as she left the room.

A moment later Georgiana came into the dining room as Elizabeth still stood, dismayed, behind her chair. "How odd that Fitzwilliam would have such urgent business, and be in such a rush to go away! He would not even wait for the carriage to be prepared."

"It was a surprise to me as well," Elizabeth answered shakily, knowing a response was expected. "I suppose you have no more information than I about what demanded his sudden attention."

"No, not at all. He merely said that he had received an important communication, and that he might be required to stay in town for some time."

He had not even left a message to tell her he was going. Elizabeth thought again of the look on Darcy's face the night before, when he had turned and left her room, and suddenly felt an almost physical pain in her chest. Her hands clenched the chair even more tightly. "Did he mention anything about our conversation last night?"

"No." Georgiana looked at her curiously. "Were you able to speak to him about Mr. Bingley?"

"We spoke of many things." Elizabeth evaded. She gazed at the seat that Darcy would normally occupy. It already looked strangely vacant and forlorn, a silent rebuke to her for her cruel words. "I am afraid your brother may indeed be away for some time."

Georgiana looked at her with an odd expression but fortunately asked nothing further, and Elizabeth ate her meal in miserable silence. Darcy had said he would never impose on her again; apparently he had not been exaggerating.

CHAPTER EIGHTEEN

Elizabeth's days now dragged by, bogged down in uncertainty over what the future might hold.

If Darcy had been any other man, she might have given up in despair over the outlook for her marriage, certain that she would be returned to her family in the near future, disgraced for the grievous injury she had caused her husband. But she had begun to understand more of the complex character of the man she had married. He might be angry, his pride deeply wounded, but he was not vengeful. She was safe, she thought, from any public displays of his contempt. But that small consolation did not wipe away the guilt she now felt over the unfair accusations she had made against him.

When she saw Darcy again she must explain not only that she now understood Wickham's real character, but also that Wickham had never made inroads on her heart. How it must have stung her husband to realize that Elizabeth had preferred Wickham's company to his at one time! She must also explain that he had not been entirely mistaken in his assessment of Jane and Bingley; or rather, that his mistaken assessment of her feelings had been understandable. Even Charlotte had not been convinced of Jane's feelings towards Bingley, and her friendship was of far longer duration than Darcy's casual acquaintance.

Above all, she must apologize for her ill-conceived words and convince Darcy that she knew she had sorely misjudged him in certain matters. She could not bear the thought that he had gone away without knowing at least that much.

However, no matter how much Elizabeth was struggling to maintain her own spirits, she soon became aware that Georgiana was struggling even more.

During her time at Pemberley, Elizabeth had fancied that Georgiana was improving in self-confidence and assurance almost daily. When Elizabeth first met her, Georgiana had been scarcely brave enough to say a monosyllable in front of her new sister, but that reticence had been disappearing as their intimacy increased. Now for the past two days, since Darcy had gone, Georgiana had lapsed into an even greater tendency to silence than previously. Whole meals passed with barely a word spoken, and Elizabeth sometimes caught a distant, pensive look on the younger girl's face when she thought nobody was watching. Had Georgiana caught wind of the quarrel between her brother and his wife? If so, she had given no sign; but unless Elizabeth asked her, there was no way of knowing what she might know or guess.

Elizabeth waited until a time when she could entice Georgiana into the garden to pick flowers, and then decided to broach the subject with care, speaking casually as she delicately worked with the shears.

"Georgiana, I could not help noticing that you have been out of spirits ever since your brother left for town. It must be very hard on you, after being used to his company every day, to be separated once again."

Georgiana started and looked at her briefly, but she did not say anything. Elizabeth continued, "Not having any brothers myself, I must admit to being surprised at the strength of the attachment between you and Mr. Darcy." There was still no response. "I wonder if there is something I might be able to do to help you in his absence."

Georgiana looked reluctant to speak, but she finally dared to look at Elizabeth and say, hesitantly, "There is something that has been weighing on my mind, but it is not an easy question to ask."

"Ask whatever you will. I will be pleased to answer you, if I can."

Georgiana took a deep breath. "Elizabeth, did Fitzwilliam leave because of me?"

The question was so unexpected that Elizabeth did not quite know how to respond. "Because of you? What do you mean?" Perhaps Georgiana knew more than she had first thought.

"I mean because of my mistake last summer."

Elizabeth looked at her, utterly mystified. "I am not aware of any mistake. What do you mean?"

"I thought perhaps Fitzwilliam--but never mind. I probably should not speak of it." She looked down again, her face flushing.

Though Elizabeth knew she should not ask, burning curiosity made her do so anyway. "Speak of what, Georgiana?"

"Last summer I met a friend of my brother's, someone I had known for many years, and I believed that he cared for me. But he did not." Georgiana stopped and Elizabeth waited for her to continue, but the younger girl was silent.

"You fell in love, and the gentleman did not return your interest? My dear sister, that is an old tale, one that has been re-told many times. I cannot imagine why you think your brother might hold it against you."

"But that is not all the story," said Georgiana, her voice wavering a little. "There is much more involved. The gentleman was only in love with my fortune, not with me." Her face flushed deeper.

"Did he speak to you of marriage, then?" This did put a different light on the matter. Elizabeth could well imagine that Darcy might be angry with his sister for accepting the attentions of a gentleman before she was out. Still, it seemed out of character for him to keep his anger against his beloved sister for long. "It was very wrong of the gentleman to speak to you in such a way when you were so young, and had not even entered society yet. I wonder that he was foolish enough to attempt it."

"Yes, we spoke of marriage," Georgiana said, and she suddenly looked so much more miserable than before that Elizabeth knew they had reached the heart of the matter. "We planned to elope together."

"Georgiana!" Elizabeth exclaimed, truly shocked. Immediately she schooled her features into something more consoling.

"I knew it was wrong. I knew I should not even be speaking of marriage with someone who had not spoken to my brother yet, but he and Fitzwilliam had been such friends that I knew he would approve eventually, and I did not care to wait. I was so flattered that he had chosen me, out of all the other girls he could have looked at, that I simply could not wait to be his wife. Oh, what was I thinking?"

Elizabeth laid a hand comfortingly on her arm. "I take it the gentleman was older than you. Was he old enough to know better?"

"Yes, but you must not blame him entirely. I did wish to marry him; he was not forcing me against my will."

"Perhaps; but he had powers of persuasion at his disposal that you had not. And had he given you any reason to distrust him?"

"No," and Georgiana looked tearful once again. "I believed his intentions were honorable."

"How, then, did you discover their true nature? That is, if you do not mind telling me."

"My brother had made an establishment for me at Ramsgate, and I was there with my previous companion last summer. It was there that the gentleman found me, while Fitzwilliam was away, and convinced me to be in love with him. We had planned to leave the house in the middle of the night, before anyone could catch us, and be halfway to Scotland before Mrs. Younge even noticed our absence. But Fitzwilliam came to Ramsgate unexpectedly just two days beforehand. I could not bear to disappoint him, after all he has done to support me, and I confessed everything to him at once. He was very angry."

"With you?"

"No, with the gentleman. They had a great row in the drawing room. Such an argument! I can still remember every word of it. Fitzwilliam threatened to denounce him publicly but he did not care. Then Fitzwilliam told him that if he married me, he would have none of my settlement until I reached my majority."

"And how did your young man respond to that?"

"He said that he could not wait that long, and that he would need to make his fortune elsewhere in that case. He left the house without a word to me, and I have never heard from him since."

Elizabeth fairly shook with the magnitude of the secret Georgiana had just confided. So, all was not as perfect as it had seemed at Pemberley! Her heart ached for the girl, carrying such a heavy burden of grief and guilt for so many months, and churned with anger towards the unknown seducer. What a lesson to learn for one of such a tender nature! But now was not the time to voice her anger. Georgiana needed consolation, not hostility. She wished she had Jane's natural talent for seeing the best in every situation. "It could have been worse," she offered. "You might have married him and then discovered what sort of man he was."

"Yes, that is what Fitzwilliam said."

"Your brother did well to cover the matter up so entirely. Not a syllable of this has ever reached my ears until now. Had Mr. Darcy chosen public exposure, your name might have been damaged irreparably; many a young woman has lost her reputation for less."

"Yes, I know. My brother is so good; truly, he is too good for me." Georgiana said tearfully.

"He would not say so," Elizabeth assured her. "To him, you are all that is perfection."

"And yet he left right after you spoke to him about Mr. Bingley--and me."

"Oh, my dear!" Truly distressed, she did not know what to say. How could she comfort Georgiana without betraying the rift in their marriage? For surely Darcy would not care to have his private business discussed with his own sister. "Mr. Darcy--your brother--had other issues weighing on his mind. Though I cannot betray his confidence, please believe me when I say that his leaving for town had nothing to do with you. He is not the least bit angry with you."

Georgiana did not look reassured. "Are you certain? It seems so strange that he would leave so quickly, immediately after you spoke to him about me not wanting to marry Mr. Bingley. I know I have been a great deal of trouble to him."

"Is this what you meant when we spoke previously, when you said that your brother had reason to question your judgment?"

"Yes." She burst into tears.

Elizabeth was dismayed. She had never dreamed that her troubles with Darcy would spill onto his sister in such a way. Here was yet another reason to regret the rash words that had driven him away. She put an arm around the girl and let her weep for a minute before she spoke again, keeping her tone as soothing as possible.

"Georgiana, if your brother were still angry about your actions from last summer, would you not have sensed that before now?"

Georgiana choked down a sob. "I suppose so."

"And you saw Mr. Darcy just before he left for town, did you not? Did he do or say anything then that led you to believe that he was angry with you?"

"No," came Georgiana's muffled response, her head against Elizabeth's shoulder. "But he looked so stern, and I wondered if you had spoken to him about me. And then when you said that you had--" her voice trailed off and she said no more.

Girls Georgiana's age, Elizabeth remembered, inexperienced in the world, did have a certain tendency to assume that every event around them was somehow connected to them. It was no wonder that Georgiana had assumed that her brother had gone because of her, without taking other possibilities into account. She spoke gently but firmly. "I can assure you, from the bottom of my heart--your brother did not leave because of you and Mr. Bingley, nor because of what happened with you and this other gentleman. Though I do not perfectly understand all his business affairs, I can at least promise you that."

"Are you certain?" Georgiana asked, still tearful. "I do not like to think that I have caused him any more distress, not after last year."

"I am certain that your brother holds nothing against you; but you ought to hear that from him, not me. Why not write and ask him directly?"

"Oh, I could never! There are some things that we do not speak about in this house. I think it makes Fitzwilliam uncomfortable."

"I see." Perhaps Darcy felt he was protecting his sister by trying to pretend the unfortunate event had never happened, but that strategy had not worked in this case. "It is your decision, of course, but I have always found that asking someone what they think, rather than assuming, is a better course of action. Your brother might not want to talk about what happened for fear of upsetting you."

Georgiana gave a tentative half smile. "I had not considered that possibility."

"And he might be waiting for you to raise the topic first. Will you at least consider writing to him? Or will you perhaps speak to him about all this when he returns? It would relieve both your minds, I think, and it will put an end to this dreadful uncertainty you are facing."

"I will consider it," Georgiana said after a moment of reflection, and Elizabeth had to be content with that. She was glad that Georgiana had chosen to confide in her; but it would take time and patience for Georgiana to work through the hurt she had sustained, and Elizabeth had driven away the one person most likely to help. Darcy and Darcy alone would be able to assure her of the strength of his affection.

Georgiana needed Darcy, and in her own way, Elizabeth did too. When would he ever return?

CHAPTER NINETEEN

Three more days went by with no communication from Darcy. Elizabeth counted those days off like beads on a rosary, clinging to some desperate hope with each one, though exactly what hope, she could not say.

On the fourth day Mrs. Reynolds brought in the afternoon post to Elizabeth and Georgiana together. Elizabeth's heart fairly leaped into her throat when the housekeeper handed her a single envelope, but sank again as soon as she saw the handwriting. It was from Charlotte Collins. She smiled sadly to herself. How odd it was to be disappointed by a letter from one of her oldest friends!

Georgiana was more fortunate. When Mrs. Reynolds gave her a letter with Darcy's fine, bold hand showing on the front, she smiled tenuously as she took it. Her smile grew broader as she opened it and began to read, and then she looked up at Elizabeth with shining eyes.

"Thank you, Elizabeth," was all she said, though the expression on her face conveyed far more. "I should have known you spoke the truth."

"About what?" asked Elizabeth.

"Fitzwilliam is writing to apologize for anything he may have done in the past to make me feel uncomfortable. He says that when the time comes for me to marry, I must follow my own inclinations. I do not have to marry Mr. Bingley or anyone else who does not engage my affections."

Elizabeth could only smile weakly. "I am very happy for you, Georgiana."

"He also regrets that I did not feel at ease speaking to him directly on this subject. He says that I am fortunate to have a sister now who can now fill the role of confidante in a way he never could."

Elizabeth wondered if Darcy wrote those words with real sincerity or in a certain bitterness of spirit. It must rankle him that Georgiana would choose to confide in her, a newcomer to the family, instead of to her own brother. She would say nothing of this to Georgiana, of course. "Your brother loves you devotedly. I was certain he would never force you into an alliance not of your choosing."

"He would never have known how I felt if you had not spoken to him for me," Georgiana answered gratefully. "I must reply to him at once.

Thank you, so very much! I will feel much more at ease now when I see him again."

Elizabeth wished heartily that she could feel the same way.

∞

"Has Fitzwilliam said when he is planning to return from town?" Georgiana asked Elizabeth the dreaded question while they shared a small dinner together. She probably assumed that the letter Elizabeth had received earlier that day was from Darcy.

Elizabeth had not heard a word from her husband, of course, but she did not want to admit that to her sister. "I am anticipating his return, though I do not know when it will be," she prevaricated. "He has not yet told me his plans."

"It must have been something particular that took him there at this time of year," Georgiana said, persisting in an opinion she had expressed several times. "He usually avoids town during the season."

"He might be waiting to meet Mr. Bingley, in order to bring him with him to Pemberley when he returns," Elizabeth offered. It was the only explanation she had been able to invent ahead of time in order to satisfy her young sister. "Perhaps they are planning on examining potential homes for Mr. Bingley while they travel north together." Georgiana nodded and appeared satisfied with this weak excuse, although Elizabeth herself certainly was not. In reality she had no idea what Darcy's plans might be in regards to Bingley's visit, or if Bingley would even come at all. The invitations for the dinner party sat, half-finished, in the top drawer of the desk in her room; she would have to make a decision on their fate soon.

Darcy's letter was also hidden away in that top drawer, untouched during the day. Each night after Elizabeth retired she removed it and read it carefully through in the lamp light, seeking answers still hidden from her in its pages, although the action was merely force of habit by now. She had already nearly memorized it, but certain phrases still puzzled her no matter how she tried to tease apart their meaning.

What did Darcy truly want from their marriage, and why had she never asked him such an important question before now? She could no longer believe what her uncle had told her, that he desired an heir and nothing more. A man with Darcy's wealth and connections could have married anywhere in order to achieve that end. Nor did he seem to want only a social hostess, someone to grace his table while he cultivated relationships with other wealthy and influential men. He showed little desire for society himself. He had only announced one dinner party so far--and that would likely not have been planned at all if Bingley had not asked to visit. If all he wanted was an older sister for Georgiana, Elizabeth could fairly say that she had fulfilled that expectation; yet she sensed he wanted more.

It seemed clear that Darcy was determined to improve her view of him, but why her regard mattered to him was more of a mystery. *I know beyond a doubt your true opinion of me*, he had said, *but I request and require as your husband that you read this letter in its entirety*. Had his pride truly been so deeply wounded? Had Darcy previously believed that she held him in much higher esteem? If so, he must have been incensed to discover her true feelings. Incensed, and perhaps hurt. *I hope after you have read it that you will at least acquit me of willful indifference to the feelings of others, if not of the arrogance and condescension which you so eagerly pointed out in my character when we spoke together.* Elizabeth pictured again the expression on Darcy's face, when he had turned and looked at her for the last time before leaving her room. There had been more than just offense and anger in that look, but the name for the emotion embedded there eluded her.

∞

It was several days later that Mrs. Reynolds announced that correspondence had arrived for Elizabeth and that it was in her room as requested. Elizabeth made her way there swiftly, both hoping and dreading that it was from her husband, but the writing on the front of the envelope indicated it was from her aunt Gardiner. Elizabeth weighed it in her hand for a moment, wondering at her aunt's punctuality. She had received a letter from Mrs. Gardiner just one week earlier, and although her aunt was a faithful correspondent, writing twice in less than a fortnight would seem to indicate something of note.

The letter began with a brief recitation of the parties and assemblies Mr. and Mrs. Gardiner had recently attended in town, and some lighthearted gossip about mutual acquaintances. But abruptly, in a new pen, her aunt started a very different topic.

My dearest Lizzy, we were astonished yesterday afternoon to receive a visit from someone we never imagined would deign to be seen in Gracechurch Street, let alone in our humble home. Can you imagine who it might have been? You have been very sly never to mention his name, but you must have known that Mr. Darcy was planning to call on us. He arrived while I was at the park with the children, and when we came back imagine my surprise to see your husband sitting in the parlor with mine!

After settling the children with the nurse I was able to join the gentlemen, and I was then struck with the difference in Mr. Darcy's manners from when we first met him in Hertfordshire. He assured us that you are quite well and gave that as his reason for calling. He made the usual inquiries into the health of your mother and sisters, and asked several times if Jane is still at Longbourn. When your uncle assured him that she is still there, he asked your uncle to let him know if there is anything that the residents of Longbourn might be lacking that would be in his power to supply. Although your uncle assured him of everyone's well-being, Mr. Darcy made it apparent that he intends to be a diligent custodian of his wife's family. Nothing, he says, is to be done for them that he will not do himself.

My dear niece, I congratulate you on the changed aspect you seem to have inspired in your husband. He would never have called on us simply for our own sake.

May I say how open and charming I found your Mr. Darcy to be? This was my first experience having a conversation of any length with him, for when he came to Hertfordshire in the spring his dealings were almost always with your uncle, alone. Perhaps my memory is faulty but he seems more open, more affable, and much less proud than I remembered him to be. He was very serious in his looks, perhaps even grave sometimes, which I gather to be his wont. He was especially serious in his manner whenever your name came up; but he exerted himself to be agreeable. We asked him to stay for dinner but he claimed a prior engagement with such obvious regret that I was compelled to ask him to come for dinner Monday next, which he gratefully accepted.

Your uncle was as much struck by the change in Mr. Darcy as was I. He has said little of it except to comment that we were perhaps much mistaken in our impressions of the gentleman.

Please do write again soon, and if it would not be too much trouble to ask, may we look forward to seeing you some day at Pemberley? Your description of the park makes me think that a walking tour might not be enough to see all of it comfortably, but I trust that you will have other means at your disposal for entertaining your guests. That is, if you think your husband would not mind. I remain

Your most loving aunt,

M. Gardiner

Elizabeth had to read her aunt's letter a number of times before she could begin to credit its contents. Never in her wildest flights of fancy had she imagined that her husband would voluntarily call on her aunt and uncle, that he would seek out the acquaintance of someone who was in trade, or that he would willingly associate with someone whose condition in life was so far beneath his own. It had been necessary for him to approach her uncle at Longbourn after her father died, in order to ask for her hand, but Elizabeth had never deceived herself into believing that Darcy would maintain a connection once the wedding took place. Everything in his prideful nature must revolt against it.

Perhaps all was not as hopeless as she had first imagined it to be. It was past time for her, Elizabeth, to take her own advice to Georgiana in relation to her marriage. For too long she had been passive, allowing her circumstances to be dictated to her instead of taking an active role in her own life. What had happened to the courage she liked to claim as part of her character? Rather than waiting for Darcy to raise the painful topic of her errors, she should reach out and apologize to him first. Before she could think too much about it, she seized a pen and paper and wrote:

To my husband, Fitzwilliam Darcy,

I am writing to express my deepest appreciation for the trouble you took in calling on my aunt and uncle Gardiner. I have just received communication from my aunt about your visit, and I can scarcely believe the lengths you went to in order to begin an acquaintance with them. I did not expect such a gesture after the unfair and unkind things I said to you before you left for town. It was more kindness than I deserved after abusing you so abominably.

You ought to know that Georgiana is much relieved by the letter she received from you a few days ago, the contents of which she shared with me. I think when you come home again, you and she will have much to discuss.

Nor is your sister the only one who has been poring over the contents of a certain letter. It is my most sincere wish that you will allow me to apologize in person much more fully than I can in writing.

I am your loyal wife,

Elizabeth Darcy

The words looked up at her accusingly after she had finally finished writing them. They were not enough, they could never be enough—but what more could she say? She sent the letter off by the next post, praying that her husband would recognize and respond favorably to the olive branch she was extending.

CHAPTER TWENTY

Edward Gardiner looked with keen curiosity at the man who had just been announced into his study; a gentleman well out of Gardiner's usual social sphere, but one who had already gone to some trouble to begin an acquaintance with him and his family. "Mr. Darcy, it is a pleasure to see you again, as always." Although that pleasure, he thought silently, could have waited until a little later in the day. It was not even ten o'clock in the morning--too early for polite social calls.

"I appreciate you seeing me at this hour of the day," Darcy responded, taking the seat indicated by the older man. "I know that you could not have been expecting me."

"We were not expecting you, but it does not follow that an unexpected visitor must be an unwelcome one." Gardiner frowned as he noticed that his visitor was fidgeting, his hands working nervously at the rim of his hat. "But Mrs. Gardiner will be sorry that she missed you. She and the nurse have taken the children to the park."

Darcy nodded. "I am aware that she is out. It is better that you and I have this conversation, if possible, without being overheard."

Gardiner nodded to his manservant, who immediately left the room, closing the door behind him. "This must be a matter of some importance. You have my attention, Mr. Darcy. How may I be of assistance?"

Darcy hesitated. "The assistance I seek is of a peculiar kind. It will no doubt sound odd, coming from your niece's husband."

Gardiner frowned as he looked at him. "Please go on."

Darcy leaned forward almost imperceptibly in his chair. "If you could, I would like for you to tell me as much as you can of a particular conversation."

"A conversation?"

"Yes--the one you had with Elizabeth in which she agreed to marry me."

∞

"Do you think Fitzwilliam will let me join the dinner party?"

Elizabeth looked up, surprised by Georgiana's question. Georgiana was keeping Elizabeth company while she made a show of considering menus for the dinner party for Bingley--the dinner party which Elizabeth was increasingly convinced would never happen. But in front of Georgiana and the servants she must continue the fiction of a satisfactory domestic life with her husband as long as possible, and it would seem odd not to have considered at least some details of the dinner party by now.

"I am not certain what he will allow. You are not out yet, but we are not in town. He might not insist that you stand on ceremony." She observed Georgiana questioningly. "Has Mr. Darcy allowed you to participate in these kinds of gatherings before?"

"I have not had the opportunity to do so. This will be the first entertaining we have carried out at Pemberley since my mother died."

"Oh!" Elizabeth looked rather blankly at the page in her hand. "I ought to have realized that. Your brother could hardly host a party without someone to act as the hostess; but what about your father? Didn't he have a sister or aunt who would fill the role for him?"

"He did not care to entertain after my mother passed. I am told that he never really recovered from her loss. They were a most devoted couple. Has Fitzwilliam never spoken of them to you?"

Elizabeth's mind went back to the first days of their marriage, to the night when she had insisted on wearing black to the recital she had attended with Darcy. He had spoken of both his parents with tenderness that night, and she had brushed him away, declining to listen to his memories or respond with any of her own. She had not been ready, then. "He mentioned them once, when we were in town."

"I wish I had known my mother." Georgiana's voice took on the same wistful quality Elizabeth remembered hearing in her husband's voice that night. "Fitzwilliam says she was very beautiful. She enjoyed laughing and teasing, but she was never cruel. She was known for laughing with people rather than laughing at them."

Elizabeth smiled slightly. "How did she meet your father?"

"Their parents introduced them."

"An arranged match?"

"Not exactly. She was the daughter of an earl, and he was from an old family, quite wealthy, but without any noble connections. Both families thought it would be an ideal pairing, but they were not told they had to marry. They were each free to seek out their own life partners, but they were fortunate enough to fall in love with each other."

Elizabeth immediately saw the parallels to how Darcy had

encouraged Bingley and Georgiana to make their own match. "A very happy pairing, then."

"It is the same kind of connection you have with Fitzwilliam, is it not?" Georgiana continued innocently. "My brother told me that he was going to ask for your hand. He said that I might be surprised by his choice because you did not come from the same kind of background that he did, but that nothing could persuade him away from you."

"Did he?" Elizabeth looked at Georgiana, wide-eyed.

"Oh yes! He was so happy to announce your engagement, and delighted that you allowed the wedding to take place so soon after your father's passing. He thought he might have to wait months and months for you."

Elizabeth was suddenly finding it difficult to breathe. When she could speak again she said, "I was of the impression that your brother had no doubt that I would accept him."

"He can sound rather high-handed at times, though I know it is not my place to criticize him," Georgiana answered, a little shame-faced, "It is only because of how much responsibility he has had to take on since our father died. So many people depend on him for their welfare!"

This was not possible, Elizabeth thought. Surely she had not mistaken her husband so badly? "Do you know, Georgiana," she said after a moment, trying to inject a note of humor into the conversation, "that when your brother and I first met in the autumn, I was under the impression that he looked at me only to criticize."

Georgiana's eyes flew open and she clapped a hand over her mouth. "I cannot believe that! He told me several times how much he admired your manners, and that he believed you to be the handsomest woman of his acquaintance!"

"I am certain he was teasing you."

"Of course not! He wrote of your clever wit, and of how much pleasure he found in your singing and playing."

"I--" Elizabeth could barely get the words out. "I was rather surprised by your brother's interest, when I first discovered it."

"I do not doubt it," Georgiana answered earnestly, "especially if that was last autumn. Fitzwilliam still had anger at himself over--the mistake that I made, and he had a difficult time finding pleasure in anything. But when he wrote to me of meeting you, I could tell at once that his spirits had improved. How did you first learn of his affection for you?"

There are moments when one look or expression, a single word or phrase, uttered at precisely the right moment, has the power to change our perception of a situation entirely. The last piece of a puzzle, once inserted, changes our view of the whole, and we clearly see things never noticed before. This was one of those moments. Georgiana looked at her with concern.

"Elizabeth, are you well?"

"I feel suddenly faint. Please allow me to excuse myself, Georgiana." The younger girl nodded and Elizabeth retreated as quickly as possible to the privacy of her room, sinking onto her bed with her hands over her inflamed cheeks. It was not possible that she had misread her husband so badly, was it? She, who prided herself on her perception and insight! It was true--Darcy had loved her from the beginning! And she had spurned him!

Memories of their wedding day and of their first private time together as husband and wife came flooding back to Elizabeth's mind now. "You are beautiful, Elizabeth," he had said. "No matter how lovely you looked in your wedding finery this morning, you are even lovelier to me now . . . I shall make you happy, Elizabeth. I swear it--and the oath shall be kept." At the time she had found ways to explain Darcy's ardor away. Lacking any basis for comparison, she had assumed that in the novelty of the event a new husband would naturally be passionate toward his bride for a time. Even her father had, for a time, maintained strong feelings for her mother, however little time they had lasted. With her parent's example and her uncle's warning, she had not expected her husband to be any different once the first flush of newness was past.

From their wedding night her mind moved to her first days in town, to her new home. She remembered how Darcy had taken care to introduce her to his family and friends, to expose her to sights of the city that she would never have otherwise seen, and to ensure that she received clothing and everything else she needed for her new station in life. In her misery over her father's passing Elizabeth had seen all this as evidence of her husband's controlling nature, until he had explained that he did it to help her. "I have purposely kept you involved with a variety of activities each day, so that you would not be focused on your loss," he had said. Darcy had even gone so far as to try to protect her from gossip by directing her not to wear full mourning in public, but he had shown an unexpectedly gentle side by listening to her objections on that matter and acceding to her wishes.

Nor had that been his only display of humility. She recalled their disagreement over the day of leaving for Pemberley, and how he had thanked her for saving him from committing a serious breach of etiquette with his aunt and uncle.

There had been unexpected moments of tenderness between them. "You must still grieve your father," Darcy had said, his eyes warm with sympathy, encouraging her to share her loss with him. "I have never seen you weep." He had lowered his own guard and spoken freely of his father's death, gently encouraging her to do the same. Instead, she had callously pushed him aside.

She could still clearly recall the night of their disagreement after Lady Catherine's visit, when Darcy had agreed with his aunt's assessment of Elizabeth's poor connections, her lack of wealth, and the indecorous behavior of her mother and sisters. He had been right on all counts. But he had also held her in his arms and soothed her anger and tears, and she had been comforted.

That had been their most serious disagreement up until now. After traveling together to Pemberley their time together had seemed almost charmed, filled with quiet walks, lively conversation, and pleasing interactions with Georgiana. Her husband had been solicitous and gallant, a sharp contrast to the man she thought she had known from her own observations in town and from Wickham. Like her aunt, she had to admit Darcy had been more open and less proud than she could ever have imagined before coming to know him so intimately. If she had seen that side of her husband's character in the first days of their acquaintance, she would have had an entirely different first impression of him. How might she have responded to his interest in her before they married, if she had been aware of it?

The night Darcy had led her out onto his balcony, when he had pointed out the comet and spoken of her father again, he had seemed closer to her than ever before. Elizabeth could still feel the touch of his hand on her waist, his warm breath in her ear as he leaned close to point to the night sky overhead. He had asked her what her deepest wish was, but she had deflected the conversation away instead. If she had chosen to confide in him at that moment, to tell him of her desire to marry for love, how would he have answered?

Looking back now, she could see the dividing moment, when awful suspicion must have entered his mind: the afternoon that they spoke about their time together in Kent. She had told him then that she had not noticed any particular regard on his part towards her before he had proposed. Everything before then had been light; everything after had been tainted with an increasing doubt and anger on his part. No wonder there had been so many questions about her reaction to his offer; little wonder that she had felt an increasing distance in his manner after that time.

What haunted her more than anything was the look on Darcy's face the night of their great quarrel, when he had followed her to her room and heard her impassioned speech condemning his high-handed and ungentlemanly behavior. When he left her room that night he had said he would never impose himself on her again; and then he had shut the door between them. Much more than a door had been closed in that moment; much more had been lost than what she had ever appreciated until now.

Her husband was a good man, and he had loved her. If, by some miracle, they could start over again in this poor marriage, so full of mistaken intentions until now, could his affection and character overcome his resentment? He had written to Georgiana but not to her; did any of his love remain? Or would Darcy prove implacable in his anger? Would their marriage end up being exactly as described by her uncle Gardiner when Darcy first proposed? Elizabeth did not know; but she resolved that when she saw Darcy again, she would not rest until she had discovered these answers for herself.

CHAPTER TWENTY ONE

If Elizabeth had counted the days before, she agonized miserably over the hours now; wondering if or when she might expect an answer from Darcy to the letter she had sent him, and wondering what that answer might be. Her brief note, written innocently, now seemed cruel in light of the tender feelings he had held for her. If she had known more, if she had understood him better, she would have done differently. She would have written more fluently, and shared more of her own heart. The die was cast; she could only wait to see how Darcy responded to what she had written.

How could she express her heart, when she hardly knew it herself? Darcy loved her; what did she feel in return? It was nearly impossible to realize that he had loved her so ardently and for so long, and not to want to return some portion of those feelings. She was concerned for his welfare. She fervently regretted every harsh word she had directed towards him. She would not willingly wound him again, and she desired to be on friendlier terms than they were now. Was that love? Was that the type of affection on which to base a marriage?

She was walking with Georgiana in the woods alongside the stream one morning several days later, trying to raise her own melancholy spirits, when a shape moving through trees a little distance away caught their attention. A man with the same coloring and nearly the same height as Darcy was walking towards them on the path that led from the house; he would intercept them in a few seconds. For a few hopeful moments Elizabeth thought that Darcy himself might have returned, but that hope was dashed as the gentleman came through a little thicket and they could see him clearly.

"Richard!" Georgiana exclaimed, rushing to embrace him as soon as he was fully in view.

It was Colonel Richard Fitzwilliam, Darcy's cousin, whom Elizabeth had met at Rosings before her father's death called her away. Later he had stood up with Darcy at their hasty wedding, but she had not seen him since that time.

"Georgiana!" the colonel answered, accepting her embrace for a moment before stepping back to look at her more fully. Elizabeth could not help feeling touched by the obvious affection between the two cousins. While they spoke together for a moment, exchanging warm greetings, Elizabeth stood back a little to enjoy the domestic tableau.

Colonel Fitzwilliam had not changed at all in the months since he had witnessed their wedding. While he could not be called a truly handsome man, his figure was as tall and dignified as ever, and his open and charming air had not diminished. At one time Elizabeth had thought the colonel more appealing than Darcy because of his superior manners; he had been as courtly as her husband seemed to be aloof. In those days she might even have welcomed him as a possible marriage partner. But now his presence and the memories it invoked simply reminded her, keenly, of her husband's continued absence. An unfamiliar ache rose in her chest as she observed the other two.

The colonel finally seemed to recall her presence.

"Miss Elizabeth," he began, turning towards her apologetically, but then he caught himself with an easy laugh. "Pardon my error, please, Mrs. Darcy. The old title dies hard. You are the wife of my very fortunate cousin, but you still remain Miss Elizabeth in my mind."

"And you are as gallant as ever," Elizabeth answered with a somewhat strained smile as she curtsied. "Your error is forgiven. Is your family well? I hope they are experiencing the best of health."

"The very best; thank you."

"I enjoyed meeting Lord Robert and Lady Eleanor in town."

"My mother was quite taken with you. In her latest letter she mentioned that she hopes you will be able to see each other again the next time you are both in London."

"Has she left town, then?"

"She and my father are on the continent, visiting friends. I have just come from London myself."

"If you came from town then you must have seen Fitzwilliam!" Georgiana cried. "What is he doing there? We have not seen him in nearly a fortnight, and he has written to me only once!"

"I have seen him," the colonel confirmed, "and he is quite wrapped up in business matters, which he is working to resolve as soon as possible. But," he added with a sudden, penetrating look for Elizabeth, "I fear that may not be for some time yet."

Was the colonel aware of their difficulties? Perhaps he had brought an answering message from her husband. "I hope Mr. Darcy is also well," she said after a somewhat awkward pause, wondering how much her husband might have confided in his cousin.

The colonel hesitated. "He is, I would say, somewhat fatigued. That is to be expected at this time of year. The heat, you know."

"Yes, of course."

Georgiana had grown impatient with the formalities. "What are you doing here, Richard?" she asked. "We had no word that you were coming. You ought to have told us to expect you."

"Can't your favorite cousin drop in unannounced, if the mood takes him?" the colonel replied, looking back at her with mock indignation. "You would not make me stand on ceremony and wait for an invitation, would you?"

"Of course not; but Fitzwilliam is not here. You usually come to see him."

"I come here to see both of you," he chided her gently. "At any rate, I decided I should look in on you for a few days before I travel north to join my regiment."

"There is no need to look in on me," Georgiana replied, playfully indignant. "I am perfectly well."

"Well, then, perhaps we shall say that your brother has sent me to make a full report of your behavior in his absence." He smiled teasingly at Georgiana, who returned his look as she took his arm. Elizabeth fell in on Georgiana's other side, and the trio began to walk slowly back to the house together.

The two cousins began to speak of mutual family and friends, which gave Elizabeth time to consider the colonel's responses to Georgiana's innocent questions. His words had been evasive; there was no need for the colonel to report on Georgiana, not if Elizabeth was already there. But if the colonel bore no message to either her or Georgiana from Darcy, then why had he come to Pemberley? Did his lighthearted manner cover a more serious intent? Perhaps after receiving her letter, Darcy had decided he no longer wanted Elizabeth to have a position of care over his sister. Perhaps he could no longer abide her presence, and had sent his cousin to relieve Elizabeth of her responsibilities while he was away.

If that was the case, she could expect to return to Longbourn in disgrace in the very near future, humiliated, her reputation shattered. It would be a painful, but not improbable, reaction on Darcy's part.

When the next pause came in the colonel's remarks to Georgiana Elizabeth spoke to him carefully, measuring every word.

"It is remarkable how much time Mr. Darcy has devoted to his business matters. We have heard so little from him."

"I myself have not had much contact with him. He is a man singularly dedicated to carrying out what he believes to be his duties, leaving little time for leisure."

"We will have to hope for a speedy conclusion to those duties, then. Could he give no further information about when he might return to Pemberley?"

If the colonel found it odd that she was asking him about her own husband's plans, he showed no sign of it. Instead he looked at her gravely over Georgiana's head. "As I said, I think it is possible that he may need to stay away for some time."

"I see." She paused. "And how long may we look forward to enjoying your presence here?"

"I will stay, assuming you are willing to have me, as long as I believe I may be of service." The colonel made a gallant little bow, which Elizabeth acknowledged by a slight nod. Despite the colonel's words about joining his regiment, it sounded as though he might be planning on a sojourn of some length.

They were passing the stables just then, and Elizabeth's attention was caught by the colonel's horse, a tall gelding with military trim on its saddle, who was being walked out. The animal was blown and sweaty, its sheen and breathing indicating it had been ridden hard. She glanced curiously back at the colonel, noticing for the first time the dust on his clothes and his overall appearance. It was nothing like his usual careful grooming. He had the look of someone who had given more care to speed in the journey than in his appearance at the end of it; it was plain that he had not even taken the time to refresh himself before seeking out the two ladies.

"When did you leave town, sir?" she asked, looking back at the animal.

The colonel's eyes followed hers. "But yesterday morning," he answered, with an air that showed his awareness of her scrutiny, and Elizabeth pondered this piece of information. It was not quite noon now.

Even if the colonel had left London early the day before, he must have kept a surprising pace to arrive at Pemberley so early on the second day; normally she would not have expected even a single mounted man to arrive until the mid-afternoon at the earliest. She looked suspiciously back at the colonel, who met her gaze evenly.

"You keep up a remarkable pace, then; you must have wanted to arrive here as soon as possible."

The colonel bowed again. "As I said, I am pleased to be at my cousin's service," leaving Elizabeth burning to ask more. But Georgiana, pointing out a colorful butterfly on the path, began to speak on a different topic, and the conversation went on with no chance for Elizabeth to ask further questions.

∞

Dinner that night was a lively affair. Elizabeth had grown accustomed to Georgiana's reserved conversation and her husband's near silence at meals, but the colonel entertained them both with gossip from town and stories of his life in military service. Georgiana responded eagerly, with more laughter and high spirits than Elizabeth had ever seen from the girl. There was a bond between Georgiana and her cousin that surpassed the bond she had with her brother. It was clear that Georgiana felt none of the reticence with Richard that she felt with Darcy. He and Georgiana spoke freely of relatives and acquaintances who Elizabeth did not know; while Elizabeth, still preoccupied over Darcy, felt at times that her presence was scarcely noticed. Then the colonel would turn to her with a generous smile and encourage her to contribute in some way, and Elizabeth began to feel more at her ease.

After dinner Georgiana went to her new piano with no urging and sat down to play at once, evidently eager to demonstrate both her skill and her new instrument to her cousin. The colonel and Elizabeth took seats on a nearby pair of small settees that were grouped together for easy conversation. When Georgiana's attention was fully absorbed in her activity and the sounds of her playing filled the air, Elizabeth noticed the colonel reaching inside his jacket, withdrawing an envelope from the pocket there, giving Elizabeth a grave look as he did so.

He leaned close and spoke to her quietly, under the cover of the complicated fugue Georgiana was playing. "I have been entrusted to give this letter to you and only you." He pressed the envelope into Elizabeth's hand.

There was another purpose for the colonel's visit! Elizabeth's heart caught in her throat. There was no writing on the outside, so she could only guess at the sender's identity. "Is this from my husband?"

"Yes. He said it would be faster and more certain of arrival if I brought it to you directly. And he wanted me to give it to you in private, if possible," he added.

"In private?"

"So as not to disturb Georgiana's peace of mind, if that can be avoided."

"Of course." Elizabeth clutched the envelope tightly, the paper fairly burning in her hand. Her letter to Darcy had not been enough, and now the colonel was fully aware of the state of their marriage. Shame stained her cheeks; their separation was entirely her own fault.

"I take it from my conversation with Georgiana this afternoon that she is unaware of recent events," the colonel went on, still speaking as quietly as the music would allow, and Elizabeth could only nod. Apparently there were no secrets with him. "She is entirely ignorant, I think, of any domestic disturbance. It is probably best that she remains that way until matters are more settled."

The letter must contain a statement of some kind from her husband about the future of their marriage. Her heart sank. "I have tried my best to protect her from any such unnecessary burden of information. I would never want to be the cause of such disruption for Georgiana," she answered, feeling the bitter sting of disappointment. "News of that sort should come from her brother, when he feels the time is right."

"I agree entirely," the colonel nodded approvingly. "Darcy also asked me to tell you that there will be no dinner party for Bingley. Your invitations, if you have sent any out, should be rescinded immediately."

"I understand." At this confirmation of her worst fears, Elizabeth's heart sank even more. The colonel watched her closely.

"Allow me to say, please, that I admire your courage under the circumstances. My mother is also strongly disposed in your favor. You can always rely on our friendship and support."

Was the entire Fitzwilliam family aware of their disagreement? Whatever Darcy had told his cousin, it must be dreadful to make the colonel speak in this way. How Lady Catherine must be rejoicing in her triumph now!

Elizabeth had to read Darcy's letter right away. She smiled wanly at the colonel. "You are very kind. If you will excuse me, I believe I feel a headache coming on."

The colonel nodded understandingly. "Of course you want to read your letter at once. If you wish to retire, I will make your excuses to Georgiana." He looked at her sympathetically as she rose and began to turn away. "Do not fear, Mrs. Darcy. All will be well."

CHAPTER TWENTY TWO

In the privacy of her room, Elizabeth held the letter with trembling fingers. Nothing on the outside of the envelope gave a hint as to its contents. This was the moment she had been dreading, the time when she would discover her husband's intentions towards her after her cruelty and indifference towards him. From this point on, there would be no doubt about his feelings towards her. She opened the envelope and sank down carefully on her bed.

My dearest Elizabeth,

I beg your pardon in addressing you thus. It has been many months since I have thought of you in any other way, and even now, when I have finally realized the paucity of your affection for me; it is a privilege I am loath to surrender, especially since this will likely be the only time I will be able to speak to you in this way.

It is clear to me now that the difficulties in which we find ourselves now began at almost our first acquaintance. It is also clear to me that the position in which we now find ourselves may be untenable.

I am ashamed beyond words, after receiving your short note, that you believe I deserve thanks for taking notice of your family--that you would go so far as to express appreciation for the trifling courtesy I paid of calling on your aunt and uncle here in town. I can only blame myself for your reaction. When I remember some of my words to you in the past-- that your family is not the equal of mine, that they were not to be invited to visit you at Pemberley, I know that my shame cannot go deep enough.

I am also painfully prompted to review my conduct with you from the day of our wedding until now, and to realize how much my behavior as a husband has been lacking. I used you as though you have no thoughts or feelings of your own; I cannot view my actions without reprehension.

I love you, Elizabeth. I ought to have told you this many months ago, and left you in no doubt of my true feelings. The estrangement between us now is entirely of my own making.

On our first evening at Pemberley you stated that you would criticize only where you saw a real defect of character, and that you would say nothing of me which I did not deserve. Little did I know how prophetic your words would be.

If I could give you your previous life back, if I could return you to that state of happiness that was your dwelling before your father's death and my proposal, I would do so at once. But what was done cannot be well undone now. Returning to Longbourn, as you probably realize, is almost certainly out of the question. In Meryton and its environs you would be subject to every manner of gossip and speculation imaginable once the nature of our union became known. Staying at Pemberley must also be odious to you, except perhaps for the companionship of my sister.

Your happiness is my only desire. To that end I am arranging for an establishment to be set up for you in a neighboring county, in whatever sort of home you choose, where you may live in comfort as long as you want. Your mother and sisters can join you there if you desire. My arrangements for their maintenance will not change; your mother will still receive her allowance, and your sisters will experience no changes in their fortune. If you decide that you prefer to have them remain in their present state at Longbourn, their situation there will stay the same. You need never fear that a permanent break between us will affect them in any way. My only request would be that you still allow for some small amount of contact between you and my sister, as I know how fond of you she has become. Beyond this, I ask for nothing.

If, in some small part of your heart, you find that you may perhaps learn to tolerate my presence one day, I beg most humbly for the chance to earn the love and devotion that I have so far failed to inspire in you.

These, then, are the choices before you: to move to a location of your choosing, renouncing your position as Mrs. Darcy in the eyes of society if not in law; or, if you prefer, to continue at Pemberley as my wife, the mistress of my home, a trusted guide and companion for my sister, and the mother of my children. Whatever choice you make, you will always be in my heart.

In that same conversation we had on the night when I first brought you to Pemberley, you told me that I ought to have married a fashionable young woman, not one who is likely to speak her mind. I hope that you can recall my response to you. I told you I did not regret my choice, for your criticism has always been tempered with charity. I pray for that charity now.

After I conclude my business in town, when or how I return to

Pemberley will depend on your answer. One word from you on this subject will silence me forever. If you can give me some token of hope, no matter how small, I will fly to your side. If, however, you are irrevocably set against me and have no wish to continue in this marriage, then tell me so at once. I will abide by your decision.

Until I hear from you again, I remain

Your devoted husband,

Fitzwilliam Darcy

Elizabeth held the letter in her hands for a moment when she finished reading it, feeling the sting of tears in her eyes. Then she folded the pages together carefully, as if they were precious, and held them close to her heart.

She had not expected such unwavering assertions of affection, nor such an outpouring of remorse.

How much had it cost Darcy's pride to make his generous, self-sacrificing offer? She could not even imagine. He was willing to to set aside his own wishes and desires, to give up so much for her comfort and her peace of mind, and yet to ask for so little in return. The kindness and humility expressed here put all her former feelings against her husband to shame. She had already given over her resentment and anger; but if she had still harbored any such feelings, they would have disappeared under the assault of these heartfelt words.

Relief washed over her like a wave, and in its wake the emotion she had tried to deny for some time came forward, demanding recognition. It grew, swelling and spreading, until she felt it in the deepest fibers of her being.

She must write to Darcy at once, though she doubted any words could capture the feelings in her heart at this moment. There were some emotions too delicate for words, too fragile to commit to paper. But she would do her best, because whenever she did see him again she wanted to see the answering love-light in his eyes even as she confessed her love for him.

Love. Was that what this was? Yes, it was--a warm love filling her completely!

Half weeping, half laughing, she took up pen and paper.

My dearest Fitzwilliam,

You have made an honorable offer and asked for an honest answer, and so I feel compelled to respond to you at once. I choose not to leave Pemberley.

She paused, weighing her words carefully. There was a peculiar feeling in her chest, a lightness and warmth that had never been present before when she thought about her husband.

Although I have come to know and appreciate this home, and although I have developed a deep and abiding affection for Georgiana, in coming to this decision I believe I have thought only of you.

The feelings that I expressed on your last evening here have changed completely from what they were then. They are, in fact, now quite the opposite.

No. This would never do. The nascent tenderness in her heart was still cautious, unwilling to risk further hurt, but if ever there were a time to throw caution to the wind, it was now. She must let her heart speak for her.

If you were here in person, now, I would say so much more. I would apologize more fully for the abuse you suffered at my hands, and assure you of my desire to correct every misunderstanding between us. There is only so much that can be expressed in writing. There are not enough pages in the world to hold my regret for the past, my hopes for the future, or the regard I have come to have for you.

What gift can a woman give to a man who already owns so much? The only token that I can send you, the best and truest token in my possession, is my heart. If you still want it, it is yours.

Please come home. I am your loving wife,
Elizabeth Darcy

Gazing at her signature on the page, Elizabeth wanted to dance, to spin wildly about the room in joy. Instead, she must seal the letter and make ready to send it at once. Even a moment's delay would be too much.

As she rose to her feet, a motion by her bedroom window caught her attention, a brief fluttering of the curtain, and she moved closer to investigate. Some careless servant had opened the window to air the room during the day and neglected to close it again. Now, in the early dusk of a summer's eve, the curtain had caught the warm breeze and was blowing lightly, drawing her towards it. Elizabeth lifted her hand to rearrange the curtain and close the window, but as she looked out she caught her breath in wonder and delight. The night was warm and humid, with clouds obscuring the moon just as they had on the night she had stood on the balcony with her husband. In the east the clouds were rolling away, revealing a sliver of starry sky. Just beyond their edge, visible even in the early dark, Darcy's comet was shining.

CHAPTER TWENTY THREE

It was impossible to guess how many times Elizabeth re-read her letter from Darcy that night. She sat in the window seat for hours, using the light of the comet to recite Darcy's tender words to her over and over. She savored every sweet sensation his endearments engendered, and when she finally yielded to sleep she kept the letter under her pillow, where her hand rested on it all night. It was not the letter itself that brought her comfort; it was the reassurance that all would be well, that her husband would return to her and that they could make a happy marriage after all.

She knew that the future with Darcy would still be fraught with difficulties. They still had many misunderstandings to work through; and painful memories, like scars, would need time to fade away. But they would face them together from now on, and she felt no fear. She felt only gratitude for the worth of the man she had married, and hope that Darcy would be able to return to her as soon as possible.

The sun awoke her the next morning, shining brilliantly across her pillow. Elizabeth laughed at her own carelessness when she looked out the window and saw the position of the sun in the sky. In the excitement of reading Darcy's letter she had stayed up far too late, and now the day was nearly half gone. She rang for Cora and the girl responded at once.

"Good morning, ma'am."

"Good morning, Cora. I would like to dress and do my hair right away, please."

"Of course, ma'am."

"How long have I slept?"

"Quite late, ma'am."

"Has the morning post been taken to Lambton?"

"It was gone an hour ago, ma'am. Is there something you would like added?"

"Perhaps--no, never mind. I have a letter to send, but I think I can find someone who might be willing to take it to town for me. Is Colonel Fitzwilliam up?"

"He's been up since dawn. He likes to keep his army hours, he said."

If she had risen just an hour earlier, her answering letter for Darcy might already be on its way, but this might be even better. She would emulate her husband and send her letter by the hand of someone he knew and trusted, rather than by the common post. Elizabeth smiled confidently at herself in the mirror while Cora arranged her hair, practicing what she would say to the colonel.

Clearly Colonel Fitzwilliam had feared the worst when he gave her the letter the night before. Elizabeth found it surprising that Darcy, such a private man, would have confided so much about his marriage to his cousin, but apparently she had misjudged her husband yet again. She still did not understand why the colonel had felt so rushed in his journey to Pemberley, but perhaps he was simply trying to be of service to his cousin. He must have been aware of the choice that Darcy would offer his wife. Even now he might be lingering downstairs, waiting to see Elizabeth and wondering what her decision would be. If she could convince him, without violating her own privacy too much, that a happy reunion was in the offing, perhaps he might volunteer to bring her answer back to Darcy himself.

But when Elizabeth came downstairs, looking eagerly about her, the colonel was nowhere to be seen. The sound of the pianoforte from the music room betrayed Georgiana's location, but a quick look inside did not show him there either. "I understand the colonel is an early riser," she said to Mrs. Reynolds, as the housekeeper passed her in the hallway. "Is he still in the house?"

"He rose very early, ma'am, and has been gone for some time."

"Do you know where he went?"

"He generally rides about the estate in the cool of the day, before the sun grows hot. By now he would be in Lambton, if he follows his usual pattern. Would you like me to locate him for you?"

Elizabeth shook her head. "No, that will not be necessary; but I would appreciate it if you would let me know when he returns."

"Certainly, Mrs. Darcy."

Elizabeth took food from the sideboard and ate her own hasty meal, then settled in the parlor to wait for the colonel. The upcoming interview with Colonel Fitzwilliam had her in a state of suppressed excitement. She earnestly hoped that the colonel would agree to return to London at once with her letter for Darcy, once he understood its importance. He had mentioned traveling north to join his regiment, but she felt sure that had been a ruse, an excuse to stop at Pemberley without exciting Georgiana's curiosity. Now that she had reason to hope, she was painfully impatient, anxious for the return of the person who would be the means of ending this separation from her husband.

An hour passed with no sign of the colonel. Restlessly Elizabeth took up a book and tried to read, but she had too much nervous energy to allow her to focus on more than a half page at a time. In other circumstances she might have spent her agitation on a long walk, but she did not want to risk being out of sight of the house; so instead she took out a pen and paper and began to write.

Elizabeth had first neglected and then avoided answering her sister's most recent letter, which had arrived the day of her argument with Darcy. She had planned to respond right away, but was delayed by Georgiana's dilemma. After that she had been too disturbed in her spirits to write rationally, and then too worried about what the future might hold. The time had now come when she could begin to bare her heart.

My dearest Jane,

I have sadly neglected you, I fear, not to have written to you for so long. I hope that this letter will, by its novelty, atone for the delay; and that it might well forever after hold me blameless from any charges of oversight or indifference.

I have astonishing news, Jane; news that I know will please you, even if you have a hard time crediting it at first. My heart is truly engaged for the first time in my life, and the object of my affection is none other than my very own husband, Fitzwilliam Darcy!

I know you will protest. I know you will say that you know I do not even like him, and that I need not sacrifice any more for my family by voicing sentiments which are not my own. But those feelings are all in the past now, and this is the last time I shall ever speak of them. Though I have sometimes been accused of professing opinions which are not my own, I can tell you now, in all seriousness, that I have come to love my husband.

I have not always felt this way, as you know. He is not an easy man to understand. I have mistaken his intentions since nearly the first day of our acquaintance, interpreting his silences as disapproval, imputing the worst of motives to almost every action he has taken, and misjudging him in every way possible. We were crossed in our understanding of each other at nearly every turn.

I know now that he is a good man. There is a gentleness in the way he treats those who are most dependent on his goodwill--his servants, his sister, and me. He is an exemplary brother and friend, and he does what he thinks is right regardless of the cost to him. Truly, Jane, despite my previous assertions to the contrary, he has no improper pride. He is the best man that I know.

Whatever would Papa say, if he knew of all this? Surely he would never have dreamed of such an outcome to this unlikely match! I like to think that he is watching, and that he approves this most unexpected development.

Unfortunately we have been in some difficulties here. I spoke to my husband in anger about matters I did not fully understand, and regretted it almost at once. He is in town now and I do not know when he will return. But when he does, I intend to open my heart to him fully, make amends where I can, and show him all the faith and affection I should have had for him from the beginning. Until then I will pray every day that he can forgive me, and that we can have a new start in our relationship and in this marriage.

In her improved mood, Elizabeth could not resist teasing her sister somewhat.

Finally, my dear sister, if everything I have written here does not convince you of the truth of my newfound affection for Mr. Darcy, perhaps I should describe again the glories of Pemberley. You would have no trouble believing me then! I hope that you may see them for yourself one day.

If she and Darcy could reconcile, Elizabeth thought with a smile as she continued writing, was it possible that Bingley could also reconcile with Jane? Surely Darcy would no longer look down on Jane as a possible match for his friend. Perhaps Jane could join her at Pemberley when Bingley arrived--but then Elizabeth caught herself with a frown. Darcy had said there would be no dinner party for Bingley. She would have to ask the colonel if he had any further information on what Darcy had meant by that.

She must not forget to address the troubling issues Jane had brought up in her letter.

Speaking of Mama, her plan to send Lydia to Brighton sounds as monstrously ill-conceived as any of her other schemes. I can only hope that some great disaster, such as a lack of suitable dresses or bonnets, may have kept our sister at home for the summer instead. If she has indeed gone with Mrs. Forster, as you thought she might, I doubt much worse could happen to her there then at home. After all, although my husband's generosity has improved our family's prospects considerably, the Bennets of Hertfordshire still can not be considered rich. I cannot imagine that any of our younger sisters would be an attractive target simply for their own charms. Perhaps if Lydia does go to Brighton and makes herself ridiculous flirting with all the officers, she will return home a little more conscious of her lack of consequence to anyone in the world.

Perhaps, Elizabeth thought as she continued writing, just perhaps, in the future, Darcy would consent to allowing Jane or even one of her younger sisters to visit Pemberley, where they could be better supervised. Georgiana would benefit from the exposure to more young people her own age, and Mary and Kitty could only improve by exposure to such superior society. Now that she was certain of Darcy's feelings for her and her own in return, nothing seemed impossible.

She was about to close and seal the letter when she remembered one final, important communication.

By the by, there is still one more piece of information which is probably not needed now, but I will relate it anyway in hopes that it might possibly prove useful. If Wickham is still anywhere near Meryton, you ought to do everything in your power to avoid him, and to tell others of your acquaintance to do the same. I am afraid that he is not a man to be trusted; we have been entirely deceived in his character.

The front door had just opened, and Elizabeth heard the colonel's voice speaking to the servants in the hallway. Hastily she finished.

I hope to write again soon, more promptly and more fully, after Mr. Darcy has returned from town. Until then I am your affectionate sister

She signed the letter and sealed it. As she did so, Colonel Fitzwilliam came striding into the room. When he saw her he came directly to her and bowed. "Good morning, Mrs. Darcy. May I ask after your health today?"

Elizabeth smiled radiantly at him. "I am entirely better, thank you."

"Your headache is quite relieved then?"

"It was a trifling thing; it disappeared as quickly as it came."

"I am glad to hear it," he answered, observing her cautiously.

"And I believe that I may have you to thank for my improved health."

He tilted his head to one side, considering her words. "How is that, madam?"

"Why, you cured my headache by bringing me the most potent medicine in the world--my husband's letter."

"Indeed!" The colonel gave a short laugh. "I had not anticipated such an immediate, beneficial effect!"

"I can safely say, colonel, the only tonic more restorative than a letter from my husband would be his presence here with me."

The colonel looked at her with pleased satisfaction. "As I said once before, my cousin was most fortunate in his choice of a bride."

Elizabeth acknowledged the compliment with a slight bow of her head and then asked if he was hungry, knowing that his breakfast had been some hours ago. Upon receiving his affirmative reply, she rang the bell and called for refreshments to be served. The colonel brightened at the prospect of food and immediately sat down to wait with her. They chatted on inconsequential subjects for several minutes while plates of fruit were brought in and arranged before them; and then Elizabeth decided to broach the subject of her letter.

"I wonder if I might ask a favor of you, if it is not too much trouble."

"It would be my pleasure to help you if I can."

"I think we both know that you have no immediate plans to join your regiment in the north." Elizabeth raised a questioning eyebrow as she said this, and the colonel had the grace to look a little embarrassed.

"You are correct, of course. I had to come up with some reason to visit Pemberley, some motive that would not sound suspicious to

Georgiana. Traveling to join my regiment seemed like a convenient excuse."

"Your excuse was unnecessary, since Georgiana has been unaware of anything amiss. All is set right now, and I have an important communication to send back to my husband. I wonder if I might be able to impose on you to take it yourself."

The colonel looked at her, tilting his head slightly as if puzzled. "I do not have the pleasure of understanding you. What has been set right?"

Elizabeth was a little flustered. Without knowing exactly how much the colonel knew, she was reluctant to mention any specifics. "The difficulties which have been keeping my husband in town have been resolved. I expect he will return here as soon as he receives my letter."

The colonel frowned. "I am unaware of any changes in the situation at hand."

Elizabeth raised her chin. "The situation has completely changed."

"In what way, exactly?"

Such a direct question took her aback. For a moment Elizabeth floundered, struggling to devise a response, but before she could say anything, the colonel went on.

"When I last saw Darcy, Lady Catherine was being as obstinate as ever."

"Lady Catherine!"

"There was no change of status at that time. Darcy asked me to come here specifically to protect you and Georgiana."

Elizabeth was now thoroughly confounded. "Protect us from what?"

"Why, from Lady Catherine and her schemes, of course."

"Her schemes?"

"Yes, of course." He saw her look of astonishment. "Darcy sent me here to prevent Lady Catherine from removing Georgiana from Pemberley."

CHAPTER TWENTY FOUR

"Whatever do you mean?" Elizabeth exclaimed, shocked beyond the point of courtesy.

The colonel stared back at her, equally surprised. "Did Darcy not tell you anything about this?"

"Mr. Darcy has not said a word to me about Lady Catherine."

"But I thought Darcy's letter to you--" the colonel started, and then stopped. "What else would Darcy write about, if not his aunt?"

"Never mind that now; pray tell me what is happening this instant."

The colonel shook his head. "I see that I have blundered into some sort of error. If Darcy did not choose to tell you then I should not either."

"But why would my husband not share something of such importance with me?"

"I cannot say. He must have had some reason."

Elizabeth fixed him with her firmest expression. "Colonel, you must know that I cannot rest until I know all the particulars."

"Your curiosity does not disturb me. I am not obligated to satisfy it."

"But I am obligated to protect my sister, and I cannot do so when I am wholly in ignorance of any threats against her."

The colonel looked at her for a moment, and then shook his head. "That is true, but I am not inclined to speak more on this subject without asking Darcy first." The look on the colonel's face said that he considered the matter settled.

Elizabeth decided to try a different tack. "Did my husband expressly forbid you from speaking of this with me?"

"He did not, but there must be a good reason why he has not done so himself."

"But is it not logical to think that, if my husband had wanted you to keep it a secret, he would have told you so? And since he did not mention it, it would not be wrong to tell me."

The colonel looked at her again, hesitating, and Elizabeth could see that he was wavering. She tried one last approach. "Colonel, I shall use all the resources at my disposal to find out what is happening, with or without your help; and then I will do whatever I think necessary to protect Georgiana. But it would be so much easier if you would share what you know now."

The colonel frowned at her unhappily, considering her response. "Well, Darcy is not here and I must do as I think best," he finally said. "And if you are truly uninformed about any of this, I suppose I will have to tell you everything from the beginning." He settled back into his chair as if preparing for a long stay.

"Lady Catherine wrote to Darcy shortly after you arrived at Pemberley," the colonel began, speaking earnestly, "threatening to do everything in her power to have him repudiate his marriage to you. You know how determined she is, once her mind is set on a plan. Darcy has been fighting her ever since."

Elizabeth gasped in disbelief. "Repudiate his marriage? I do not understand."

"She threatened you in town with having your marriage annulled, did she not? I thought I understood from Darcy that she had."

Elizabeth recalled her forceful encounter with Lady Catherine at Darcy House. "You might say that we had a spirited discussion. She did say something about finding an error in the marriage contract, but Mr. Darcy assured me that he would never go along with such a plan."

"Of course he would not! The man is utterly devoted to those he loves, and besides, this would not be the conduct of a gentleman. He told Lady Catherine that he has no intention of breaking his marriage vows to you, now or ever."

Darcy's letter, resting inside her sleeve where she had hidden it for safekeeping, became even more poignant. "They must have had this conversation when he returned her call to me at Darcy House, the night before we left town."

"Indeed. Lady Catherine told him then that she would do everything in her power to see his 'degrading' marriage ended. Darcy lost his temper entirely and told her that she would never be welcome at Pemberley again, unless by some miracle she found it in her heart to beg your forgiveness and recognize you from then on as Mrs. Darcy."

So Darcy had been her champion that night after all! Elizabeth's heart leaped. "Go on."

"Her ladyship was quite disturbed, as you can imagine. I cannot recall the last time anyone defied Lady Catherine de Bourgh so thoroughly! She became incensed and made wild accusations against your character. The servants told me it was quite a scene."

Elizabeth recalled her own interview with the strong-willed matriarch. "Creating scenes seems to be a particular talent of hers."

The colonel nodded. "She finally threatened to have Georgiana removed from Darcy's care entirely unless he did as she wished. At that point Darcy turned and left the house."

No wonder Darcy had been so grim and preoccupied at the table that evening! "I knew that he was disturbed by his meeting with her, but he would not give me any of the particulars."

The colonel snorted. "I am not surprised. Darcy has an inordinate sense of responsibility. He believes it is his duty to shield those he loves from unpleasantness around them, no matter how futile the effort. It is at once one of his best qualities and one of his worst, for how can one man carry such a heavy burden his whole life? But I digress.

"Darcy did not believe that Lady Catherine was serious in her threats. As you have seen for yourself, she has often tried to intimidate others into doing what she wants. Because of her title and wealth, most people acquiesce very quickly, and so her threats have never turned into anything more. This time was different. Almost from the moment you left town, she began to contact other family members, trying to bring pressure to bear on him."

"Is that why he went to town so hastily?"

The colonel shook his head. "I gather from Darcy that some other matter drove him to town, though he would not say exactly what." Here he glanced at her uncertainly. "But after he arrived he found that Lady Catherine had begun agitating against him with the other members of the family."

All this time she had been unaware of the turmoil weighing on her husband. "But she could not succeed! Was not Mr. Darcy's guardianship of his sister laid out in their father's will? How can a will be overturned?"

"It cannot be overturned, but it can be ignored."

"And how does she mean for it to be ignored? What is it that she means to do?"

The colonel hesitated before he answered. "Lady Catherine thinks that if enough family pressure is brought to bear on Darcy, he will give you up rather than risk losing his sister."

"I see." Her heart sank as the implications of the colonel's statement hit home. Her thoughts floundered, drowning in a sea of doubt. Though she was now convinced of Darcy's devotion to her, he was also devoted to his sister. Which affection would carry more weight with him, if put to the test? Yet the letter Elizabeth had read last night seemed to say that he had already made his choice. The colonel saw the look on her face and spoke gently.

"Never fear, Mrs. Darcy. Lady Catherine's scheme has no chance of success without Darcy's cooperation, which he will never give. Men like my cousin do not surrender their hearts easily; and once given, there is no chance of it being recalled. Darcy will find a way to rally the family to his side and keep you and Georgiana."

Elizabeth took a deep breath. The colonel had put her feet on solid ground again. "How does your aunt mean to bring this pressure?"

"By telling everyone in the family about your low connections, as she calls them; your lack of fortune, and your 'utter unsuitability,' as she terms it, to have any influence upon Georgiana. She believes that if Darcy is forced to choose between you and his sister, he will choose her; and then he will offer you a discreet settlement in order to end the marriage. At that point, she believes, Darcy will finally marry her own daughter."

"What an evil, despicable woman!" Elizabeth cried. "To separate a brother and sister who love each other, merely for the sake of advancing her own daughter!"

"To say nothing of separating a devoted husband and wife," the colonel said with a quick, inquisitive look, leaving Elizabeth to wonder if he had guessed more than he was saying. She wished he would not be so prescient, but she would admit nothing. She raised her chin proudly.

"I trust you have no plans to take Georgiana away with you. If you do, you must know that I would never go along with such a scheme."

"Of course not! I could take her with me, as her other guardian, and nobody would contest my right to do so. But I will not. She is happy here at Pemberley, with her brother and you. And," he added with a half-smile, "I see no harm from her association with the 'headstrong, impertinent girl' which my aunt described meeting. In fact, I can see that your lively spirits have been very good for her."

Elizabeth barely noticed the compliment. "Then why are you at Pemberley? Would it not be better for you to stay in town, to stand with my husband against his aunt?"

"For two reasons. First, to see for myself how Georgiana is doing with you. Darcy gave me nothing but glowing reports on her progress, but I had to see for myself. And secondly, he thought it best for me to be here in case Lady Catherine tries to take matters into her own hands."

Elizabeth thought of the colonel's hasty ride from town, of the fatigued animal outside the stable. "You mean in case Lady Catherine sends someone to collect Georgiana without my husband's consent."

"Exactly." Seeing her look of horror, he added, "Never fear, Mrs. Darcy. It is only a precaution. Darcy has retained the services of the best solicitor in the city, and he is working day and night to stop this foolishness and make Lady Catherine give up her objections forever. He is fighting for you--and Georgiana--even as we speak. Mrs. Darcy, where are you going?" he added, for Elizabeth had risen and was making her way to the door.

"I beg your pardon, colonel. Please forgive me for taking my leave of you, but it is imperative that my husband receives this letter as soon as possible."

"But--this very instant?" he said in amazement to her retreating back, and Elizabeth forced herself to turn around.

"Though I am not at liberty to give you further details, I can assure you that Mr. Darcy has great need of the information I am sending him."

"Then I will not detain you for a moment, but allow me to secure the services of a trustworthy member of this household. We can ensure that Darcy hears from you as soon as possible. I will speak with Mrs. Reynolds right now to find someone, if you wish."

Elizabeth thanked him, and the colonel, ever obliging, left to do as he said. In the meantime Elizabeth stood contemplatively, studying her letter to Darcy as it lay in her hand. She ran her fingers thoughtfully over the seal. Her husband was defying his aunt, he was bearing with the scrutiny of his family, and he was risking losing his beloved sister; all for the sake of a woman who had never even declared her affection for him--except in this letter. Should she open the letter and add to it, letting her husband know that she was aware of the forces he faced?

No, she decided. It was better for him to believe she was acting of her own free will, without undue influence; which was certainly the truth, for she had been entirely ignorant of Lady Catherine's machinations until now. That, she suddenly realized, was probably the reason Darcy had held back this information--he wanted to be certain that, if she chose to stay at Pemberley, it would be for himself, not for consideration of Georgiana or anything else. She would do him the same honor and let her words stand as they were. This was not the time to do anything to make Darcy doubt her motives or her faith in him, just when their relationship might finally be on a secure footing.

With the colonel's assistance and a recommendation from Mrs. Reynolds she was soon able to secure the services of one of the under grooms, who was happy to travel to town for the handsome bonus she promised. She commissioned the letter to his care, bidding him to take it to her husband with all possible speed; and hoping he might return with an answer from her husband, or even, possibly, with Darcy himself. With luck her letter would be in his hands late the following day. All she could do now was wait.

CHAPTER TWENTY FIVE

Two days passed by quietly at Pemberley, with nothing of note occurring. By unspoken agreement Elizabeth and the colonel arranged their activities so that one or the other of them was within easy sight of Georgiana at all times, and they deliberately kept their walks about the estate as close to the house as possible without arousing suspicion. The colonel had arranged that news of any unusual arrivals or visitors to Lambton be brought to him right away, and he kept a wary eye out for anyone making unexpected deliveries to the house. All of this was an elaborate precaution, the colonel assured Elizabeth, as the real battle was being fought in town; but he was following Darcy's admonition to be thorough. Colonel Fitzwilliam threw himself into the task so much that Elizabeth suspected he rather relished the opportunity to play soldier at home, rather than fighting foreigners across the sea.

Elizabeth, of course, had her own reason to look out for any deliveries coming to the house. Her answering letter to Darcy must have reached him by now, and she could expect a response, one way or the other, within a day or two--depending on how he chose to reply. He might send an answering letter back to her, but she rather hoped she would look out the window and see either his carriage or himself on horseback riding up the lane at any moment. What he would say to her, and how she would respond to him, were questions that preoccupied her constantly. She longed to see the smile he saved only for her, to hear his deep voice speak her name, to feel his admiring gaze on her once again. It had been too, too long.

With Georgiana's constant presence it was difficult for Elizabeth to speak privately with Colonel Fitzwilliam again, but in the afternoon of the second day she did manage a few quiet moments in the midst of a spirited discussion on the contents of a certain novel. Georgiana and the colonel each had a different recollection of a certain key event in the story, which Elizabeth had never read; and so at length Georgiana announced that she would go to the library to find the book and prove which person had the better memory. She left the room with the air of determination that had become more characteristic of her in the last few weeks.

The colonel watched her leave the room with an air of satisfaction.

"It is remarkable what a change you have brought about in her," he said, when he was certain Georgiana was out of earshot. "She is still shy at times, but your self-possession has certainly begun to make its mark on her."

"I have grown very fond of Georgiana," Elizabeth answered with an affectionate smile. "Her improvements have been her own making, however. She has come to the age where self-assurance naturally begins to grow as young ladies are exposed to more society; and over time, I believe you will see her confidence improve even more."

"Hmph! I do not agree. She told me that she told you all about her sad business last summer, and that you spoke to Darcy on her behalf. You must have worked some kind of magic, I think, to win her trust so easily. She said her mind has been remarkably free from worry since that time, and for that I must thank you."

"And I thank you, but you still give me too much credit. It is merely the effect of having the listening ear of an understanding sister, I think. One cannot confide everything in an older brother, no matter how affectionate and devoted he may be."

"Nevertheless, I will be sure to let the rest of the family know of the beneficial effect you have had on her. It may be of some small assistance in counteracting Lady Catherine's plans."

Elizabeth was glad the colonel had raised the subject of his aunt once again, for she still had many questions about the topic they had discussed two days before. The colonel would not have the same dispensation her husband had received, she decided. He was the only person who could answer the questions she had in mind, and she intended to ask them all. "There are still many things which I do not understand about Lady Catherine's designs," she began, making the most of her opportunity. "Please explain, if you can, how Lady Catherine expects her plan to work when it depends so much on the actions of others. Mr. Darcy and I would both have to agree to dissolve a legally contracted marriage, and there is the little matter of my family and the objections they would make! There is the scandal that would attach not just to Georgiana, but to Miss de Bourgh. Surely Lady Catherine does not want that for her daughter."

"My dear Mrs. Darcy, your naivete is refreshing. Scandals occur quite often in the Ton, and if the family is wealthy or important enough, the damage never lasts for too long. However, as I said previously, this is not something that should cause you great concern. Her plan has no chance of succeeding."

"Why not?"

"Because the worst charge Lady Catherine has laid at your doorstep is that of being from a family that is not--" he paused tactfully, "as well off as her own."

Elizabeth saw no need for delicacy. "You may speak plainly, colonel: my family is not rich."

The colonel looked at her gratefully. "Not to put too fine a point on it, but yes. You are not wealthy, but my family cares nothing for that. If Darcy had married someone who was truly unacceptable for some reason, someone who was compromised in some way, things might be different; but your character is unimpeachable, your reputation untarnished. It is impossible for Georgiana to be tainted through her association with you, as her ladyship insists, and everyone who has had the pleasure of making your acquaintance knows that."

It was the most forceful statement the colonel had yet made in her favor, and Elizabeth warmed to the compliment. But she could not resist teasing.

"Everyone knows it except for Lady Catherine," she pointed out, and the colonel smiled grimly.

"Indeed, everyone but Lady Catherine; but my aunt sees only what is convenient for her and her plans."

"A quality she shares with many others I could name."

"Whom I could name as well."

"Is Lady Catherine really so convinced that my family and I could be swayed by money, that we would subject ourselves to such humiliation simply for financial advantage?"

"Many families have been swayed for less," the colonel answered with a rueful half-smile. "She does not know that your case would be any different."

Elizabeth recalled the letters from her mother and Kitty and admitted to herself that, at least in her mother's situation, if it came to the test, Lady Catherine might be right. Greed had always ruled the day there. She quickly pushed the unworthy thought out of her mind.

"It is almost a shame, then, that her ladyship will never have a chance to discover her error. I am not as used to the ways of society as you are, colonel, but I do know my husband. I believe I can safely say that Mr. Darcy will never allow anyone to dictate terms to him."

"You are entirely correct. Darcy will not accept blackmail, and he can always be trusted to put his principles before his inclination. Even if our entire family disapproved of you, which they do not, he would not bend from his duty. He is having his solicitor review all the documents to ensure that everything is in order, and he has solicited the assistance of his uncle to use his influence on the rest of the family. My family will receive confirmation of your character in time, and there will be an end to the matter."

Elizabeth took some comfort in these observations, not only in what the colonel was saying but in the easy confidence with which he spoke. He was right, of course. She herself had seen that Lady Catherine held no real influence over her nephew; and her strategy, based as it was on mistaken assumptions about Elizabeth's character, had no basis in reality.

"I had the privilege of meeting your uncle, Mr. Gardiner, in town once, not long before coming here," the colonel added casually, while Elizabeth continued with her own thoughts. "You bear a strong resemblance to him, you know."

"You have met my uncle?" Elizabeth said, amazed.

"Yes. Darcy introduced us when I met with him to discuss this business. He is a fine gentleman."

"I knew that Mr. Darcy was invited to dinner at my uncle's, but I was unaware of any further acquaintance between them. My uncle was at Darcy House?"

"Oh yes! They appear to be on very easy terms. I gather that Darcy has come to enjoy Mr. Gardiner's company."

"I would not have imagined such an outcome just six months ago," Elizabeth said, with equal parts pleasure and pride. Her husband had become friends with a man who was in trade--all for her sake.

"Nor I. Love has a way of overturning our expectations, does it not? One can never be sure where it may lead."

Elizabeth smiled reflectively. The colonel had unknowingly voiced a thought in her own head.

"Do you know," he went on humorously after a moment, "that you and Darcy have one remarkable trait in common?"

"Besides being married to each other?"

The colonel smiled. "You are the only two people I know who have ever stood up to Lady Catherine de Bourgh!"

The unexpected observation drew a laugh from Elizabeth just as Georgiana returned with the novel under discussion, and so the conversation with Colonel Fitzwilliam ended on a happy note.

CHAPTER TWENTY SIX

Late in the morning of the fourth day Elizabeth felt her heart pound hard when, looking down from an upper window, she saw an approaching rider making his way up the lane to Pemberley. By the distant outline of the form on the horse, she could see at once that It was not Darcy. After a few more seconds she could also see that it was not the groom she had commissioned with her letter; but a response from her husband might well be carried by another messenger. She could barely contain her impatience as she went down the stairs to the front entry, where Mrs. Reynolds was paying the carrier, and took the envelope eagerly into her hand.

Her name was written in Jane's careful writing. The letter was not from Darcy.

Despite the disappointment that swept over her, a letter from Jane could never be a cause for regret. Elizabeth took the letter to the parlor and called for tea, then prepared to sit and read at her leisure. She noted the dates on each page as she removed them from the envelope, for apparently the letter had been written over a period of several days. There were half a dozen pages or so, written quite through, and the envelope was full. Elizabeth therefore found the earliest date and began her reading there.

My dearest sister,

I fear that I may have written to you too quickly last time, and given you information that led to an inaccurate portrayal of Mr. Bingley and his intentions. Either our information was wrong, or we were greatly deceived. Mr. Bingley is not leaving Netherfield!

We discovered this news in the following manner: yesterday afternoon Mama received word when she stopped at the butcher's that Mr. Bingley had sent orders for Netherfield to be opened up again. He was planning to return to Meryton no later than today; and the housekeeper, Mrs. Nicholls, was directed to recall what furniture she could from storage and put at least the master's chamber in readiness since he would have need of it right away. Poor Mrs. Nicholls was nearly distracted by her master's sudden change of heart, trying to arrange the house, bring back the other servants, and have everything prepared as it should be in time for his arrival.

For very different reasons our mother is also nearly distracted. I must admit that it is rather embarrassing to hear her proclaim to everyone in the house, including the servants' listening ears, how she believes Mr. Bingley is returning to Netherfield for the sole purpose of making an offer to me, and how she thinks I could not be, as she says, so beautiful for nothing. She keeps on in this loud manner no matter how many times I ask her to lower her voice. Her greatest fear, she says, is that, with Papa gone, she has no way of calling on Mr. Bingley in order to invite him to call on us.

She need not concern herself; it is by no means certain that he has come for my sake at all. The lease is not yet up, and a gentleman might have many reasons for visiting a property still in his possession. My only fear is that such unseemly speculation may be heard by Mr. Bingley if he does choose to call.

Dearest, most deserving Jane, Elizabeth thought with a rush of pleasure as she came to the end of the page. The mystery of why Bingley would not be coming to Pemberley any time soon was solved; and it looked likely to be solved in the most agreeable manner possible. Little wonder Darcy had sent word that there would be no dinner party for Bingley after all. It could not be a coincidence that Bingley had decided to return from town to Netherfield not long after Darcy had gone to town himself; his sudden removal to Meryton hinted strongly at her husband's involvement.

She turned the page in her hand and saw that Jane had continued on the opposite side. It was dated from Longbourn the succeeding afternoon.

Lizzy, Mr. Bingley came this morning! Just one day after arriving at Netherfield, he came riding up our driveway, straight to the house, which made Mama call for Hill to help her find the smelling salts. I was reading in the garden, or rather hiding, hoping I might be overlooked; but Mama discovered me and nearly dragged me into the parlor, where Mr. Bingley had already been admitted. I had barely a chance to straighten my dress before being pushed into his presence. Mary and Kitty were already sitting with him, and when Mama and I entered he rose politely and asked after my health, to which I responded in the usual manner. We then sat down. He earnestly extended his regrets on the death of our father, which I accepted, and he very courteously asked after you and Lydia. The whole time he was speaking Kitty giggled while Mary looked down at her own hands and refused to say a word. Oh Lizzy! You have no idea how exceedingly awkward it was!

For a minute or two there was an uncomfortable silence while we all looked at each other and at Mr. Bingley, and Mama simpered in the corner. Finally Mr. Bingley stood and asked if he might have our mother's permission to walk to Oakham Mount with me, if I was agreeable to such a plan. Mama fairly leaped at the suggestion and assigned Kitty to accompany us, though she disappeared from sight almost as soon as we left the house.

You cannot imagine the state I was in, Lizzy. My heart was beating so that I thought even Mr. Bingley might hear it. I could not bear to look at his handsome face as we walked down the lane together, nor could I bear to look entirely away, so I settled on staring at the buttons on his coat; and then he began to speak. He begged my forgiveness for leaving so suddenly last winter without sending word, saying that he had most unwisely surrendered his own judgment in favor of another's at the time, and learned only recently to see his folly. Of course I could not withhold pardon under the circumstances; and after I had given it, Mr. Bingley asked if I could ever learn to think well of him again and if I might possibly be able to feel affection for him one day. Lizzy, I could not breathe or make any sensible response, not until he had knelt in front of me and forced me to meet his eyes. Then he said that he had loved me almost since the first time we met, and asked if I would do him the honor of agreeing to be his wife.

Lizzy, I accepted him. When he spoke so touchingly of his feelings for me, and begged for the chance to redeem himself, what else could I do? Please do not tease me by asking for more of the particulars of the scene. Let it be enough to read that the lane to Oakham Mount heard many declarations of our sentiments towards each other, and that he expressed himself as well as any man violently in love can be supposed to do.

So, dearest Lizzy, we have arrived at an understanding. We have already decided that we are to be the happiest couple in England, if having this title awarded to us will not be the means of diminishing the happiness of others. Charles will speak with Mama tomorrow, and what joy my family will then experience! I can scarcely imagine it. I wanted to write to you first, you who have been first in my affections until now, knowing that you will rejoice with us more than anyone else.

Such happiness is too much for me--I can scarcely contain it! What bliss is mine, to know that my affection was returned through all these long, hard months! I wish Papa were here to see this happy and unexpected ending! Surely he is looking down from heaven tonight, smiling on his oldest daughter, and laughing that all of Mama's predictions came true in the end.

The only possible source of any regret I may feel now is the awareness that you, my dearest sister, are not as happily united with your husband as I will be with mine. Oh Lizzy! If there is any possible chance of finding love with your Mr. Darcy, I beg you to not throw away the opportunity. Do anything rather than remain in a union solely because of duty. If you can find a way to set aside the very natural resentment at the circumstances of your marriage, I hope that you will one day find the same unlimited joy in your new situation in life that I do, and in the companionship of your dear husband.

Adieu. I must close this letter, as I am writing to my uncle tonight to let him know of Charles' intentions. When everything is settled and we are able to agree on a date, I will write to you again. Until then I am

Your loving sister
Jane

It was just like Jane to pause even in the moment of her greatest delight to consider the feelings of those around her. To think that the uncertainty, the anxiety, and the misery that had shadowed Jane for much of a year was now over! How neatly Jane's arrival at happiness had paralleled Elizabeth's change in feelings towards her own husband! Fervently she hoped that her own letter describing this momentous change would be in Jane's hands very soon, thus removing this last barrier to her total felicity.

Taking up the next page in happy anticipation, she saw that it was dated two days after the first. Elizabeth unfolded it eagerly, expecting it to contain details of her mother's acceptance of the match and, perhaps, the setting of the date for the ceremony. Instead, the very first paragraph caused her to sit forward in her chair, her eyebrows knitting together in concern.

Dearest Lizzy,

I must take up the pen again to write ill tidings that came not long after closing my previous communication to you. To save the time and expense of two letters, I will put all these pages into the same envelope, so that they will reach you as quickly as possible. I trust that this will not prove troublesome for you.

There is no easy way to break this unhappy truth. Be at ease--we are all well. But Lydia is missing from Brighton and we have reason to believe that she has run away. To own the truth, we believe she may have run away with Mr. Wickham!

"Merciful God!" exclaimed Elizabeth aloud.

It was past eleven o'clock last evening when we received a post from Captain Forster in Brighton asking if we had any knowledge of Lydia's whereabouts. She had been missed at breakfast and when inquiries were made, it was discovered that she had been seen getting into a hired coach with an unknown gentleman. From Wickham's sudden absence from his regiment and a note left in Lydia's room it was soon obvious that they left together. They have eloped!

Dear Lizzy, can you imagine a more imprudent match? She so young, and he so unsettled in the world! But as bad a match as it might be, we are now forced to imagine something worse: that they may not be married at all!

After Colonel Forster had determined that the two runaways left together, he was approached by Wickham's friend Denny, who told him that Wickham had said something about not going to Scotland at all, but rather to London! It was Denny's dismal conclusion that Wickham therefore had no plan to marry Lydia, now or ever. The colonel instantly took alarm and followed their trail, stopping in every inn along the way to make inquiries. The fugitives made it as far as Clapham before changing horses, and then the colonel lost their trail. All we know for sure is that they were last seen on the London road; they are certainly not gone to Scotland.

"Poor Lydia!" Elizabeth cried out. "Poor, stupid Lydia!"

I have sent messages to my uncle Gardiner in town to ask for his assistance, and I am hopeful that, with Colonel Forster's help, the fugitives will be found quickly.

Colonel Forster seems determined to think the worst, but I cannot agree. I cannot believe that Wickham, who himself has known such hardship and deprivation, would have such a base scheme in mind as seduction without the promise of matrimony. Even if he does, our uncle will soon convince him otherwise. Lydia is not friendless, nor unprotected in the world. Her youth and liveliness, combined with the funds settled on her by your husband, should be inducement enough to marry under the circumstances. I expect to hear at any moment that they are living in town as husband and wife.

Elizabeth shook her head, tears beginning to well in her eyes.

Shall I own that I long for your presence, Lizzy? The house is in a state of wild disarray. Mama has taken to her bed and weeps nearly all day, insisting that if Wickham were going to marry Lydia, he would have done so already; and lamenting that there is nobody to fight for Lydia's honor. Mary and Kitty, rather than walking to Meryton, stay inside for fear of what neighbors might say; and Mr. Bingley only called once since the dreadful news was made known in the neighborhood. I had to send him away, as it is not seemly for him to continue calling under the circumstances. There is not a servant in the house, or perhaps in the entire neighborhood, who does not know the whole story.

If Mr. Darcy can spare your presence for a few weeks, until the present crisis is past, we would be deeply indebted to him. However, do not raise the subject if you have reason to think he will not be amenable to such a request from you. If that should be the case I ask only that you acknowledge the receipt of this communication; but I hope to hear instead that you are on your way to us. I am your loving sister

Jane

CHAPTER TWENTY SEVEN

"Oh, where is Colonel Fitzwilliam? I must speak to him immediately!" Elizabeth cried, darting from her seat, and was surprised to see Georgiana and the colonel himself coming through the doorway just as she said the words.

"Elizabeth! Whatever is the matter?" Georgiana exclaimed, coming to an abrupt stop when she saw Elizabeth's face.

"Good God, Mrs. Darcy, what has happened?" the colonel exclaimed from behind, not as formally as his cousin.

Elizabeth could not fault him for his response. She was gasping for air, and she knew she must have a wild, desperate look about her. She had to grip a chair for support before she could begin to form any words. "I beg your pardon, but I must leave Pemberley as soon as it can be arranged. I have not a moment to lose."

"For what purpose?" the colonel cried. "Where are you going?"

"I must return to Longbourn at once," Elizabeth answered, and burst into tears as she did so.

There were exclamations of wonder and dismay. Georgiana stepped forward and embraced her sister while the colonel stood helplessly by, observing in wretched silence. At length Georgiana stepped back to look at her and said, urgently, "Elizabeth, you must tell us what has happened. Has there been some news from home? Is your family well?"

Elizabeth tried to catch her breath, gasping before speaking again. "I will tell you all that I can, but first, I must call my maid to start packing my things. If you would be so good as to ring the bell for Mrs. Reynolds, I would be obliged."

"We will do no such thing," the colonel answered firmly, coming forward to take her elbow, and leading her to a chair. "We will not delay you, of course, but you are not well. Sit down for a moment, and let us discuss what has disturbed you so. A few minutes to organize your thoughts will not harm your purpose."

"Perhaps--a glass of wine?" Georgiana offered, trying to be consoling.

"You are kind, so very kind," Elizabeth said, with a brave if tearful smile, "but wine will not help me. I have received dreadful news from Longbourn. My youngest sister has disappeared--she has run away from home." Her lips trembled as she said these words, and she could not hold back another choked sob.

"My dear sister!" Georgiana exclaimed. She sat down next to her, taking her hand in one of her own. "Is this Lydia you are speaking of?"

"It is."

"I believe you said she is younger than I am."

"She is just sixteen--the youngest and most foolish of my family."

"This is a tragedy!" the colonel cried. "But if she is so young, and alone, she cannot have gone far. Has anyone any notion of where she might be?"

"We have too much idea," Elizabeth responded, dreading what she must say next. "She did not run away on her own."

"Then with whom?" Georgiana asked, her eyes widening.

"She has run off--eloped--with someone you know well. She has thrown herself into the power of George Wickham. We believe they are in London."

Georgiana and the colonel were speechless, staring at her. "When I think," she continued, speaking passionately, "how I knew what he was, and did nothing to stop him! I could have told my family weeks ago of his true nature! But it is too late now."

"Are you certain?" the colonel cried, recovering his powers of speech. "Are you certain it was the George Wickham we know, and no other?"

"There can be no other. We met him last autumn, when his regiment was stationed nearby, though I was not aware of his true character until recently. Mr. Darcy disclosed his history with the man just before he left for town, but I did not tell my family of what I knew until just a few days ago, after Lydia was already in Brighton. Wretched, wretched mistake!"

Beside her, Georgiana had gone stiff, pulling her hands away from Elizabeth's and clenching them together in her own lap. Elizabeth, caught in her own anguish, scarcely noticed.

"I do not understand," the colonel said, pulling up a chair to sit across from her, and looking at her with a face of utter sympathy. "I thought your family was from Hertfordshire."

"And so they are, but Lydia went to visit friends in Brighton right after Mr. Wickham's regiment removed there a few weeks ago."

"She went there to follow the regiment?"

"Yes." Shame stained Elizabeth's cheeks.

The colonel looked shocked. "And your mother permitted this? Was she not with her daughter?"

"No," she answered, as her cheeks flushed even deeper. "My sister went by herself."

The colonel shook his head disapprovingly. "That was not well done, I am afraid. Was she not aware of the danger? She allowed your sister, only sixteen years old, to follow the army when it moved away, and without the supervision of family?"

"She permitted it--she encouraged it," Elizabeth answered, staring down at her hands while tears pooled in her eyes. "She could not see the impropriety in such behavior."

The colonel's lips tightened, but he made no response. Elizabeth continued, "Lydia left a note saying that she was running off to get married, but we have since discovered that Mr. Wickham had no plans for matrimony. Jane writes that she hopes he can be prevailed upon to marry her now, but I can see no hope of it."

"But she does have some dowry, thanks to my cousin," the colonel pointed out. "He ought to be able to see the advantages of marrying your sister."

Now it was Elizabeth's turn to shake her head. "It is as my mother said--if he had wanted to marry Lydia, why would he not have done so already? He certainly had the opportunity. They did not go to Scotland-- they were last seen on the London road. She is lost to us--she is ruined forever."

There was a stony silence for response.

"It is hard to think," Elizabeth went on, "that my own sister could be so lost to every notion of decent behavior, to believe she would be so careless with her reputation. But it is so. Jane wants me to come home, to help support her in this crisis, and of course I must go. But there is nothing that can be done. I know very well that nothing can be done!"

"Though it pains me to say it, I have to agree with you," the colonel answered, his voice low and angry. "But I would not blame your sister too much. Now that I think on it, I doubt that Wickham's motive in this case had anything to do with money. He has a much lower motive."

There was an odd intensity in the colonel's voice that made Elizabeth quickly look up at him. His eyes were flashing with an unexpected anger, his lips clenched tightly together.

"Then what--?" she asked, and was surprised to see him glance at Georgiana, who stood abruptly and walked across the room.

"This is about me," Georgiana said unexpectedly, her voice containing a note of bitterness that Elizabeth had never heard in her young sister before. The girl stood with her back to Elizabeth, hands clasped behind her, staring out the window at the grounds of Pemberley in a pose reminiscent of her brother. "Mr. Wickham is taking revenge on our family by working through yours."

Elizabeth stared. "I do not understand. You believe Mr. Wickham is taking his revenge on your brother for denying him the living?"

The colonel glanced quickly, questioningly at Elizabeth, then rose and went to Georgiana's side. He placed a gentle hand on one arm. "Georgie," he said, using a diminutive Elizabeth had never heard before, "You do not have to speak of this if you do not want to."

"No!" Georgiana contradicted him. "It is important for Elizabeth to understand what is happening. She knows what happened to me last summer, but she does not know this part. I never thought to tell her. Elizabeth," she said, turning to face her sister once again, "Mr. Wickham is the man who--" she paused painfully for a moment, "who tried to convince me to run away with him last year."

Elizabeth did not know what to say. It was her turn to stare, dumbstruck, as the words hit home.

"Wickham used his previous friendship with Darcy to worm himself into Georgiana's affections," the colonel said, his words clipped and angry, "and prevailed on her to think herself in love. She consented to an elopement, and if Darcy had not returned a day early from his trip, they would have run off together the next day."

"If not for my brother, I would have been tied forever to a man who only wanted my fortune."

Elizabeth covered her mouth with her hand, tears of sympathy welling in her eyes, as she silently contemplated what such a future would have been like for the young girl. The thought was nearly unbearable.

"So you see, you mustn't be too hard on poor Lydia. She is only doing what any other girl might have done." With those words Georgiana's face crumpled, and her voice ended in a sob. "Will that man never stop intruding into our lives?" she cried. The colonel pulled her into the circle of his arms as she wept freely while Elizabeth watched silently, tears on her own cheeks.

There was nothing she could do here; no comfort she could offer, no soothing words. Her very presence was a painful reminder to Georgiana and the colonel of what they most wanted to forget. "If you will excuse me, I must prepare to leave Pemberley," she said quietly, and rose to her feet. Neither of the other two attempted to stop her as she silently left the room.

CHAPTER TWENTY EIGHT

Elizabeth walked slowly to her room, her feet leaden--her heart numb. When she reached her chamber she threw herself full length on the bed and wept until she had no more tears. Then she stood resolutely and looked slowly around the room.

In one corner of the room stood her wardrobe, filled with dresses and other finery Darcy had provided for her. In another corner her brush and small hand mirror, engraved with her initials, sat primly in their place on the dresser. They too had been a gift from her husband, along with a book he had thought she would like, now lying face down next to them. On one wall hung the watercolor that Georgiana had painted and then had hung in her room after Elizabeth's admiring comments. Everywhere she looked the evidence of the love and care offered to her as Elizabeth Darcy looked back at her, mocking her. None of it could be hers now, thanks to the machinations of George Wickham and Lady Catherine.

If they had planned this assault together, their victory would not have been more assured. Their separate attacks had united at the worst time, in awful harmony.

Lady Catherine had based her criticisms of Elizabeth on her family's lack of fortune, connections, and decorum. The first two items could not be denied; but Elizabeth had rather hoped that on the third point, her family, unimportant and remote, would escape criticism. But this--this lamentable behavior on Lydia's part and the permissive behavior which led to it--this would provide all the ammunition Lady Catherine needed to double the family pressure on Darcy. Her triumph was sure. It had all played out in front of the colonel; he was privy to her mother's failings and her sister's folly. Why, oh why had she not held her tongue in his presence? He was not vicious; he would not go out of his way to cast aspersions on her character, but if he was asked now there was no hope for it. He would have to answer, truthfully, that Elizabeth's family was seriously lacking in decency and decorum.

And Wickham! If he had planned on seducing Lydia and then leaving her, unmarried, as an attack against Darcy, his revenge would be complete indeed. Unmarried, the shame would be great. Lydia's name would not be spoken again in polite society, and her family would not be allowed into the circles they had long occupied. The disgrace of one would become the disgrace of all. Her sisters' marriage prospects would be materially damaged as a result of Lydia's infamy, perhaps even affecting Jane's engagement to Bingley. It was too soon to speculate how far the damage would go; but whatever the result, it was certain to be felt for years to come.

If Lydia married Wickham, the situation could hardly be any better. Whatever affection Darcy felt for Elizabeth would be sorely tested in the face of becoming Wickham's brother. How much more unacceptable would Elizabeth be to Lady Catherine as Wickham's sister? If any members of Darcy's family had been wavering in their support of him, they would not back him now. Georgiana, too, would be forced into an alliance with the very man who had wounded her so deeply! No, it was too much. She would not bring such distress on the two people she loved so dearly--Darcy and Georgiana.

The only solution was to leave. She must cut the ties between her and Darcy and she must do so quickly, irretrievably, like a surgeon severing a poisoned limb. If Darcy returned from town while she was yet preparing, she might lose her nerve. When Darcy heard the news about Lydia he would feel conflicted, torn between his duty to his wife and his responsibility for his sister. There might be a long, protracted scene while he tried to convince Elizabeth to stay, but she could not allow him to make such a sacrifice for her. She must make the decision for him, saving him and Georgiana from the taint of a connection with the Bennets of Hertfordshire. Duty demanded it of her.

It was important that neither the colonel nor Georgiana suspect her true intent, which was to leave Pemberley and never return. A painful scene of separation would follow—and this she must avoid at all costs.

Fortunately, she saw no need to remove most of the belongings she had accumulated in her short time at Pemberley. She had left many of her things behind her at Longbourn when she married Darcy, knowing they would not fit into her new life just as surely as she knew her new wardrobe would not fit into her old one. She would leave all but two or three of the plainest dresses behind, along with the costly mirror and brush and various other notions. Perhaps Georgiana would like to have them. Above all, she wanted no painful reminder of the life she had so briefly tasted when she had experienced Darcy's love.

She rang the bell for Cora and directed her to pack the items she pointed out, and then made her way to the stables, where she directed the head groom to prepare the carriage for travel to Hertfordshire the next day. It was too late to make a start now.

On her way out of the stables she nearly collided with the boy who had carried her letter to Darcy in town, apparently just returning from his errand; and they stopped short as each recognized the other. The boy was the first to speak.

"I got your letter to Mr. Darcy like you said, ma'am," he said, weary but eager for her approval.

Elizabeth smiled sadly. It hardly mattered now. "How did my husband look? Was he well?"

"I couldn't say, ma'am. He seemed the same as always to me."

"And did he send any answering message for me?"

"No, ma'am. I waited like you said but he finally told me to get a bite to eat in the kitchens, and that I might go back to Pemberley the next day."

"He had nothing else to say?"

"No, ma'am. He just frowned and sent me away."

Perhaps Darcy would not be as conflicted as she had thought. "I thank you for the information, and I will echo my husband's advice. It is a long trip to town and back. Go to the kitchens for a good meal before you return to your duties, and I will see that you receive your extra coins right away."

The boy straightened up, brightening, and Elizabeth returned to her room, walking slowly through the silent halls of Pemberley. Other than the servants, it was empty as a tomb. Neither Georgiana nor the colonel was seen anywhere. She was glad, for it made her next task easier to perform.

In her room, she sat wearily at her desk and took up pen and paper for what she knew would be her final communication to her husband. Tears blurred her vision; it would be a miracle if the final product were legible enough to serve its purpose.

Mr. Darcy,

Upon further reflection, I have reconsidered my previous response to the offer of separation you made in your letter, and I have now decided to accept it. I am returning to Longbourn with the full expectation that any connection between us will be severed as soon as the legalities can be worked out. I neither expect nor desire any financial consideration as compensation--simply a return to the former status I enjoyed as Elizabeth Bennet of Meryton. I appreciate every instance of your past kindness to me and extend my gratitude for your generosity in offering to allow me to continue to live at Pemberley; however, please consider that offer definitely declined. Your solicitors should communicate with Mr. Gardiner in town as you take action to dissolve our union.

Sincerely,
Elizabeth Bennet

CHAPTER TWENTY NIINE

"Georgiana, Colonel Fitzwilliam, I am leaving this morning for home," Elizabeth announced without preamble as she entered the breakfast room the next morning. She had been relieved to find the two of them together, making her painful task of separation easier to carry out. Today would be difficult enough without having to repeat her arguments to each of them.

Georgiana's hand with its burden of toast, halfway between plate and mouth, stopped in mid-air. "You mustn't leave," she said, her voice tremulous.

The colonel shook his head emphatically no. "I believe you ought to stay here at Pemberley, Mrs. Darcy. There is nothing you can do for your family at home."

"I can comfort them in their time of distress and support my sister Jane, which is all that matters," Elizabeth answered as firmly as she could. "I have already spoken to the driver and made arrangements for the journey, and I hope to be off in half an hour."

"But that is so soon!" Georgiana said, beginning to rise from her seat in alarm. She remembered the toast in her hand and placed it on the plate in front of her before standing awkwardly before Elizabeth. "You cannot possibly have made arrangements so quickly! Who will go with you? Where will you stay on the way to Hertfordshire? Is it not several days' journey?"

"If all goes well, two days," Elizabeth said, trying not to think too much about the trip ahead. "The driver assured me he knows the best stops along the way, and my maid Cora will go with me. I will not be alone, nor unprotected. You need have no worry for me."

"But Hertfordshire! Fitzwilliam is in town and now you will be in Hertfordshire, and I don't know when I will see either of you again."

"You have your cousin here, and your brother will return as soon as he can, I am sure," Elizabeth said, evading the implied question about her own plans. She would prefer to leave Pemberley without the sin of deceit on her conscience. "My company is not needed."

Georgiana looked imploringly at her cousin. "Richard, please don't let her go."

The colonel put down his napkin and stood to his feet as well. "Georgiana is right. There is no time to prepare for a journey of this sort properly. At the very least we ought to send word ahead to the inns Darcy normally patronizes, to prepare for your arrival; and I should speak to the driver and make sure the carriage is in good repair. Darcy would not thank me if I did any less."

"Mr. Furness informed me yesterday that the carriage is ready, and my things are already packed. There is no need to go to any trouble for my sake."

The colonel tilted his head slightly as he looked at her. "What are your travel plans? Will you go to London first, to speak to Darcy?"

"I have written him a letter which I would like to entrust to your care. I prefer not to slow my journey by stopping anywhere else." She placed the envelope into his hand, and he took it reluctantly, studying her face as if measuring her words. "Will you see that Mr. Darcy receives it?"

His eyes flashed for a moment. "It would be better if you delivered it yourself."

"Believe me, it will be better this way," Elizabeth persisted, holding back the emotion in her voice only with supreme effort.

The colonel frowned at her for a moment, his scowl deepening, and then spun around on one heel and marched out of the room, her letter in hand.

Elizabeth watched his retreating back helplessly. "I did not mean to cause any trouble for Colonel Fitzwilliam," she said, more to herself than to her companion.

"He is not angry with you," Georgiana answered, in a low voice. "This is my fault."

Elizabeth looked at her questioningly. "How could you possibly be responsible for such foolish behavior on the part of others?"

"I neglected to tell you Mr. Wickham's name when I told you about my failing last summer. If I had not been so reticent, you would have known to warn your family about him and none of this would be happening."

"Georgiana, I do not believe the colonel would agree with you on that. Did he actually tell you that you are to blame?"

"No, but it is logical to conclude." Her eyes were pools of misery. "You have to leave us because of what I did wrong."

"None of this is your fault, Georgiana," Elizabeth answered sadly. How little the girl really understood of the situations all around her! "If you must blame anyone, blame me for not telling my sisters what I learned as soon as I knew of it. My place now is at their side."

"But you will return, won't you?" Georgiana asked plaintively.

What a question! "When all of this is resolved," she said evasively, hoping the girl would not press for details. In time, she would come to understand.

Georgiana looked away, and for a minute Elizabeth thought she might begin to weep again. Instead, she said, "If you must leave, please at least allow me to have Mrs. Reynolds make up a basket for your journey. It will be a long ride to your first stop."

Elizabeth was touched by the thoughtful gesture. "I would like that," she answered, and Georgiana left the room to speak with the housekeeper. Elizabeth picked half-heartedly at the fruit on the sideboard for a few minutes while she waited, her emotions too stirred for an appetite, until the colonel came back without warning.

"You will not be able to leave today," he announced with a note of triumph in his voice. Elizabeth thought she saw a gleam of satisfaction in his eyes. "The carriage is not fit to use."

The carriage had been in excellent condition just the day before. "What exactly has happened to it?"

"One of the carriage wheels has cracked down the middle and I have ordered it removed from the vehicle. You cannot travel with only three wheels, and fashioning a new wheel will take some time." This time there was no mistaking his pleased expression.

She raised a skeptical eyebrow. "How much time will be needed to fashion a new wheel?"

"It could be several days. You will have no choice, now, but to wait here and see what transpires in that time. Perhaps circumstances will change and you will not find it necessary to leave Pemberley at all."

Elizabeth sighed. "Colonel, deceit, however kindly meant, does not become you. I recall quite clearly from my visit to the carriage house yesterday that there were several spare wheels mounted on the wall above the harnesses. If one wheel is truly damaged, which I doubt, replacing it should be easily accomplished."

The colonel looked back at her in frustration. "I should have known you could not be fooled," he finally said. "I apologize for my attempt at trickery; but you must understand that I do not believe that this action of yours will please my cousin. I have not been blessed enough to experience the married state for myself, and the mysteries of husband and wife are unknown to me, but I know an unnatural separation when I see one. I simply cannot allow you to leave when I am certain that Darcy is expecting you to be here when he returns."

Once again, she wished he would not be so prescient. "You have made your opinion clear, but I must do as I think best," she answered as she lifted her chin bravely, knowing her fears of a difficult scene were being realized. She must leave now, or risk losing her courage altogether.

The colonel crossed his arms. "You cannot seriously believe that Lydia's situation will change anything between you and Darcy!"

Elizabeth's eyes filled with tears as she looked at him. "My decision has been made. You must not try to stop me, for it will serve no purpose."

The colonel uncrossed his arms and stepped towards her, looking ready to argue the point, but Georgiana came into the room just then. He closed his mouth and stepped away, frustration showing in every line. He made no further objection, however, when Georgiana stated that the basket of food for her journey was being prepared and would be ready very soon. He and Georgiana walked solemnly with Elizabeth out the front door of the house, and they both stood silently by as she summoned the carriage.

It was not many minutes until the carriage stood before her; the same carriage that had first brought her to Pemberley, its dark polish gleaming in the morning sun. It took several minutes for her trunk, small though it was, to be brought and strapped to the back. While this was going on, the colonel moved to the front of the carriage and spoke privately with the driver. Elizabeth could not hear his words, but she had no doubt he was giving painstaking instructions on the safest route to take and which inns to patronize.

Just as he was finishing his directions Mrs. Reynolds hurried out the door of the house with the requested basket, apologizing that she had not had time to prepare more. The basket and Elizabeth's small bag containing a few personal items were stowed inside the compartment. Cora in her traveling clothes went in next, and then it was time for Elizabeth to take the steps.

She turned to Georgiana.

This was the moment, and her chest ached painfully as Georgiana threw herself into her arms. "I wish you did not have to go!" she exclaimed, and Elizabeth finally let her own tears flow. After all, she reasoned, she was supposed to be upset over Lydia's situation. Tears would not betray her secret--that this would be the last time she ever had contact with Georgiana, or Pemberley. Or Darcy, her heart silently cried.

"You will write very often, I hope," Georgiana pleaded, and Elizabeth nodded mutely. Darcy would have to explain everything to his sister when the time was right.

When she and Georgiana finally stepped away from each other, she turned to face the colonel Unable to meet his eyes she embraced him instead and felt his stiff surprise as he returned the gesture. Then, with his face full of regret, he gave her his hand and assisted her into the carriage.

The door closed, the colonel spoke briefly once more to the driver, and then the wheels began to turn. Elizabeth looked straight ahead as the carriage turned in the driveway and moved away from the house. She would not turn to see the warm windows of Pemberley pass by, the gardens and walks she enjoyed so much, the colonel's troubled gaze, nor Georgiana's imploring look that resembled Darcy so strongly. Never would she allow herself to look back at all, for never would she allow herself to bring such misery to those she loved.

∞

The first day of travel went by slowly and painfully, the carriage seeming to creep along the road while other, swifter vehicles passed them by. Cora fell asleep almost immediately; and there was little to do except look out the window and wonder what Darcy would think when he found out that Elizabeth had gone. Would he accept the statements she made in her letter at face value, or would he suspect that she had gone in order to protect him? When would he even receive her letter? Perhaps the colonel would send it to town right away rather than waiting for Darcy to return to Pemberley, but it would make no difference. She would be beyond Darcy's reach by the time he received it. At first, she doubted not, he would be hurt, perhaps even angry at her precipitous departure. But in time he would come to realize this was for the best and would forgive her. Perhaps he might even think well of her again some day.

The miserable thought made her hide her face in her handkerchief, and her sobs threatened to awaken her companion.

∞

There were several unscheduled stops along the way, the driver pulling aside, he said, due to concerns with the road. Looking out the small window Elizabeth could not agree with him. The road appeared to be free of debris and the weather was clear, though the sky was somewhat overcast. To speed their lingering journey she instructed the driver not to stop for a noon meal, instead distributing the contents of Mrs. Reynold's basket between Cora and him. Nevertheless, after hours of tedious travel it was nearly six o'clock in the evening before they reached the first inn. The driver secured a room for Elizabeth and Cora, and then carried their things in while they followed closely behind. They walked into the building, up the stairs, and into the last room along the narrow hallway; and then the innkeeper stood anxiously by while Cora inspected the room carefully and finally pronounced it acceptable for her mistress.

"Although it's a good thing we'll only be here the one night," Cora added, after the door had closed behind the innkeeper, glancing at the single bed and small cot that had been arranged for them. "This will do well enough for temporary lodgings, but it's hard not to be at Pemberley, when all is said and done. Will you be wanting a bath, ma'am? I imagine I could get someone to bring up water for you."

"No bath, please," Elizabeth answered. "In a little while, perhaps, I might want to see what is available for supper. I am too weary to think of eating just now."

"'Tis early yet for supper," Cora responded, "but I can see what they're planning for a meal downstairs. If you will excuse me, ma'am, I'll be back when I can." She looked at her mistress carefully in the dim light of the curtained room. "Perhaps you'd like to lie down and rest, ma'am, while you wait."

If she looked half as weary as she felt, she must be a sight. "My head is aching," she said, grateful that Cora had slept most of the way to the inn. Hopefully she did not realize that her mistress's aching head was caused by an aching heart. "Perhaps I will stretch out on the bed while you see what can be arranged for a meal to be served here." Lying down in her clothes would surely cause wrinkles, but she did not plan on going below stairs before the next morning. "I will latch the door behind you when you leave; when you come back, knock, and I will open it for you."

1 7 0

Cora left the room eagerly, and Elizabeth suspected that she was ready to stretch her legs after being jostled in the carriage all day. She herself was eager to be still and rest after the emotional leave-taking of the morning, to lay her throbbing head on the pillow and let the peace and stillness of the remote room wash over her.

∞

It felt like only a few minutes had passed when a firm knock came on the door.

Startled, Elizabeth sat up quickly and looked about her in surprise. Her first thought was that, judging by the shadows in the room, an hour or so had passed since Cora left. Her second thought was that her headache had diminished, though she still felt fatigued. She should not have given up all thought of eating during the day. Perhaps a good meal would restore her energy; and after that she might ask the driver to accompany her and Cora into town for a short walk. First she must let Cora with her burden of food into the room.

The rap came again, and Elizabeth called, "I am coming!" impatiently as she stood. It was not like Cora to be so imperious. She ran her hands over her hair and then tried to smooth her skirts into some kind of order before taking the short steps to the door. "Have patience," she said, as she began to lift the latch. "I am as eager to eat as you must be."

But when she pulled the latch up and the door swung open, it revealed not Cora, but the last person she had expected to see in this remote location.

"Mr. Darcy!"

CHAPTER THIRTY

Darcy's eyes, enormous and dark, bored into hers as she gazed back at him, drinking in the sight of his face. He was thin, she noted instantly, thinner than when he had gone to town, and he looked haggard, as if he had spent a long day traveling.

"Elizabeth," he said formally, his voice hoarse. "May I come in?"

Instinctively she stepped aside and allowed him to step past her. Almost at once she regretted her mistake. How could she convince him that she must leave him when her heart melted just to hear his voice? She should have refused to speak to him, turned him away. Instead she turned towards him slowly, keeping her eyes on his cravat, and they faced each other from a distance of several feet.

"Elizabeth," Darcy said, breathing out her name like a prayer, not taking his eyes from her face. He moved forward to take both her hands in his. "My own sweetest, dearest Elizabeth."

Elizabeth flinched against the unexpected endearment. At all costs, she must endeavor to keep her distance from this man, lest she lose her resolve. She pulled her hands away and took a step back, crossing her arms.

"You have caught me by surprise, Mr. Darcy! I had no idea of running into you on the road. How did you know where I was?"

"I received a message from Colonel Fitzwilliam that you were on your way to Hertfordshire. He gave me your route and urged me to find you before it was too late."

"But you could not have heard from the colonel and made it here from town all in one day."

"I was not in town. I was barely half a day's journey from Pemberley, on my way to see you." He took a step closer to her. "I am thankful beyond words that the colonel's messenger was able to find me so swiftly."

"I see." She turned away from him, barricading herself against the feelings that had built up in her for weeks. "What a shame that the colonel chose to substitute his own message to you for the one I asked him to deliver. If you had read my message, you could have saved yourself an unnecessary journey."

"Elizabeth, look at me." Darcy's voice, quiet but intense, made her turn around slowly to face him, meeting his eyes warily. The desire she saw there sent a shock through her. "After the letter I received from you four days ago, do you think anything could have kept me from coming to you?"

She bit her lip as she looked at him. Leaving him would be much harder than she had feared.

"I will admit," Darcy went on, "that this most recent action has left me somewhat confused. But nothing," he said forcefully, "nothing could keep me from your side, not after you said your feelings towards me had changed. Not a bitter argument, nor angry words spoken in haste, not a separation of weeks--not even your letter this morning could keep me from you, once I knew that I had hope."

Arm's length was not far enough. She walked to the other side of the small room before turning to speak to him from a safe distance. "You are mistaken, Mr. Darcy." She let the words lash out at him. "As I said, I have changed my mind. It is best for us to separate."

"Why?" he demanded. "Is it because you have no feelings for me?"

Elizabeth could not answer. She blinked hard and looked away from him.

"Or is it because of your sister? Do you think her situation is enough to make us part forever?"

"It is more than enough! If Lydia is so unfortunate as to remain unmarried, the disgrace will pass on to you through me. If she is even more unfortunate and marries Wickham, the shame will be even greater. You do not want to be Wickham's brother."

Darcy's face softened and he took a step towards her. "I would accept far more than that to be with you."

"And there is Georgiana to consider," she continued. "The last thing she needs is to be reminded every day of her foolish mistake with that man. Surely she would be relieved to have our connection severed."

"There you are mistaken," he corrected her. "She will be heartbroken to think that her situation may have caused even more grief and misery for me than it did last year. And she would miss you for your own sake. You are the sister she has never had." He took another step.

Elizabeth clasped her hands before her, looking down at the floor. Darcy was taking her carefully constructed arguments and destroying them one by one. But she still had her one insurmountable weapon.

"Lady Catherine is desperate. There is nothing she will not do, no lengths to which she will not go, in order to see you bend to her will. I know she is already urging your family to have you put me away, and that she is threatening to take Georgiana from you. If you persist in this path, she will make you choose between Georgiana and me. I will not be the one to bring that upon you."

"What is Lady Catherine to me?" he exclaimed passionately. "What have I to do with her? She is my aunt, nothing more. She is neither parent nor guardian. I owe her nothing but the familial affection and loyalty due to her as my mother's sister, and even that she has ruined with her recent conduct. She will not dictate my choices in life, nor will I allow her to control my destiny."

"But she can take away that which you hold most dear!" Elizabeth cried, and suddenly tears stood in her eyes. With a muffled exclamation Darcy crossed the remaining divide and took her hands in his again.

"She can only succeed if you allow her to, for what I hold most dear is here with me, in this room. We can speak of the rest of this later. Right now I need to know--I must know, Elizabeth--what are your feelings towards me?"

"I told you in my letter this morning."

"You did not. You said nothing of your feelings, just that you wanted to separate."

"Let me go!" She struggled for a moment, trying to free her hands, but Darcy would not yield. "I must return to Longbourn."

"I will give you your freedom, if that is your true desire," he said, looking grim. "But if we are to part, we must do so honestly. I want--no, I need to hear you say what you want for yourself."

Elizabeth was silent, trying to gather the courage to speak over the growing lump in her throat. Darcy put one hand under her chin, forcing her to look up. "Elizabeth, do you want to go?"

Elizabeth slowly lifted her eyes to his. What she saw there destroyed her resolve to be brave. "I do not wish to go," she whispered.

Darcy did not answer. Instead he framed her face with his hands, his eyes fairly burning through her. Elizabeth closed her eyes as his lips gently made contact with hers. As he pulled her close to him, she forgot everything except the strength of his arms, the tenderness of his touch, and the way her heart beat faster, threatening to leap out of her chest. To her surprise she found that her own arms were around him, drawing him close, and Darcy made a sound deep in his throat as she returned his kiss. At length he pulled away.

"Elizabeth, I beg of you, forgive me for the many ways I have hurt you since we married. I cannot think of my conduct as a husband thus far in our marriage without acknowledging that my actions deserve the severest reproof."

"Your failings?" She looked at him with a feeling of mortification. "I cannot recall any failings of yours which compare to the great disservice I did to you. I should never have spoken to you the way I did on the night we quarreled."

"What did you say that I did not deserve? My motives were good--I wanted to make you happy. But in my arrogance I assumed what you needed and wanted, rather than asking. I took for granted that I had won your heart when you gave me your hand. I should never have been so presumptive."

"And I," said Elizabeth, "never gave you the chance to show me your affection after we were married. I held you off, convinced you had married me for only the basest of motives. If I had opened myself to you sooner, I might have fallen in love with you much more quickly."

Darcy's face softened. "Do you truly love me, Elizabeth? Is it possible that you have the same feelings for me that I have had for you all along?"

"My feelings-- " Elizabeth looked down in embarrassment. "My feelings betray my tongue sometimes--I find it difficult to say what is in my heart. But I believe that my feelings may, indeed, have come to mirror yours." As she said these words, she managed to look up at him, and the heartfelt expression on his face rewarded her small effort on his behalf.

"I have so many questions, but there is only one that matters now." Darcy released her slowly, gathering both her hands into his while he looked at her with the tender look she had missed for so long--ever since that night on the balcony, she remembered. "Will you return to Pemberley with me, Elizabeth? Will you consent to be my wife, my best and truest companion, the mother of my children?"

She nodded mutely.

"And will you stay with me forever?"

"Yes, William, I will."

"William." Darcy repeated the name wonderingly as he caressed her face, his eyes beginning to glow. "You have never called me William before."

"I will address you differently if you like, but Fitzwilliam is too affected for me. I much prefer William."

"William is what my mother called me," Darcy told her. "I would be pleased if you also used it."

"Then, sir, Elizabeth Bennet of Hertfordshire is proud to be the wife of Mr. Darcy of Pemberley."

"Elizabeth Darcy," Darcy corrected her, as he bent his head towards her once more.

CHAPTER THIRTY ONE

Darcy and Elizabeth remained locked in an embrace for many minutes, murmuring endearments to each other, until Elizabeth pulled back to look at Darcy, her eyes tracing his beloved features once again.

"Why did you not answer the letter I sent you, when I told you my feelings had changed? How did you learn about Lydia? Did Colonel Fitzwilliam tell you about her situation?"

"There are many things we need to discuss," Darcy said, his look suddenly turning serious, "but first things first. Your hands are cold, and your maid told me you have not eaten all day. Do you feel you can eat now?"

"Cora!" Elizabeth exclaimed. "I sent her off some time ago! Where has she gone? Is she the reason you knew to come to this room?"

"Do not be too hard on your maid, please. The colonel directed me to this inn, and when I came inside I found Cora coming back from the kitchens. She directed me to your door, and I asked her not to disturb us until we called her. Would you like to have her bring dinner to us here? I find I am not in a mood to share you with everyone in the common room tonight." Elizabeth nodded. "Then let me go find her, and I shall return as quickly as possible. After we eat, we can talk. And Elizabeth," he added with a mischievous smile, "do not even think about leaving this room until I return, lest I be forced to track you down again."

Elizabeth smiled back, warmed by his open affection. "I will not go anywhere without you," she promised, and Darcy left the room quickly. While he was gone, Elizabeth took a moment to look at herself in the small mirror hanging on the wall. Her dress was mussed beyond repair, and her hair, despite her earlier attentions, had started to fall out of its pins. None of this had seemed to matter to Darcy, however, and she decided she would not let it trouble her either.

In a few minutes Darcy came back with Cora close behind. Husband and wife stood silently and a little awkwardly while their food was set out before them; and then Cora left them with a promise to return in an hour or so.

It had been so long since Elizabeth had sat at a table and shared a meal with her husband. She could not help looking at Darcy with a feeling of unreality, wondering if she had begun to imagine what her senses were now taking in. If this was a dream, she decided as Darcy pulled out her chair for her, she would prefer not to awaken. Cora had set their places across from each other at the small table, but after seating his wife Darcy moved his own chair around to be closer to her, and he did not hesitate to touch her hand lingeringly whenever they passed the simple dishes between them. The meal did not take long; and when he was done Darcy pushed his plate away from him with a satisfied sigh, and then turned to look at her again with his old admiring gaze. Elizabeth was the first to speak, however.

"You have not been eating well," she said, looking closely at the new hollows in his cheeks.

"I would say the same of you," Darcy responded, reaching out gently to enfold one of her hands in his. She started at the unexpected touch, which he instantly noted.

"Does this not please you?" he asked, letting his thumb caress her palm in a small circle. "I will be more reserved in my attentions if you prefer."

"It does not displease me," she answered, her cheeks flushing slightly. "But you are so different from what I recall. When we were first married, you were so very reserved and stern that I did not know what to make of you. You seemed so cold. I assumed you had no feelings for me, or you would have made them known at that time."

"Dearest Elizabeth, not telling you how I felt was the first of many mistakes I made in our marriage. It is an error I intend to correct every day from now on." He raised her hand to his lips to leave a delicate kiss. "Rest assured that I have never regarded you with anything but the warmest affection."

The light touch on her fingers had proven surprisingly distracting. She forced herself to say, "I wish I had realized earlier that you married me for love, not because of duty. I would have approached our marriage quite differently had I known."

"I can easily comprehend why you were so confused. Considering the differences in our circumstances in life, in our connections and in other matters which society values, I thought you would realize that only the deepest, most abiding affection would allow me to overcome such barriers and make you an offer of marriage. But I was mistaken, of course."

Elizabeth thought she understood. "It was a sad misunderstanding, then, on both our parts."

"No, Elizabeth." Darcy shook his head. "Call it what it was--another instance of my arrogance and presumption. I should never have assumed that you would fall in love with me simply because I was in love with you."

"And I should have realized early on that there was a reason you chose me to marry, out of all the women you were more likely to favor."

Darcy reached to take both of her hands, enveloping them completely between his own. "Your hands are warmer now," he said softly, looking at them intently. He seemed to be measuring them, bringing her fingertips in line with his one by one before twining his fingers between hers. Elizabeth did not disturb his silent perusal; and finally he looked in her face again, bringing their palms together as he spoke.

"Do you think we can talk, now, about the real reasons why we married? Or would you prefer to wait on this conversation? You have already had a long, tiring day."

"I think," Elizabeth responded, "considering our wretched beginning, that we have waited too long already. Any more delay might be more disastrous than it has already been!"

Darcy's eyes brightened. "Then let us begin now."

∞

For ease of conversation, they moved from the small table to the settee that sat opposite the bed. Once they were settled Darcy began to speak, his voice steady and reassuring.

"The easiest way to start this, I suppose, is from the beginning. Would you agree?" At Elizabeth's encouraging nod, he went on.

"Within a matter of days after our wedding, I could see that you were not your usual vivacious self. You were more subdued than I was used to seeing, your smiles not as rich as they had once been. Considering what had just transpired in your life, this did not greatly surprise nor trouble me. She is grieving for her father, I told myself. She has had a great deal of upheaval in a short time. Even if the more recent changes in her life have been pleasant, they have still been rapid, and anyone would need a short while to accommodate themselves to a new home, a new title, and so many new responsibilities. I hoped that the healing air of Pemberley, away from the pressures of town, would benefit you once we removed there. And for a short while, it seemed that my wishes were answered."

"You were very kind, but I did not always appreciate your concern," Elizabeth interjected, wanting to shoulder her share of blame from the beginning, but Darcy gently quieted her.

"I must beg your indulgence to speak my piece without interruption, Elizabeth. I will do better if I can say everything at once." Elizabeth gave her consent, reluctantly, and he went on.

"Once we were at Pemberley, I made it my mission to raise your spirits as much as possible to their former level, and to help you acclimate to your new station. I spent as much time as I could with you, and I encouraged a friendship between you and Georgiana, thinking that the presence of one new sister might ease your sense of loss over those you had left behind, especially Jane.

"How I enjoyed those days, Elizabeth! Showing Pemberley to you made me see my home, long familiar to me, through new eyes; watching you grow closer to Georgiana warmed my heart; seeing how quickly you learned your new duties only made me admire you more. But even though you improved somewhat, there still seemed to be something missing.

"Little by little it began to grow on me that you were not sharing yourself with me in the same way in which I tried to share myself with you. Any attempts at serious conversation, to confide intimate memories or deep feelings, you turned aside with a laugh or a change in topic. I could not penetrate a certain reserve that I sensed in you--you were a shadow without a substance. And yet you did seem to enjoy my company at times--I flattered myself that not all of your smiles were given with an effort."

"I did start to enjoy your company, after we came to Pemberley," she said, unable to contain herself any longer. "I began to look forward to our afternoon walks, at least. You were not deceived."

"Did you?" Darcy half smiled. "That is good to know." He paused as if to savor the memory once again, and then sighed heavily.

"But it wasn't until the day we walked in the garden, while Georgiana's gift was being delivered and I mentioned our courtship, that I began to be truly puzzled. You claimed to have no memory of us courting. How could a series of events that had meant so much to me have gone unnoticed by you? There had not been many encounters with you in Kent, that was true; but every one of them was significant to me. Could you truly have been unaware of my interest in you? Was it possible I had been so deceived? Yet you spoke with all sincerity; I did not doubt that you said only the truth as you saw it. I was still mulling over the mystery when I noticed the comet appear outside my window.

"I am not an overly romantic man, Elizabeth. Passionate poems, grand gestures of affection, and sentimental effusions do not flow from me as they do other men. But even I could see the romantic possibilities in standing outside on a dark summer night, staring at the stars and the overhead sky. If any setting were likely to help you open yourself to me, I thought, it would be at a time when we could view such a perfect union of beauty and mystery together."

"I remember," Elizabeth said guiltily, amazed she had not realized this before. How much of her husband was hidden from her all this time?

"That encounter, Elizabeth, opened my eyes to many things. If there were any setting where you would be likely to speak freely and confide in me, perhaps about your father, it would be there, in the stillness of the night and the intimate setting. But you thought my most tender thoughts were for my sister! It was obvious, even to my deluded wishes, that you did what I asked--engaging in conversation with me, coming to my bed-- simply because I requested it of you, not because you wanted it. I had your compliance, your willing obedience, but I had not secured what I most wanted--your very heart."

"Stop! Please stop," Elizabeth begged, putting one hand across her eyes, as if to shield them from the light. "I cannot bear to think of how I treated you then."

Darcy stood and began to pace across the room restlessly, his hands clasped firmly behind his back. His words came more quickly now. "After that I avoided you. I concluded that you, like all the other women of my acquaintance would do, had married me simply for my wealth; but I could not bear to ask you such a direct question, when I might receive an unimaginable answer. It was cowardly of me to avoid the topic. I even stooped so low as to blame you for having tricked me into marriage--you, who had never tried to attract my attention in any way, who had seemed almost to rebuff me at times! In my worst moments I came to believe these actions had all been carried out in a clever scheme to excite my interest, in order to gain a proposal. I blamed myself for falling victim to the supposed trickery, but I blamed you more."

Elizabeth winced. "No wonder you were angry with me when I came to speak to you on Georgiana's behalf."

"Yes, I was angry, or I would never have responded in the way I did. You came to me to ask that I not push Georgiana into an unwanted alliance with Bingley. You were doing exactly as I had hoped you would-- performing the offices of a friend and trusted confidante for my sister; but all I could think of was my own hurt. In my selfishness, I impugned your motives. Though I thought myself cool and collected at the time, I have since become convinced that I spoke in a dreadful fit of temper."

Darcy stopped pacing to stand directly in front of her, his face a study in contrition. "I want you to know, Elizabeth, that I know you did not marry me for my money. When I came to my senses I realized that much at least. You are the least mercenary person I know."

Elizabeth's face was awash in shame; she forced herself to look up at her husband's eyes, swallowing hard before answering. "If we are to be totally honest with each other, as painful as it is, I must admit that you were not entirely wrong in your accusation. I married you because of the security you could provide for my family. If that was mercenary, then I am as guilty as anyone else."

Darcy sat down next to her again and took her hands in his again. "I will not allow you to berate yourself. You married me because you had no choice, given your desperate circumstances, not strictly for my money. You are not to be blamed for that."

"But there is very little difference between that and marrying for wealth," she protested, forcing herself to the excruciating truth. "You made an honorable offer which would protect my family, and I took it. You may choose to deny it, but I was, in fact, as cold and calculating as any lady of the Ton."

"Elizabeth, listen to me," Darcy said, earnestly. "Before your father died, would you have even considered marriage to me? Would you have tolerated a union with someone you did not love, someone you did not even respect, unless pushed to an extreme? You did not accept the offer of marriage from your cousin Collins, did you?"

"That does not signify!" Elizabeth exclaimed, amazed that Darcy knew the story. "You are nothing like him! I could never have married that man, no matter what the consequences!"

"But you could marry me, when the circumstances were right," Darcy pointed out. "And your uncle made me see that you were motivated by love--a motive I understand completely, though it took me some time to understand the magnitude of the sacrifice you made. I will forever be grateful that you gave me a chance to win your affection." He lifted his free hand to caress her cheek lightly.

"You did win my affection, and it is not fair at all to compare yourself to Mr. Collins," Elizabeth said, half amused and half offended. It was difficult to think clearly when he was being so demonstrative. "You must know that between you and him, you would be the more desirable option. And Mr. Collins had already married my friend before my father died."

"How very fortunate for me!" Darcy exclaimed, his mouth curling up mischievously. Elizabeth, sitting so close to him, could not help observing how very handsome he was, especially when he looked at her that way. He leaned in to kiss her, but Elizabeth playfully pulled away.

"You have avoided my curiosity long enough, sir," she said, with a trace of her former impertinence. "Ever since I first knew of it, I have been longing to ask about your acquaintance with my uncle. How did you come to call on him in town? And why did you do it?"

"It was the closest I could come to you," he replied simply, not taking his eyes from her. "I did not think you would welcome me again, if I were to return home."

Elizabeth felt her heart leap at the unexpected revelation.

"And I had also decided to find out, if I could, the truth about why you married me, once and for all. To do so it seemed to make sense for me to speak to the man who had been most involved in forwarding our marriage, to ask him how he had presented my proposal to you. The results of that conversation were--enlightening." He paused, searching for words. "To use your own turn of phrase, you might say that your uncle and I had a spirited conversation."

"Indeed." Elizabeth raised one eyebrow. Despite the gravity of the moment, she could not help a small smile. "It must have ended well, since you are now on easy terms."

"We are now, but it did not look hopeful at first. Your uncle reminded me that when I first asked him for your hand, I said nothing of love. I spoke of an early wedding date and of the arrangements to care for your family, and that was what he had relayed to you. He said nothing of love or affection to you because I had said nothing about it to him. He told you what he believed a man in my position expected from a marriage. I hope you know by now that I am not a typical man of the Ton."

Darcy put both of his hands to her face, letting his thumbs lightly trace her cheekbones while he gazed into her eyes. "I wanted something quite different from our relationship."

He bent his head towards her once again, but a discreet knock sounded on the door at just that moment. Elizabeth, suddenly fearful, rose at once. "That must be Cora, coming for our dinner things," she said, sounding a little breathless even to her own ears. "I should let her in."

She opened the door swiftly and Cora entered without comment, silently arranging the plates, bowls and cutlery into a neat pile, and taking a moment to wipe off the table. While she did this Darcy and Elizabeth stood quietly by, observing each other gravely over her back. Darcy's eyes, dark and impenetrable, gave no hint of his thoughts. Did he know everything that her uncle had told her to expect from their marriage? If he did not, how would he react when she told him? For there was no choice, now, but to be completely honest about the relationship she had thought they would have.

Cora finished her task, readying the items to return downstairs, and then she looked at Elizabeth expectantly.

"Shall I turn the bed down for you, ma'am?"

As one, Darcy and Elizabeth turned their heads to look at the bed in the center of the room, a larger version of the cot set up in one corner. The question of their sleeping arrangements for the night had not been addressed. The bed with its single pillow and heavy counterpane was large enough for one person but not for two; and if one of them, presumably Darcy, chose to use the cot, where would Cora stay? Darcy cleared his throat.

"I don't suppose there is another room available in this establishment for accommodations this evening, do you think?" He addressed Cora, who shook her head.

"No, sir. I heard the innkeeper saying in the kitchens how he was all filled tonight. Even in the commons there'll be precious little room to sit up. There's a fair in town tomorrow, you see."

"Then all the rooms in the town are likely to be taken as well." He frowned, looking at Elizabeth. "I do not like to leave you alone."

"You may leave the bed for now, Cora," Elizabeth directed. "If you would be so good as to take our dinner things downstairs and then return, we will let you know what our plans are for the night."

Cora curtsied and left, her arms filled as she pulled the door shut behind her. Darcy looked at Elizabeth gravely. "Where do you want to go tomorrow, Elizabeth?"

"To go?" she repeated, not understanding the question.

"Would you prefer to go on to Meryton, or would you be willing to return to Pemberley?"

"I thought you had come to take me back to Pemberley with you."

"I came to be with you, wherever you are," he replied. "If you still feel that you are needed at Longbourn, I will be pleased to accompany you. But if it is possible, I would prefer to go back to Pemberley. It will be easier for me to work with my solicitors from a distance from there."

Elizabeth frowned, hesitating. "I would like to support Jane, if possible. She has asked for my presence."

"She has Bingley to help her, and she does not need you in the same way that I do." His smile was humble but hopeful.

"But if you know that Mr. Bingley has gone back to Netherfield, you must also know that Jane had to send him away after Lydia disappeared."

"It appears that I have more current information than you do in that regard. Bingley has learned from his mistake last winter, when he let others tell him what to do. He was planning to go back to your sister and speak to her again, and he said that this time he would let nothing dissuade him. By now, I am sure, he has persuaded your sister never to send him away again."

"I suppose I have you to thank for this remarkable change in your friend."

"We can talk about that tomorrow, on our way to wherever you decide." He took quick steps across the room and enfolded her in his arms again, pulling her close to him. "Where do you want to go?"

"If you are sure that Jane is in good hands, I will return to Pemberley with you." She shyly placed her hands on his shoulders as he looked down at her. "But there are still many things we need to talk about. My sister, your aunt--and other things."

"Later," he murmured as he began to return her tentative gesture with breathtaking kisses, his arms tightening around her waist. "Later."

CHAPTER THIRTY TWO

It was early the next morning when Elizabeth first heard her husband's light knock on the bedroom door at the inn. The sound of his footsteps in the hall had penetrated her awareness first; and then, after Cora answered his rapping, she heard him asking if Mrs. Darcy was awake yet, and how soon she thought they would be down for breakfast.

They had not shared the small room the night before, though Darcy had clearly wanted to remain; but the conditions at the inn would not allow it. Elizabeth was not sure whether to be sorry or grateful for the impediment. Not that she did not feel any affection or desire for her husband, now that they had a better understanding of each other--far from it. She thrilled to his presence, now, in a way that she had never done before in their marriage. But until all matters were set right between them she would not feel honest sharing herself with him again. To yield such intimacies to him in the marriage bed and yet not share recollections she knew would hurt him would feel almost like another betrayal.

That conversation would have to come soon. Elizabeth blushed to remember how Cora had interrupted them again last night, just when her husband's passion had begun to make her forget her surroundings. Cora had to knock on the door several times before she and Darcy disengaged; and when she finally opened the door, there was no disguising her dishevelment, nor the fact that her hair was completely let down so that Darcy's hands could run through it. Elizabeth and Darcy were both breathless, and without a doubt Cora had at least some suspicion of what had been transpiring during her absence from the room. As a well-trained servant, of course, she had kept her thoughts to herself.

Now it was the next morning. They would return to Pemberley today to face, together, the yet-unresolved problems of both Lady Catherine and Lydia. To get there Elizabeth and Darcy would share the carriage, his horse tied behind the vehicle, with Cora and the driver sitting outside. With no one to overhear and few opportunities for interruption, there would be no avoiding the painful conversation she knew had to come.

They met at the breakfast table in the common area of the inn, and Elizabeth blushed when she saw his eyes fixed on her as she advanced into the room. This morning he was more reticent than he had been the night before. He gave her his arm to escort her to her chair, but beyond a somewhat reserved smile, pulling out her chair for her, and then sitting next to her at the table, he gave no hint of the passion that had stirred him the night before.

"I hope you slept well last night, Mr. Darcy," she said, frowning, as she began to help herself to the food, ignoring the curious looks from other guests. No doubt they were wondering at a husband and wife who came to the table separately.

"I slept little, and that very ill," he answered, his look serious. "I have you to thank for it."

"Me? I cannot imagine what you mean."

He leaned close to speak into her. "Dreams of you kept me awake," he said softly.

"Mr. Darcy!" she said, her cheeks suddenly flaming. She looked around quickly and was relieved to see that nobody appeared to be paying them any attention. "I am sorry that you had to stay up in the common room all night. I would have shared a room with you, if possible, but of course my maid could not stay in the commons by herself." Surely he did not blame her for the arrangements; perhaps he simply could not be in public what he was in private. If so, then she should probably be more restrained as well.

"Of course not. Nevertheless, I am afraid I might be poor company on the way back to Pemberley." He looked at her soberly. "If I fall asleep along the way, it is no reflection on you, merely a result of my own weakness."

"If you would prefer, I could go ahead of you in a different carriage, so that you can have the carriage to yourself and not suffer through any disturbances I might create for your rest." She raised one eyebrow at him, wondering how he would respond.

"Unless you are with me, my dearest Elizabeth, I shall have no rest at all." His hand lightly brushed hers under the table and then pulled away again, leaving her with a distinct feeling of loss.

∞

Then they were on the road back to Pemberley, the carriage swaying gently as it made its way along the smooth road, now crowded with travelers on foot and in carriages and wagons all going the opposite way.

Elizabeth marveled to find herself happily retracing the steps she had taken just a day earlier, with far different emotions. Then she had been tearful, distraught; certain that she was turning her back on happiness, knowing that her life would never be as full as the time she had enjoyed while she was the wife of Fitzwilliam Darcy. She had been fleeing, knowing that every step would bring her closer to her own disgrace, but willing to pay the price for the chance to atone, in some small way, for the hurt she had caused the man she loved.

This morning they were reconciled, but he was closer to the reserved husband of Pemberley than the ardent lover of the previous night. Would she ever truly understand this man?

Darcy, looking out the window, sensed her perusal and turned to look at her, smiling slightly when he caught her eye. "It will be a long ride home."

"Not as long as it took to get here, I think, even with this crowd. The driver made remarkably poor time yesterday."

"He was following the colonel's instructions, of course. My cousin was doing everything he could to make sure I would catch up to you as quickly as possible."

"Yes, I worked that out for myself last night, after you left the room. It would seem I owe him a great debt."

"So do I. Without his intervention, who knows when I might have found you again?" One corner of his mouth tipped up endearingly. "I might have had to follow you all the way to Longbourn."

The thought intrigued her. "Would you truly have taken so much trouble?" she asked. "Would you have gone so far in pursuit of a woman who might have rejected you once again?"

"I have a confession to make, Elizabeth."

Elizabeth looked at him curiously, her eyes trying to read his in the darkened light inside the carriage. His expression looked more wistful than guilty. "What confession would that be, sir?"

"I was not entirely truthful in the letter I sent you from town, where I offered to give you your freedom."

"Were you not? I thought you were a man of your word, sir."

"I am a man of honor. I would have released you, if that had been your desire. But I promised you that one word from you would silence me forever, and that is far from the truth. I could never have let you just walk out of my life."

Elizabeth waited, looking at him expectantly.

"If you had chosen to return to Longbourn, I would have followed you and made my case to you there, for as long as it took to change your mind."

The warm look in his eyes, shining even through the darkness of the carriage, wiped away the uneasiness she had felt all morning. As if in a dream Darcy extended his hand to her, and she took it carefully, moving slowly but without hesitation towards him. He made room on the bench as she seated herself next to him, putting his arm around her so that she could rest her head on his shoulder. She felt the slow move of his lips on her hair and closed her eyes to enjoy the sensation as he took her free hand in his. For a long time all was quiet in the carriage except for the sounds of the road and the creaking of the wheels.

"I am glad you are not pushing me away again," Elizabeth finally said, sounding relieved even to her own ears. "I was a little concerned earlier, when I realized that the William I met at the inn last night was much more demonstrative than the Mr. Darcy I met at breakfast."

"Forgive me, my dearest," Darcy answered, his deep voice rumbling in his chest pressed against her ear. "Making free with my feelings is not something that comes easily to me. It may take me some time to become accustomed to the sort of openness you seem to prefer."

"Yet you showed me your affection last night rather unmistakably!"

"Yes. Your uncle told me that I would have little chance at winning your affections unless I let you see mine first. Last night, after leaving you, I wondered if I had perhaps overwhelmed you with my attentions. I do not wish to be any less the gentleman just because we are married."

"You could never be that," Elizabeth assured him, wondering guiltily if he was thinking of the night of their quarrel, when she had accused him of less than gentlemanly behavior. She had seen him wince in reaction to that charge. To change the subject she said, "My uncle has been of infinite use, which no doubt makes him very happy, for he loves to be of use. Not as much as your aunt, fortunately."

"My aunt is going to learn that it would be better for her not to be so involved in my life," Darcy answered, with a grimness that took her by surprise. She twisted her head to look up at him, but could make out little of his features in the dim interior light of the carriage.

"If I did not know better, I might think that you are plotting some nefarious scheme against Lady Catherine!"

"I am indeed. Her behavior towards you in town was intolerable, but her behavior towards me ever since has been even worse. It is time someone in the family puts an end to her constant interference, and it seems the task will fall to me, if nobody else will do it."

"And how will you stop her? What can you possibly say to her that will make her stop her attack on my character?"

"That, my dearest, remains to be seen." His arm tightened around her shoulder. "I would rather not say until I hear from my solicitor in town. He has been engaged in a particular line of inquiry that I suggested to him, and I should hear back from him shortly. Besides, I did nearly all the talking last night. Today I would like to hear your recollections. When did you first realize that I did not marry you simply out of duty? Was it when you received my letter from town?"

"No; by then I already knew. It was when your sister told me that you were happy that I had accepted you at once and allowed a rapid wedding. She said you were afraid you might have to wait months for me. She also mentioned that you had admired my playing and singing, and that your spirits had risen once you met me, after your anger over her near elopement just a few months previously."

"All true, and all things I ought to have told you myself."

"And then I recalled when you said that the reason you married me no longer mattered in light of my feelings for you. It was as if a screen had been removed from before me, and suddenly I could see everything clearly, from our engagement right up until the night of our quarrel."

"Did you not sense my affection for you before then, when I paid you so much attention? Could you not see that I was trying to please you?" The hurt in his voice was plain.

"I ought to have, but I invented other reasons to explain those things."

Darcy said nothing, and she sensed that he would not be satisfied with her feeble excuse. Sighing, she resolved to face the unpleasant subject without further delay. There would never be a better time than now, in the circle of his arms, when she would not have to meet his eyes as she made her confession.

"This will be difficult. Like you, I do not always say what is in my heart."

"So I have noticed," Darcy said, and this time Elizabeth heard the smile in his voice.

"Please, William, let me have my say. Just as you needed to speak without interruption last night, I need to speak freely today."

Elizabeth felt his lips press to her forehead. Taking that as his agreement, she took a deep breath and began to speak.

"First, I want you to know that I have never had any affection for George Wickham."

She sensed Darcy tense next to her. "Never?" he asked.

"You may have thought so from what I said to you on the night that we argued, but he never made inroads on my heart. Only you have ever done that."

Darcy exhaled, and Elizabeth thought she felt him relax.

"But I did listen to him last winter, when he began to tell me how you had wronged him. I allowed myself to be flattered by the attention he paid me, especially after you had declared me not handsome enough to tempt you, and I was angry when I thought that you did not approve of my family. I was ready to hear whatever he had to say, but I was only diverted by him, never enamored.

"Then Mr. Bingley left Netherfield, and I was certain that you and his sisters had convinced him to forget Jane. After that happened I could not think of you without resentment. Jane lost her spirits for many weeks, and even when I went to Kent and she was in town, she had not fully recovered. When I met you at your aunt's home I was determined to provoke and annoy you, perhaps to pay you back, in some small way, for what I felt sure you had done to her. I never once imagined that you had developed any kind of attachment to me. As angry as I was, I still would not have encouraged your addresses if I had known what you were thinking. If I had known you planned to make me an offer, I would have refused you plainly and told you the truth--you were the last man in the world I could ever be prevailed upon to marry."

She expected some kind of response at this point, but Darcy remained silent. Only his quick intake of breath let her know he was listening.

"I didn't know you then," she continued, half-desperately. "If I had known you then as I do now, I would have welcomed your courtship--and your offer of marriage. But I had no chance to learn to appreciate you. I received the message that my father was near death, and the next thing I knew, he was gone.

"After that I was in a kind of a blur. My family was going to be uprooted, we had no means to support ourselves, and I had no future to look forward to. Then you appeared. When my uncle came to tell me that you had made an offer, it seemed utterly unreal."

"I wish I had been able to comfort you at that time," Darcy spoke unexpectedly.

Elizabeth clung more tightly to the hand which held hers, wondering if he would say something more, but he did not.

"After we married, everything Wickham said seemed to be true, at first. So many of your actions seemed to confirm that you thought I was beneath you--when you told me not to wear mourning for my father, the way you arranged my days, when you agreed with your aunt about my family's behavior. But I had to admit that you had reasons for doing as you did and saying what you said, and there were times when your presence was comforting to me. When we came to Pemberley, I began to see the affection and loyalty you inspire in those around you. Even your servants praised you. My anger began to fade. I wanted to spend time with you, to tell you about the events of my day. Then you announced that Mr. Bingley was coming to visit, and all of my previous prejudices rose in my mind again.

"After our quarrel, when I read your letter, I had to face myself for the first time. I wanted to speak to you and apologize for my prepossession and pride, but you were already gone."

She paused to catch her breath, and in the silence Darcy asked, "Is that all?" His voice was so quiet it was almost a whisper.

"No." They had come to the most difficult part. "When I accepted your offer I had a completely different idea of what our marriage would be like. My uncle said that you wanted to marry me not despite the differences in our station, but because of them. He said that you had chosen me to marry so that I, out of awareness of my inferior status, would make no demands on you; that I would be content with whatever small luxuries came my way. He said that I would be required to produce an heir and very little more."

She gulped, trying to take in fresh air to choke out the next words.

"And he said that I should not be surprised when you decided to take your mistress to your bed instead of me."

Another painful pause ensued.

"I did not want to believe him at first, but he seemed so certain, and his words had certain logic to them. I had heard of such marriages before in the Ton, and I assumed that he spoke the truth. He also said that, if you followed the pattern he expected, my life would be my own to live after giving you an heir, and I would be permitted to--pursue other relationships."

There was absolutely no reaction from Darcy. The silence was more dreadful to her ears than any outburst would have been.

"Please understand that I realized very quickly that you are not that sort of man. Your conduct at Pemberley was so far above reproach, and your concern for your sister was so exemplary, that I soon began to discredit much of what my uncle had said. It did not seem possible that one who took such care for those around him, even his tenants, would ever treat his wife in such a dishonorable way. And I never wanted to live in such a disreputable manner myself."

Still there was no response from her husband. Was he determined to say nothing at all? Was it possible that his rage was building, that he would pull away from her at any moment?

"That night on the balcony, when we looked at the stars together, you asked me what wish I would make if I could. I told you that I wished to see a falling star for myself, but that was not true."

Darcy still did not speak, and Elizabeth suddenly realized that he had not moved for several minutes. The only motion anywhere around her came from the movement of the carriage on the road, and the only sound besides the sounds of travel was the beating of his heart. "William--are you awake?"

She pushed herself a little away from him in order to look at his face, and was relieved to see his eyes focused on her, relaxed but open. "Is there anything else?" he asked.

"You already know the rest. I resolved to marry you in order to protect my family, and to make the best of the circumstances in which I found myself. Can you forgive me for marrying you under false pretenses, for being so willing to think badly of you when I hardly knew you?"

"Can you forgive me for behaving in a way that seemed to justify what your uncle said?"

Just like that, he was willing to forgive her. "I have already forgiven and forgotten. In a case such as this, a good memory would be unpardonable."

"Then we will put this behind us forever. The only thing I want you to remember now, Elizabeth, is what I told you when we married."

In the half-light coming in through the window, Darcy took both her hands in his as he had during their wedding. He looked at her solemnly, his eyes gazing into hers. "I, Fitzwilliam Darcy, will love you, comfort you, honor and keep you," he paused, "and forsaking all others, will keep only to you, for as long as I shall live."

Deeply moved, she responded, "And I, Elizabeth, will love, honor and cherish you, forsaking all others, for as long as we both shall live." She wanted to say more but could not speak over the lump in her throat. Instead she looked at him, willing him to see her in her eyes all the tenderness that was in her heart.

Darcy must have seen understood some of her unspoken message, for after a moment he brought his hands to her face, framing it gently with his fingers, still looking at her with his intent, loving gaze. "What God hath joined together," he said softly, "let no man put asunder."

CHAPTER THIRTY THREE

Afterwards Elizabeth would never remember how long she and Darcy had remained in a passionate embrace, her husband kissing and holding her as their desire for each other mounted. She only knew that she wanted to be with her husband with a fervency she had never felt before, and from the way Darcy murmured her name while he pressed kisses to her lips and neck, she knew he felt the same. Eventually he pulled away, releasing her reluctantly.

"It would not be appropriate to continue this here," he said, his voice shaky, and Elizabeth was forced to agree with him.

"But, Elizabeth--" he paused for a moment, "tonight, when we are at Pemberley, will you come to my bed?"

"Of course, if that is your wish."

"No." He shook his head in frustration. "I mean, yes, of course it is my wish, but I want it to be your desire as well. I want you to want to be with me, not merely to tolerate my advances."

Elizabeth felt her cheeks flame, but she answered with the impudence he seemed to enjoy. "I will do my best to come to your bed only thinking of my own desire. I will take no notice of yours at all."

Darcy's lips curved into a smile and he let his forehead rest against hers for a moment. Then he exhaled deeply. "May I sleep with you?"

"I believe we just resolved that issue, Mr. Darcy," Elizabeth could not help teasing once again.

"I mean, may I go to sleep with you now? I was not jesting when I told you that I had little rest in the commons last night. Of course I have no pillow here, but I might do well if you will allow me to rest on your shoulder."

Elizabeth's heart swelled. "Perhaps you would prefer to lie down instead, and place your head in my lap," she suggested. "It might be more comfortable."

Darcy wasted no time in taking her up on her offer, stretching out on the bench as much as possible. Elizabeth moved over to one side as far as she could and sighed as Darcy laid his head down.

"You are a very handsome man, Mr. Darcy," she added, removing a glove to stroke her fingers through his thick hair. She had often wondered what his hair would feel like under her fingertips, but had never allowed herself to make free with it before. Now she relished the fine, smooth texture against her palm.

Darcy grasped her hand in his to give it a quick kiss. "I love you Elizabeth," he said just before closing his eyes and relaxing deeply.

"Sweet dreams, William," Elizabeth answered, and felt herself relax as well.

∞

It was hours later when Elizabeth woke once again, feeling the change in the carriage's motion as it made a sharp turn to the left and began moving over a smoother surface. The passing foliage outside the window looked familiar somehow, and as she saw the great wrought iron gates of Pemberley go by, she realized--they were home.

"William," she said gently, hating to disturb his rest. For a few moments she simply enjoyed the sensation of watching him in his sleep, her hands lightly caressing his face. "William, wake up. We are at Pemberley."

Darcy opened his eyes but he seemed in no hurry to sit up. He reached to her instead, pulling her head down to his, somewhat awkwardly, for a kiss. "How very beautiful you are, my dearest."

Elizabeth could not resist teasing. "Am I correct in thinking that you now find me handsome enough to tempt you?"

"It has been many months since I first thought of you as the most handsome woman of my acquaintance." He kissed her again, just to make his point; and then sat up, still looking somewhat the worse for wear. He and Elizabeth managed to restore their appearances to normal as much as possible before the carriage stopped in front of Pemberley.

Georgiana and Colonel Fitzwilliam came out of the house together as the carriage came to a stop, and as the steps were placed and the door opened, Elizabeth could see them anxiously trying to peer inside the vehicle. They both smiled in relief when Elizabeth appeared in the carriage's doorway, but they smiled even more when Darcy followed closely behind her. The colonel gave them both a knowing look.

"Mrs. Darcy, it is good to see you again--so soon," he said pointedly, and Elizabeth laughed in response.

"Colonel! As if I did not know that you spoke to the driver behind my back! Surely you knew I would uncover your clever misdirection sooner or later."

"But not until it was too late to avoid Darcy, which was precisely my goal."

"Your assistance has been invaluable, cousin," Darcy told him, shaking his hand heartily, "and I am grateful. Without your help I might have had to travel all the way to Meryton."

"Your happiness is my best reward," the colonel answered with a gallant little bow, and Elizabeth felt, from his pleased expression, that his pleasure at their reunion was sincere.

Georgiana had already embraced Elizabeth, and then moved to do the same with her brother while this conversation went on. "But I do not understand," she said, stepping back and looking between the two in confusion. "I thought Elizabeth was needed at home, to comfort her family."

"Other issues took priority, and our plans have changed," Darcy answered, volunteering no details.

"Yes," said Elizabeth. "I realized it would be better if I stayed at my husband's side so that we can work through this crisis together. Besides, I am assured that Jane, at least, probably has no need of my poor support at the moment."

"Your timing is fortuitous," the colonel said, still beaming his pleasure at their presence. "The afternoon post came but two hours ago, and there was a letter in it for Mrs. Darcy. We were just debating whether to send it on to Longbourn for you or not, but it would seem odd to return it so quickly to the place where it originated."

"It is from Longbourn?" Elizabeth asked. "Then perhaps Lydia has been discovered. I hope Jane wrote to tell us that she and Wickham are now married."

It was news of a very different wedding which surprised her when she entered the house, briefly refreshed herself, and then joined the rest of the family in the parlor. She took her letter from Georgiana and read eagerly, turning each page rapidly and with a growing smile, and then looked at her husband with shining eyes.

"You were right," she told him. "Jane and Mr. Bingley are to be married; they may be married already."

Exclamations of surprise and pleasure rose all around, and Elizabeth was happy to note that of them all, Georgiana was the loudest in her approval, though her eyes were wide with amazement. "Was Mr. Bingley already attached to your sister?" she asked. "How did this come about so quickly?"

Elizabeth reminded herself that Georgiana knew nothing of the aborted courtship between Bingley and Jane. "They met last autumn in Hertfordshire," she told her now, "and they were on the point of announcing their engagement when Lydia disappeared." Georgiana appeared satisfied by this brief explanation, and Elizabeth turned her attention back to the pages in her hand.

"The letter is from my sister Mary," she said. "I suppose Jane was too busy to write herself."

My dear sister, Elizabeth began.

I have been commissioned by our eldest sister Jane, and compelled by the bonds of sisterly love, to inform you of what has happened in this household since she last wrote and told you of Lydia's elopement. It would appear that when you write back, you will have to address me, your younger sister, as Miss Bennet, since Jane will have resigned the title by that time.

The precipitous event came about in this manner: but three days ago, the day following Jane's last letter to you (so she tells me), Mr. Bingley arrived to call before ten in the morning. The hour being unconscionably early, Hill absolutely refused to admit him; but he would not listen to her. He claimed the rights of an engaged man and positively pushed his way past her, then seated himself in the parlor and refused to leave until he had spoken with Jane himself!

There being no plan to deal with a guest who refused to leave where he was not even invited, the house was thrown into confusion. Our mother, who had been sick in her bed until then, suddenly found new life and rose long enough to insist that Jane meet with her betrothed. Jane tried to tell her that their engagement was now ended because of Lydia, but Mama said that certainly Mr. Bingley would not come all the way from Netherfield in the rain if his intent was to break off the match; and anyway that Jane is too beautiful for anyone to think of breaking an engagement. This observation did not strike me as entirely logical, but overwhelming logic has never been our mother's most distinguishing characteristic. At any rate, it was apparent that Jane felt she had no choice but to obey. She went into the room with Mr. Bingley, quite slowly, and then closed the door behind her.

Mama then directed me to listen at the keyhole and report every word said to her.

Bingley, as it turned out, had not come to break off the engagement. On the contrary, he had come to hasten its fulfillment. He told Jane that he thought it imperative that they marry as quickly as possible, because he simply could not stand another day away from her when their separation might be ended so easily, and with so much benefit to all concerned. He presented several arguments in favor of the scheme. He had already procured a special license before he left town, and still had it in his possession; if they could marry very quickly, it might divert attention from the neighborhood gossip about Lydia; and in this present trouble he could be of much more use to her and the rest of us as her husband, not merely her betrothed. Whatever Jane's answer might have been we will never know, for at that point Mama came flying down the stairs in her dressing gown, crying, "You WILL marry Mr. Bingley! You will marry him at once! I absolutely insist upon it!" Poor Jane had no choice at all after that, but I do not believe she was displeased with the development.

This all happened three days ago, and we have not had a moment of peace since then. Jane wanted to write and tell you all of this herself, but she is at the dressmaker's with Mama and Aunt Phillips, so that she can have a gown ready to wear the day after tomorrow.

I have never had a lover. Until now they seemed like very tiresome things, not worth the trouble and distraction from more worthwhile pursuits, such as books and music. But I begin to believe that if I can find a lover like Mr. Bingley, it might be a very pleasant thing indeed; especially this Mr. Bingley, who seems a highly improved version of the gentleman we first met last autumn. I have every reason to think that he and our sister will get on as well as most couples generally do. Even if they do not I hope to make excellent use of the library and music room at Netherfield after Jane goes to live there.

Jane, I am sure, will write to you as soon as she can after the ceremony is held, to let you know that you may start addressing her as Mrs. Bingley. Until then I am your own dutiful sister

Miss Mary Bennet

N.B. Jane said to convey her appreciation for the beautiful planting *sent to her by you and Mr. Darcy.*

Mary's letter was such a mix of pretension, absurdity and genuine good will that Elizabeth could not help laughing as she read it aloud. The others laughed with her, and then she looked thoughtfully at her husband once again.

"*You* are responsible for this change in Mr. Bingley." It was a statement, not a question, but Darcy shook his head.

"I had nothing to do with it. I merely confessed to him my fault of interference with his life, and told him that I had reason to believe that your sister still held affection for him."

"But then you told him he should go back to Netherfield."

"I did not. I told him that if he truly loved your sister, he would not allow any barrier to come between them ever again, not my opinion nor anyone else's; and that he should not rest until he had made her his own. He decided for himself that he should return to court Miss Bennet."

"How can I ever thank you enough?"

At this point the colonel gave a self-conscious cough and extended his arm to Georgiana. She looked at him in confusion for a moment, but then her face cleared and she allowed him to escort her from the room. Elizabeth looked at her husband once again.

"Mr. Bingley has been a good friend to you, and he is so easily guided that his value is inestimable. I thank you for giving him such sound advice. My sister will be very happy."

"Truthfully, I was speaking more to myself than to him. I had already decided that I should return to Pemberley, to try to patch up our marriage and begin our relationship again. I wanted only courage, and saying the words I did to Bingley gave me the portion I needed."

Elizabeth felt her face soften as she looked at him. "Then I thank you for giving yourself the advice, and for following it so quickly. You have made me very happy."

Darcy fairly glowed as he looked back at her. "Your happiness is all I have ever wanted, Elizabeth."

CHAPTER THIRTY FOUR

Elizabeth Darcy took a deep breath that evening as she stood before the communicating door between her room and that of her husband. Darcy had asked her to come to his bed, and she knew that she would be more than welcome, but it was still the first time that they would truly be together as husband and wife since being reunited. Besides this, it was the first time that she was going to him out of desire, not just a sense of duty. Nothing could possibly feel more right. She raised her hand and knocked firmly on the door. Darcy answered immediately.

He stood for a moment in the open doorway, his hand still on the doorknob, to gaze at her from head to foot. She was wearing the same white nightgown she had worn on their wedding night, a lifetime ago. "You are beautiful, Elizabeth."

She licked her lips nervously. "Thank you, sir."

"No matter how lovely you were on the day we married, or on all the multiple days between that day and this, you are even lovelier to me now." They were almost the same words he had spoken to her on their wedding night. How had she missed their significance the first time?

She surveyed her husband up and down as well, noting that he, too, was wearing the garments he had worn the night of their wedding. "I find you quite attractive as well."

Darcy put his arms around her, slowly drawing her to him, and as she came closer he bent to kiss the curve of her neck. "I shall make you happy, Elizabeth. I swear it--and the oath shall be kept."

"You said that to me once before," she reminded him mischievously, although she was already beginning to melt under the tender touch of his caresses.

"I meant it then, too," he murmured into her ear, continuing to kiss her softly. Then he stopped, pulling back slightly to look her in the face.

"Shall we?" he asked, motioning towards his bed with one hand, just as he had on their first night together. But in contrast to that time, when she nodded her agreement he swept her off her feet and into his arms, kicking the door shut as he did so. He quickly crossed the room with her but hesitated before placing her on the bed, looking at her seriously.

"If we come together now, Elizabeth, I want to be certain that it is because it is your earnest desire. I want no compulsion between us, no sense of obligation. Are you truly here because you want to be here, and for no other reason?"

"It is my earnest desire to be here," she assured him, feeling all the significance of the moment. This would truly be a new beginning to their marriage. "There is no place that I would rather be." He bent to kiss her, and she placed her arms around his neck, drawing him to her as he lowered her down onto the mattress. And although they had been together in this way many times previously, for both of them, it was the first time.

∞

Afterwards they lay together quietly, Elizabeth's head nestled against Darcy's shoulder. They were silent but not still, each keenly aware of the other's presence as they breathed in each other's essence. At length Elizabeth felt Darcy's free hand move across her waist until it came to rest on her stomach. "Elizabeth, may I ask a question?" His voice was deep, calming.

"Of course, William--anything."

"Is there any chance that you are with child?"

Elizabeth's eyes, which had been drifting closed, opened wide. "Why do you choose to ask that *now*?"

"It is important to me," he insisted, leaning up on one elbow to look down at her intently. "Please tell me if you are."

Her courses had just come the week before. "No, I do not believe that I am."

Darcy exhaled, a sigh of relief, and lay back on the pillow again. Elizabeth looked at him, puzzled. "I do not understand. Do you not want children, sir?"

Darcy took one of her hands in his to drop kisses on her fingertips. "I would dearly love to have children one day, as many as you are willing to give me. But I was afraid that you being with child might have played a role in deciding whether to stay with me or not."

"You mean that if I were with child, I could not have gone back to Longbourn."

Darcy nodded, the light from the one burning candle in the room playing across his fine features.

"If I had been with child," she answered slowly, "when you made your offer to give me my freedom, I suppose you are right. It would have been no choice at all; I would have had to remain with you. Please understand that my decision to stay with you was made before I received your offer. As soon as I realized that you truly loved me, I knew that I owed you a much more thorough apology than the weak words I had already written to you; and that I wanted, more than anything, a second chance to make our marriage work."

"And when did you discover that you loved me as well?"

"I don't know, exactly," she said, pretending to be seriously considering the question. "Perhaps when I first saw Pemberley and realized the wealth which would be at my disposal as Mrs. Darcy."

She had thought to make him laugh, but he pressed a tentative kiss to her forehead instead, and she understood that this, too, was important to him. "I believe I was already falling in love with you after we came to Pemberley, as I began to see your better nature and how much you cared for those around you. But I did not entirely admit it to myself until I faced the prospect of leaving you. Then I began to realize how empty my life would be unless you were in it."

Darcy held her a little closer and relaxed again, and she understood that her answer had pleased him. "But now, sir, since you have asked me the question, I must also ask you in return: when did you first realize that you loved me?"

His answer was immediate. "'I cannot fix on the hour, or the spot, or the look, or the words, which laid the foundation. It is too long ago. I was in the middle before I knew that I had begun."

"No, sir," she playfully pushed him away as he tried to kiss her. "You forced me to answer the question; it is my turn to have an honest answer from you."

"I will not pretend to an honesty I do not own; I can only tell you that it was certainly before you went to Kent, and most probably during the weeks you spent at Netherfield. But the love I have developed for you since we married, and especially since our great argument, dwarfs my previous emotions for you. By you I have been properly humbled. Until I saw myself through your eyes, I never knew myself at all. You showed me how insufficient were all my pretensions to please a woman worthy of being pleased."

As he spoke, the single candle in the room, already dimming, fluttered and went out. Darcy began to stir himself, but Elizabeth said, "You need not bother. There is no reason to light another."

"I have a better idea." Rising briefly, he went to the double doors that separated his room from the balcony outside and threw them open. The sky outside was almost completely clouded over, obscuring any stars, but the light from the moon still shone clearly through.

"Delightful," Elizabeth murmured as Darcy took his place beside her again. The sultry air from outside carried the scent of the trees and water, and the quiet rippling of the stream could be heard plainly. "I might not ever want a lamp in this room again. It is a shame that your comet is not visible tonight, but it is nearly as bright with just the moon glow."

Darcy pulled her back into the circle of his arms again, cradling her head against his chest. "Elizabeth, I have another question to ask you."

"William! No more questions, please!" She attempted to bury her head in his neck, but he refused to be diverted.

"As delightful as our reunion has been, I still feel that there is a part of you that is holding back from me."

Elizabeth went very still. "I cannot imagine what you mean, sir."

"I mean specifically with--this." He waved a hand vaguely over the bed, and Elizabeth understood that he was speaking of their marital intimacies. "I know you came to me willingly, but I do not think you enjoy our time together as much as I do. Pleasure should be shared, Elizabeth, not just given from one partner to the other. Do you feel any pleasure when we come together?"

Elizabeth was glad, now, of the darkened room and the cover it gave for her blushing cheeks. "Ladies are not raised to speak of such things, sir."

"You are not just a lady; you are my wife, and I am asking as your husband, in the intimacy of our bedchamber, not in polite conversation over the dinner table. Surely we can speak of such things here. Have you ever felt any pleasure for yourself when we were together?"

"It has not been exactly *un*pleasant," she hedged.

"But nothing more?"

How could she answer? She did not entirely know what pleasure he thought she should have. "Is it not enough to feel delight at being able to please the one you love?"

"No, it is not." Darcy pulled his arms from around her, sitting up straight in bed so that he could look down at her face. His expression, even in the dark, was almost painfully earnest. "Elizabeth, I want you to feel the same joy that I do when we come together, the same thrill, the same delightful sensations which have enthralled me ever since our wedding night. I do not know how to give you those sensations if we cannot talk about it. I have never been with another woman, you know," he added, almost as an afterthought.

"What!" Elizabeth sat up as well, wanting to meet his gaze as an equal. "I assumed you--my uncle said that you-- "

"Yes, I know what your uncle told you." He smiled humorlessly. "He told me your entire conversation with him."

"You knew what I believed about you already! Then why did you ask me to repeat the conversation to you?"

"I thought it was important that we talk about it for ourselves. I want you to know that I have never had another woman in my bed besides you. This experience has been as new for me as it has been for you."

"You have not? Why?" Rarely had Elizabeth been so startled. Although she had accepted that Darcy had no mistress, she had still assumed that he, like most men of his class, would have had some experience at some point in his life.

"What kind of hypocrite would I be, demanding innocence from my wife but not from myself? I know it is not the way of the world, that men are expected to have taken this step long before they are married. Certainly it is the way of the Ton. But as I told you earlier, I am not a typical man of the Ton."

"And so you had no idea what to expect on our wedding night?" Elizabeth could not help asking.

"I had some idea," Darcy told her, with a slow smile. "When men gather in the clubs, there is talk of course. But I never wanted to share that experience with anyone but the woman I married."

Stunned, Elizabeth leaned back against the pillows. Then she began to laugh. "What is so amusing?" her husband asked.

"Here all this time, I was counting on you to show me how this is done, to let me know if the marital bed was supposed to be more than the duty that Hill described to me before we married."

"Your housekeeper told you what to expect?" The shock in Darcy's voice was palpable; then he began to laugh as well. For several minutes they laughed together, amused at the misunderstandings under which they had both labored. Then Darcy sobered.

"Elizabeth, when we come together again, do you think you can tell me what brings you pleasure? Or will you be embarrassed, too ashamed to speak of such things? I will never know how to improve the experience without your help."

Oddly, she no longer felt any shame. "My courage rises with every attempt to intimidate me, sir. If you can bear with the unspeakable impropriety of such a forward wife, I will do my best to communicate with you."

"Then let us begin now." Darcy reached for her gently but eagerly, finding his way with Elizabeth's encouragement. And together, they went to the stars.

CHAPTER THIRTY FIVE

They rose rather later than usual the next morning; so late, in fact, that the morning post had been delivered by the time they came downstairs. A letter sat at Elizabeth's place at the table when she and Darcy came down together to eat breakfast.

"From my uncle!" she said with surprise. "Perhaps it is news of Lydia."

The letter was short, only one page:

My dear niece,

I have waited too long to write you this letter. I fear that I rendered you a serious disservice at the time that I arranged your marriage to Darcy, and I write now to ask your pardon, knowing that no words may serve to undo the pain I undoubtedly caused both of you.

At the time I first relayed Darcy's proposal of marriage to you, I made many assumptions about his character and his views of marriage, based on my own limited exposure to members of what is considered fashionable society. These assumptions were gravely mistaken. As I have come to spend more time with Darcy in town, I have realized how different he is from the typical men of society, a sharp contrast to the man I described to you on the day of your engagement to him. His character and disposition are above reproach. He is grave sometimes, quiet when he ought to speak, and occasionally awkward when he tries to convey what is in his heart. But make no mistake--though it may be hard for you to see right now, there is no finer man in the kingdom.

I have already asked most humbly for Darcy's pardon, and now I ask for yours. It is my belief that once the two of you resolve your mistaken impressions of each other, you may make one of the happiest couples in England. May you learn to love each other, and to live in the happiness that you both so richly deserve.

I am your sincerely repentant uncle,
Edward Gardiner

Elizabeth folded the note gently, tenderly, and replaced it in the envelope as Darcy watched. "Is there news of your sister?" he asked.

"No." She shook her head, a small smile playing on her lips. "My uncle wrote only to tell me what I already knew--that I should have realized much earlier the worth of the man I married."

"Did he?" Darcy looked at her with a bemused expression.

"Yes, but do not ask me to repeat what he said, lest I be guilty of flattering you unnecessarily. I shall cherish these words and remind myself of them at some future time when I need to remember not to let mistaken impressions rule the day." They gazed happily at each other for a moment before Elizabeth tucked the letter into her sleeve, resolving to read it again that night.

"For now," she continued more briskly, "there are other matters we need to address. For instance, now that Jane and Mr. Bingley are married, do you think there is a chance that the talk about Lydia and Wickham will go away?"

Darcy accepted the redirection gracefully. "I applaud Bingley for his actions regarding your sister," he answered, "but the talk about Lydia and Wickham will not entirely disappear. They must marry, and it must not be widely known that they were together in London beforehand. Nothing else will do. When I left town I gave Mr. Gardiner certain information about Wickham's former haunts that may help him in his efforts to locate them. I hope we will hear shortly that he has been successful."

"Then what? How do we convince Wickham to marry Lydia?"

"All it takes is money. There is nothing he will not do if the price is right."

Elizabeth said nothing, but her mouth twisted down as she looked at her husband. Her uncle had no money, certainly not in the amount it would take to convince Wickham to do the right thing, and Darcy well knew it; so he must be planning to pay for the match himself. Darcy saw the look on her face and reached out to touch her hand gently.

"Do not fret about the price; I am a wealthy man, and whatever Wickham demands, we will be able to afford it."

"I suppose I have no choice but to accept the situation, but it goes hard against the grain to think that my husband and uncle will have to bribe one of the most worthless men in England for the privilege of naming him as a relative!"

"We will do what must be done," Darcy responded, seeming to shrug it off. "I am more concerned about the situation with my aunt. Wickham will succumb to a bribe, but Lady Catherine is not so easily managed."

"You said on the way home that you had some plan in mind for dealing with her."

"It is more of a hope, really; an idea that came to my mind while I was in town. I do not know if it will bear fruit. I asked my solicitor to seek out some information for me regarding Lady Catherine and Sir Lewis."

"Information about what?"

Darcy leaned back in his chair, the corners of his mouth turning down as he frowned in thought. "There has long been talk in the family of something irregular in their marriage, some sort of scandal which was quickly hushed up."

"A scandal involving Lady Catherine? This cannot be." She waited, but her husband said nothing more. "You cannot possibly think I will be satisfied with just that tidbit of information!"

"I truly have little to add to it. My father disliked gossip and I have always avoided it, trying to follow his lead; but Lady Catherine is a special case. The only way she will leave us alone is if she thinks we hold the upper hand in some way. For this reason I am willing to delve into the family secrets, if secrets there be."

"And what secrets do you expect to find?"

"Perhaps something significant, or perhaps nothing at all. It would be folly to speculate too much on matters about which I know nothing. Until I hear something more, I have a great deal of work to catch up with now that I am back at Pemberley. I am afraid I will have to be closeted with my steward for some time this morning. Do you mind?"

"Not at all. I have my responsibilities as well, and I am sure Georgiana and I will find something to occupy our time. But after that, perhaps I can interest you in an afternoon walk in the gardens?" She smiled invitingly at him.

"You may depend on it," Darcy said, answering her smile with one of his own. "I shall come and find you then."

∞

Several hours later, they realized that the walk in the gardens would not happen. The skies had opened and a veritable deluge begun.

Darcy, taking a small break from his work, stood observing in front of his study window, marveling at how quickly the smooth driveway in front of Pemberley had filled with hundreds of small streams and puddles. The great branches of the Spanish chestnuts seemed to bend under the weight of the onslaught, only to bend again as the high winds of the storm caught at them and pulled. Darcy wondered if the colonel, bent on his usual ride around the park, had returned to the house before the storm broke.

"It is invigorating, don't you think?" Elizabeth said. She and Georgiana, unnoticed, had entered the room and come to stand at his side, drawn by the sight of the pounding rain. "The air will be cleared after this is gone, for a while. I was tiring of the constant oppressiveness."

Darcy acknowledged their entrance with a welcoming smile. "The crops will certainly benefit from it. My steward was saying this morning that we needed a good rain, and I believe this fits the bill admirably. The tenants are no doubt rejoicing even as we speak."

"I think I see one of your tenant families now," Elizabeth said, mischief in her voice. She nodded to where a mother duck was leading her brood happily across the driveway towards the stream, craning her neck and stretching her wings to try to catch as much of the moisture as possible. Her offspring imitated her in their diminutive way. "Tell me, Mr. Darcy, how much do you charge them to live on your property? I am sure they find no fault with their landlord!"

Darcy and Georgiana both smiled, amused, but their smiles changed to looks of concern as a single rider on horseback came into their field of vision, his hat low on his head to shield him from the rain. Elizabeth eyes followed their gaze. "A messenger from town," Darcy commented, his curiosity piqued. "He must have something in particular to share, given these conditions."

"He will certainly have need of drying off, lest Mrs. Reynolds scold him for making a mess in the entry," Elizabeth answered.

"I will see that he is let in right away," Georgiana offered, and rang the bell to have the butler alerted.

It was not long before the rider had entered the house and been made comfortable, and then he was shown to the study and presented to Darcy. Darcy paid him while Elizabeth and Georgiana stood anxiously by, and then swiftly opened the envelope. He was mildly surprised when not one but two letters fell into his hand.

"One of these is from my solicitor and the other from Mr. Gardiner. They are both addressed to me."

Elizabeth frowned. "Which one will you read first?"

Darcy hesitated, and then took up the envelope with the oversized letter G on the seal.

"Shall I leave?" Georgiana asked.

Darcy and Elizabeth exchanged a look, and then Elizabeth smiled at her. "Of course not. This concerns you as well as us."

Darcy read aloud:

My dear sir,

I am happy to report that everything has gone just as you hoped it would when you left the matter of my niece Lydia and Wickham in my hands. Following the information you gave me, I located them in the boarding house of Mrs. Younge, a disorderly, slatternly woman in a neighborhood that matches her appearance.

"He has found them!" Elizabeth exclaimed. "Are they married?"

Lydia is well, and not at all concerned for the disgrace she has caused herself and others. She and Wickham are not married, nor can I find that there was ever much intention of being married; but if you will agree to the arrangements that I have ventured to make on your behalf, I hope that the ceremony will be carried out soon. All that is required is the surrender of Lydia's dowry, the payment of Wickham's debts, and the purchase of a commission in the army."

"Her dowry, his debts, and a commission?" Elizabeth repeated, shaking her head. She was overcome by the greed and general want of decency on display.

"I am not surprised," was her husband's cool answer. "I would be astonished if he were to ask for anything less."

Georgiana's eyes filled with pity. "He is still seeking women to make his fortune. Your poor sister."

We have already purchased a license and the ceremony can take place as soon as we hear back from you that these arrangements are to your satisfaction. Lydia will be married from our home, and then they will be sent to join his regiment in the north, unless you object. I am including the pertinent documents for your review and signature.

I am also including a communication from your solicitor, whom I saw yesterday in the course of my negotiations with Wickham. When he heard that I was sending you an immediate message he begged me to include a letter from him as well, saying that you will benefit from the information it contains. I hope that it will prove to be as helpful as he seems to think it will be.

Trusting in an immediate response from you, I am your obedient servant

Edward Gardiner

"To think that marriage to Wickham is the best that can be hoped for Lydia!" Georgiana exclaimed. She was struck by the disgrace and helplessness of Lydia's position, even if Lydia herself was not. "He will spend every farthing she has in a fortnight, and then he will abandon her once the money is gone. And yet they must marry!"

"Yes, they must marry; there is nothing we can do about it," Elizabeth answered, wishing herself wrong. "By law all that a wife has is her husband's as soon as they are married, and he is free to spend it as he likes. There is no way to stop Wickham from doing what we know he will do. I never thought one of my father's daughters might end up the victim of a fortune hunter!"

Darcy sat back down at his desk, frowning thoughtfully as he considered the pages before him. "There actually *could* be a way around it," he said, speaking almost to himself. "We could have her dowry transferred to a trust, one managed by a reliable, discreet administrator sworn to spend it only on Lydia's behalf. Such things are done sometimes, you know. It would not stop Wickham's gaming and wasteful spending, but at least he would not be wasting *her* money."

"I have heard of such trusts before, but I am not overly familiar with them. Protecting ourselves from fortune hunters was never a concern before now. But trusts, I believe, take time to set up, and Wickham and Lydia have to marry right away."

"They do indeed. There is no delay possible on that point." Darcy mulled this over in silence for a few more seconds before looking at his sister. "Georgiana, do you happen to know where the colonel is?"

"No," she said, surprised. "But I can ask Mrs. Reynolds."

"If you would not mind," he answered, and Georgiana left the room to find her cousin at once. Darcy turned to answer Elizabeth's inquiring look.

"If the colonel is willing to help, I believe we can put Lydia's dowry out of Wickham's reach with a much simpler solution."

She raised one eyebrow. "I am curious to hear what you have in mind."

He told her briefly, earning an approving nod.

"An excellent plan. I will almost feel sorry for Wickham, once he realizes the trap laid for him! I am glad you thought of involving the colonel."

"So am I." They exchanged an amused look before Darcy took up the other letter. "It might be better to read this while Georgiana is out of hearing."

Elizabeth waited impatiently while her husband unsealed the envelope and then watched as his face registered his reaction to the first few lines. The look in his eyes changed rapidly from curiosity to shock, from shock to disbelief, and finally to something like hope. Quickly he perused the other pages of the letter, his eyes lingering for a moment on certain lines; and then he looked at Elizabeth. "I think you should read this, my dearest." Elizabeth did not need a second invitation.

"It appears to be a copy of a church register--nothing terribly interesting," she said after a minute, disappointed. "I do not understand."

"Read the first page," he urged her. "And then here," he said, pointing, "and here."

As she read the parts he indicated understanding began to dawn; she looked at her husband with eyes that were widening by the moment. "Can this be true?"

"I do not see how it can be denied."

Dazed, she looked at the words on the page again. "If this is true--" she began, hardly daring to hope.

"If this is true," Darcy finished, a smile beginning to cross his face, "then we have found a way to stop Lady Catherine speaking against you, once and for all."

CHAPTER THIRTY SIX

Five days later, in the mid-afternoon, a chaise and four made its way swiftly up the driveway of Pemberley and came to an abrupt stop before the front doors. The regal lady inside took her time about leaving the vehicle, forcing the footman to stand at rigid attention for long minutes before she finally descended the carefully placed stairs. Once on the ground, she looked down her nose at the surroundings--the stream, the trees, the wide steps leading inside, and even the house itself--and sniffed. Then she lifted her chin proudly and extended one arm.

"Attend to me, John," she commanded, waiting until the footman took his place behind her and a little to one side. "I am expected inside."

There was certainly no sign that she was expected; the front door of Pemberley remained stubbornly shut even as she approached it. With great dignity the footman rapped on the door for her, and the door swung solemnly open. Lady Catherine crossed the threshold with all the dignity of a king on royal tour.

The butler inside the house took her hat and spencer, and then Mrs. Reynolds appeared and curtsied before the august visitor. "If you will, madam," she said, and turned away with no further communication.

Lady Catherine followed the housekeeper through the halls of Pemberley, looking from side to side as she went, keeping up a running monologue as she went.

"I can write my name in the dust on that pianoforte; such shoddy housekeeping would not be tolerated at Rosings for one instant! The wallpaper will do for now, I suppose. The lamps appear not to have been trimmed for months! At Rosings we make our help earn their keep, not sit idle and gossip all day. I see that it will take some time to remove the marks of vulgar taste that have been afflicted on this home. Anne will remedy all this when she is mistress!" Mrs. Reynolds, ahead of Lady Catherine, managed not to roll her eyes as she announced the visitor into the parlor, but it was only because of her years of training as a discreet employee.

Darcy was waiting in his study when Lady Catherine came in, his face grim. He did not rise as courtesy demanded, and she took a seat across from him without waiting to be asked.

"Please, make yourself comfortable," said Darcy, although she certainly needed no invitation. "We may be here for some time."

"I came as soon as I received your message," Lady Catherine answered. "I am, I suppose, relieved that you are finally willing to honor your obligations to your family, although it would have been easier if you had not been entrapped by that Miss Bennet first."

"Elizabeth is Mrs. Darcy now," Darcy answered, his lips tightening almost imperceptibly.

"For the moment, perhaps," his aunt said, coldly.

Darcy made an impatient motion with his hands. "Let us come straight to the point. It is time that we resolve the matter of your interference with my marriage."

"Excellent. I assume you have already made the proper overtures to that woman's mother and that you will soon be free to marry Anne."

"On the contrary. I asked you to come to Pemberley so that we could resolve our impasse. I did not give any indication how I thought it would be resolved."

Lady Catherine frowned at him. "You led me to believe that a settlement was imminent! I did not travel all the way from town simply to hear you say that you are determined to continue on this course! If you are not willing to do the right thing, my trip here has been a waste of time."

"Matters will indeed be settled, but perhaps not in the way you expected."

Lady Catherine fixed him with her most intimidating glare. "Tell me, Darcy--is that woman gone from your house yet? For if not, then we have nothing to speak of. Have you managed to send her back to Longbourn?"

Darcy met her eyes evenly. "No."

Lady Catherine's face began to flush. "Will you promise me that it will be done as soon as possible?"

"I will not."

Lady Catherine's eyes grew wide as Darcy leaned forward in his chair, placing his hands on the desk for emphasis.

"Why should I do as you ask, Lady Catherine? Why should I set aside my wife, a woman with the finest character and disposition, merely to take up one of your choosing? Do you truly believe your status as my aunt gives you the right to dictate my behavior?"

"I claim such rights as your elder, Darcy, and as your mother's only sister. Besides this, I am the widow of Sir Lewis de Bourgh, of the S----- shire de Bourghs, and now the holder of the de Bourgh fortune!"

"The de Bourgh fortune that you hold in trust."

"Of course."

"For Anne."

"Naturally; who else?"

Darcy sat back in the chair again, appraising his aunt with a keen, shrewd look. "I have always found it curious, Lady Catherine, how much you like to emphasize your distinction of rank, your connections in society, and your title. My mother, though she was your older sister, did not find such self-promotion necessary. In my experience those who insist on their superiority the loudest are those who are least sure of owning it."

Lady Catherine did not answer, looking back at him with her lips pressed tightly together. It occurred to her that Darcy had a very different agenda than what she had assumed when she received his message.

Without taking his eyes off his aunt, Darcy said, in a somewhat louder voice, "Elizabeth, would you please bring me the letter which Wilson sent to me the other day?"

"Certainly." Elizabeth had been sitting quietly in a chair a little behind the door that Lady Catherine had used to enter the room. Now she rose and came into her field of view, and as she did so, Lady Catherine's mouth opened wide. She nearly sputtered in outrage.

"What is the meaning of this? Why have you allowed that woman to be present, and why was I not informed that she was in the room?"

"Wilson is my solicitor in town," Darcy explained, ignoring her outburst. "The documents he sent me earlier this week inspired me to ask you to come to Pemberley. I think you will find them most enlightening." Elizabeth laid the pages on the table and pushed them across to Lady Catherine, who looked at her suspiciously. She frowned, and then reluctantly picked them up. Darcy and Elizabeth remained motionless, silently watching as she began to glance through them.

"I fail to see what you think I ought to read here. This is a recitation of births and marriages from decades ago, in some parish I have never heard of."

"They are from a small parish in Scotland," Darcy told her, "in a town of little consequence to anyone. I asked my solicitor to look into some rumors I heard years ago, and this is what he found."

Lady Catherine glanced quickly, sharply at him, and then more intently at the pages in her hand, squinting slightly as her finger traced down the line of entries. Elizabeth heard her breath catch as her finger suddenly ceased its motion. "What is the meaning of this, Darcy?" she demanded.

Darcy took a deep breath before answering. "Anne is not the heir of Rosings Park," he announced calmly. "Nor are you the guardian of its fortunes."

"What!" Lady Catherine exclaimed, looking in disbelief between Darcy and the names on the page.

"Sir Lewis had a son before he married you. Despite his last name, that man, Lewis Beaufort, is the natural son of your husband, as I am sure you already know. I had heard talk once or twice before of a liaison between Sir Lewis and a low-born woman, but I had no idea of there being a child born from that union."

Lady Catherine angrily dropped the pages from her hand. "Yes, I knew of my husband's failing before we met. He gave in to his baser urges and fathered a child out of wedlock. Sir Lewis arranged for the mother and child to go live with relatives, and that was the end of the affair. What of it?"

"That child was *not* born out of wedlock," said Darcy, with preternatural calm. "Sir Lewis married the girl. My solicitor found the marriage recorded in Scotland, where the couple had fled in order to avoid the interference of his parents. Some months later, their son was born."

Although Elizabeth had known this information was coming, she still felt the shock of the words reverberate throughout the room. Lady Catherine gasped. "I do not believe it."

"I think you do. I think that you already investigated the matter and found out how Sir Lewis' parents pressured the girl to give up the match, since her family had no fortune. You discovered that her family accepted a bribe and swore there was a flaw in the marriage contract, and that is what inspired you to try the same with my marriage."

Lady Catherine stared, open-mouthed.

"This means, of course, not only that Anne is not the heir of Rosings, but that you yourself were never married to her father."

Lady Catherine found her voice again, gasping out, "You cannot prove any of this!"

"I do not have to. My solicitor had the pages from the register copied out for me, and that is all that we need. You can see the wedding date for yourself."

Lady Catherine slowly took up the pages of the register from the table again, her eyes fixing on the line in question. Her face now bore a look entirely different from the haughty, arrogant expression she had worn moments previously. Elizabeth could see her mind working furiously, trying to comprehend this new information.

"It may interest you to know," Darcy added, with feigned casualness, "that Lewis Beaufort is no longer living. He passed away of a fever several years ago; his mother is also gone."

His aunt's hands had begun to tremble. "Did he ever marry? Were there any children?"

"I do not believe so. Fortunately for you, as long as that remains the case, there is no one to step forward and dispute the inheritance." Lady Catherine closed her eyes and sighed with relief. Then she opened them again and looked at Darcy again as comprehension began to dawn. An awkward silence ensued which Elizabeth broke.

"Your poor cousin Anne," she said, laying a hand on her husband's arm. "It would be quite a shock for her, to realize that she had a brother she never knew. I do not think there is any reason to disturb her with such information now that he is gone. She cannot mourn for someone she never met."

"I tend to agree. Besides which, finding out about the occurrence of another marriage before that of her parents would be upsetting in the extreme for her to discover."

Lady Catherine looked from Darcy to Elizabeth and then back to Darcy again, her eyes battling his. "You wouldn't dare."

"Try me and see." Darcy's voice was stern, inflexible. Lady Catherine looked at the parish records again, and then licked her lips before trying another tack.

"There is still the matter of Lydia Bennet. Her living with an officer without the benefit of marriage has become generally known."

"I wonder how the news spread so quickly," Elizabeth said, with an arch look for the noble lady, "but it is no matter. Mr. Wickham and my sister are married."

"Married!" Lady Catherine exclaimed, throwing her hands in the air. "Heavens and earth! Are the shades of Pemberley to be so polluted?"

"Wickham will never have the chance to sully Pemberley with his presence," Darcy answered. "He will be joining the navy soon."

"The navy!"

"Yes." Here Darcy's features took on a smug expression. "Wickham was surprised to find that he had enlisted in the navy when he took Miss Lydia's hand in church. Perhaps he did not read the marriage contract as well as he should have beforehand, but it is too late now. He will be unable to cause much trouble for anyone for months at a time, and he will have little ability to spend his own money or Lydia's dowry. He may even be a better man for it, after a few years. So you see there is no scandal and no reason to remove Georgiana from our care. The colonel is more than willing to attest to the good influence which my wife has had on my sister."

The look on Lady Catherine's face reminded Elizabeth of a cornered deer. She slowly laid the pages of Darcy's letter back on the table and paused for a moment before speaking with obvious reluctance. "I suppose, in the end, that Miss Bennet *is* the daughter of a gentleman."

"I am indeed," Elizabeth answered, raising her chin proudly. "My connections are not as illustrious as your own, but they have served me well enough up to now."

"And as to fortune--well, we need say nothing of it. The de Bourghs have never concerned themselves with such petty matters. *I* will never stoop to greed and vulgarity!"

"I am sure that you will not," Darcy said shortly. His aunt ignored him.

"And it is gratifying to hear that the Bennet family is more respectable than I had been led to believe. I was sure that they must be, after meeting Miss Elizabeth in the spring and judging her for myself. Such a sensible young woman could only have come from a fine, sensible family."

Elizabeth had a sudden spasm in her throat that caused her to cough into her handkerchief for a moment. "You are all kindness, your ladyship."

Lady Catherine made an impatient motion with her hands, preparing to stand. "This unfortunate business has, I am afraid, taken me away from

Anne far too long. I ought to return to her at once."

"Would you like some tea before you go?" Elizabeth interjected quickly, a false brightness in her voice. "Our selection here is nearly as extensive as that of Rosings, I believe."

Lady Catherine rose to her feet and looked at Elizabeth with ill-concealed irritation. "No. If that is all the business we need to conduct today, I will take my leave. It is a long ride back to town."

"We will wish you a pleasant journey, then," Elizabeth answered, with as much politeness as she could summon.

Her ladyship had already gained the door, but she turned to look back at Darcy one last time. "Do we have an understanding?"

He met her gaze evenly. "We understand each other exceedingly well." Their eyes locked, and Lady Catherine looked away first.

"Good day to you, nephew," she said, not meeting his eyes. "Good day to you too--Mrs. Darcy." With impressive dignity she left the room, the sound of her cane echoing through the halls as she went.

Elizabeth waited until she was out of earshot before beginning to laugh. "I am not sure if I have been welcomed to the family or roundly insulted!"

"That was the warmest welcome you are ever likely to receive from my aunt," Darcy responded. "She will not dare to insult you again after today."

"I thank you for defending my honor so ably. It was almost worth being insulted to see the look of shock on her face when you said she was never married to Sir Lewis!"

"I do not foresee that Lady Catherine will ever visit Pemberley again." Darcy sounded regretful, not angry, and a shadow passed over his face.

Elizabeth immediately sobered. "Would you really wish her to do so?"

"I wish this matter had ended in a much different manner." Darcy frowned and stood, turning his back to her in order to stare out the window, his arms crossed around his chest.

Even a relative as difficult as Lady Catherine might be painful to lose, Elizabeth thought. Perhaps she should not have teased him about it. "I will see you at dinner," she said to his back, but received no response; and she left the room in silence.

∞

After dinner Darcy came to where Elizabeth was sitting in the parlor, sewing and listening to Georgiana sing while she accompanied herself on the pianoforte. He leaned down to speak for her ears only. "Will you come into the garden with me? There is something I would like to show you."

"Gladly." Elizabeth put down her sewing and went with her husband at once.

Outside, they strolled together in silence in the darkness, with Elizabeth's arm tucked securely into his; but despite their proximity Elizabeth felt as though she were walking alone. "I thought you had something you wanted to show me, Mr. Darcy?" she finally asked.

"We may have to wait a few minutes. I beg for your indulgence." He lapsed into silence once again and Elizabeth decided she had to speak.

"William, may I ask you a question?" she asked, using her gentlest voice.

"Of course," he said in surprise. "I am at your service."

"Are you angry with me for some reason?"

"Angry? Why should I be angry?" He sounded even more surprised now, and he stopped walking in order to face her fully.

"You have hardly spoken to me since the moment Lady Catherine left the premises. I thought perhaps you were upset with me for being cause of a rift between the two of you."

"My dearest, loveliest Elizabeth," Darcy said, in a tone of regret. "I apologize for behaving in a way that allowed you to think such a thing. I am not angry with you at all."

"Then what--?"

"I am angry with myself."

"Why?"

"I thought that I could make my aunt accept you fully, that she would come to see the error of her ways without having to use such a brutal tactic as blackmail. It is not how I would have chosen to resolve the situation."

"Oh. I misunderstood you then. I thought you were counting the cost of a permanent break with your aunt, and thinking that it was too much to pay in order to defend me and my family."

"Never fear that I will think that. There is no price too great to pay in order to be with you." He bent towards her and Elizabeth closed her eyes and lifted her face, savoring the moment. But he stopped after just a brief caress of his lips against hers. "Keep your eyes shut," he murmured. "Turn around." She felt his hands on her shoulders, gently pushing her to turn and face away from him. "Now you may open them."

In front of her, shooting across the sky, was a series of falling stars, their brilliance illuminating the night sky. Elizabeth gasped. "You remembered!"

"Indeed I did. And I remember that you never told me what your wish was."

"Do you truly want to know?"

"Of course."

"They say," she responded, looking at him in her half-serious, half-playful way, "that if you tell someone your wish it will never come true. But that is a chance I am willing to take."

Darcy watched her, waiting, admiring. She rose on her tiptoes to put her arms around his neck and whisper in his ear, "My wish was to be married for love."

"*You* are my wish," he whispered back, and they kissed each other under the light of the falling stars.

EPILOGUE

It was Christmastime at Pemberley, just four months later, and Jane and Elizabeth were laughing together at their husbands' antics outdoors. What had started as a lively walk along the snowy, cleared path in front of the house had turned into a bit of friendly banter between the two men, and then an outright challenge. Now the two men were a safe distance ahead of the ladies, each good-naturedly taking refuge behind a separate pile of snow as the frozen missiles crossed the area between them.

"Hello there! What's this?" Bingley's voice rose abruptly above the general sound of laughter. "Where did that come from?"

"Attack!" Colonel Fitzwilliam's figure was seen rising up suddenly, dashing madly by as he hurled snowballs in the direction of both Bingley and Darcy. His military charge was so life-like that Elizabeth would not have been surprised to see him brandishing a sword over his head. Behind him came four smaller figures, the Gardiner children, dashing headlong after their leader. Georgiana, who had been their constant attendant for the past week, followed some distance behind them, making no effort to restrain their high spirits. Snowballs flew madly in every direction. For a moment the skirmish became a general melee as Jane and Elizabeth kept their distance, delighting in the disorder.

"I never thought to see your Mr. Darcy so informal!" Jane said, her voice filled with wonder.

"But you expected to see your husband so?" Elizabeth teased. "One is hardly less astonishing than the other!"

"Charles is so easy-going that this behavior does not terribly surprise me. But Mr. Darcy!" Jane let the thought go unfinished.

"I admit to being a little startled," Elizabeth rejoined, still laughing, "but as I have come to know, Mr. Darcy is not always as reserved in private as he is in public."

"You have been good for him," Jane said with a gentle smile, and Elizabeth's heart swelled. It was still a matter of wonder to her that she and Darcy had managed to come together at last, despite all the obstacles in their way, and be truly united as husband and wife.

"Mr. Darcy might have hesitated to invite our aunt and uncle to Pemberley before this," her sister went on, which Elizabeth could not deny, "but I believe there must have been a goodness and kindness in him all along which your own nature encouraged him to demonstrate more freely."

"He is the best man that I know," Elizabeth agreed heartily. "In the essentials, he always was."

A fresh snowball went perilously close past their heads just then, flying towards the house, and they turned to watch it as it fell harmlessly against one of the windows. Elizabeth caught sight of her aunt and uncle Gardiner inside the house, watching in amusement, and they smiled at each other fondly through the glass. A strong, familiar bond had grown between the Gardiners and Darcy, a friendship she would never have dreamed possible at the time she married her husband. To have them here at Pemberley along with her beloved sister and her husband made her happiness almost complete.

Darcy now came towards Elizabeth and Jane, trying ineffectually to brush the snow off the shoulders of his heavy greatcoat as he walked. "Young master Gardiner has a good arm," he said as he rejoined Elizabeth, chuckling. "If he is not careful he may prove to be Colonel Fitzwilliam's next unwilling recruit. He will need someone to take Wickham's place."

Wickham had not lasted long in the navy. He had deserted from his ship at its first port of call, in the West Indies, and nobody had heard from him since. Lydia mourned his disappearance for a little while, but by the time the desertion posters with his name and description were posted, she was already beginning a dalliance with another officer. Darcy had to inform her bluntly that the money from her dowry, recently invested in a trust, would never be given to her unless she dropped the flirtation. Lydia had obeyed, but only sullenly and with many protests against her ill usage.

"Colonel Fitzwilliam may regret recruiting my cousins to his cause before long," Elizabeth now commented, watching the continued frolicking. "My cousins are *very* energetic." Even as she spoke, one of the Gardiner children aimed a snowball directly at the colonel's head. He fired back good-naturedly, and soon he and Bingley had joined forces to vanquish the small army of attackers. The children retreated, shrieking.

Georgiana, meanwhile, had come to stand out of the line of fire with Elizabeth and her brother.

"I have not been so diverted in years!" she stated, her eyes glowing.

"I had forgotten how entertaining children can be!"

"You might come to a different opinion soon," Darcy warned her, putting out an arm to shield her as another snowball sailed by. It struck Jane instead, landing on the side of her hood, just where the edge of it met her face. Jane stood stupefied for a moment, the snow clinging to her hood and face; then she began to smile. Bingley was at her side in an instant.

"I am sorry, my love; we should not have encouraged the children in such liberties. Allow me to help clean you off."

"You needn't," Jane began, but Bingley was already brushing the snow off her cheek and out of her eye. His hand lingered under her chin while he gazed at her, his expression tender.

"Is that better?"

"Much better, thank you." Neither moved as they stood looking at each other, and Elizabeth turned hastily away, her eyes sparkling in amusement at Darcy as she did so.

Georgiana, too, noticed the intimate moment. Embarrassed, she moved away and called to the children, admonishing them to have more care in the future. "And you have been outside long enough," she added. "It is time to go inside and warm up before supper. Go to the side door, please, so that Mrs. Reynolds can clean you off first." With encouraging words, sweetness, and a surprising amount of firmness, she cajoled them into following her commands, and then followed their footsteps into the house, leaving the two couples and Colonel Fitzwilliam together.

Elizabeth took her husband's arm as they turned back to the house, the colonel walking on her other side so that they formed a comfortable trio. Bingley and Jane trailed a little behind.

"Without a doubt, Georgiana has found her element," Elizabeth commented as they walked along, pleased at the development. "Who would have known she would have such a natural talent with young children? They are just what she needed in order to boost her own self-assurance. She will be a splendid mother one day."

"Not any time soon, I hope," said Darcy, good-naturedly. "I am not in a hurry to lose my sister."

"You must be mad, Darcy," the colonel answered, walking with his usual tall, proud, military stride. "You know that Georgiana will receive offers of marriage as soon as she comes out next year. There is no way you can hold on to her forever."

"No, but I doubt she will be inclined to accept the first offer that comes her way. She is still very young."

"Even if that first offer comes from me?" The colonel spoke so offhandedly that Elizabeth missed the significance of what he said at first. Darcy, however, did not. He stopped stock-still to stare at his cousin.

"Richard! What do you mean?"

"I realize I may not be what she wants. Twelve years older than she is, a second son, not blessed with a great fortune. But if I have your permission, I would like to court her after she comes out."

Elizabeth glanced at her husband and saw that he was struggling with the idea. Why had such a possibility not crossed her mind, Elizabeth silently admonished herself. It was only natural, now that the idea had been suggested to her.

"I will resign my commission if she accepts me," the colonel went on, "and be more than content to stay at home. I find that I quite like the idea of being a family man--but only if Georgiana will be a part of that family. And not," he added, with a touch of humor, "in the manner of a cousin." Despite his lighthearted manner, Elizabeth could see the tension in his tightly held fists, and in the guarded yet hopeful look he directed at her husband.

"How long have you felt this way, Richard?" Darcy asked after a moment, astonishment on his face. "What made you begin to see her as a woman, and not as the young girl you have always helped to protect?"

"It was seeing her this past summer, after you were married, that made me first think of it," the colonel answered. "Around Mrs. Darcy she was completely different from the shy, awkward girl I knew before. Now, after seeing you and your wife so content together, I find I want the same thing that you have. Besides," he finished with a twinkle in his eye, "I should take myself out of the running, before Lady Catherine insists on me as a match for Anne!"

Lady Catherine had begun to search for a husband for Anne soon after returning to Rosings, but no likely suitor had made his address. Neither Darcy nor Elizabeth was surprised to think that she might look to the colonel to fill the role. They were, however, surprised that the colonel's interest had turned in *this* direction.

"What do you say, Darcy?" the colonel asked. "Will you allow me to approach Georgiana and say my piece, when the time is right?"

Darcy's face wore the expression which Elizabeth had come to know meant he was grappling with a difficult decision. "Georgiana is so young," he finally said. "And she is already predisposed to look to you as her guardian. If you approach her the wrong way, she may agree for the wrong reasons. Believe me, you do not want that." He and Elizabeth exchanged a meaningful look.

Elizabeth laid her free hand on top of Darcy's, recalling the expression on Georgiana's face when the colonel had appeared on the path outside Pemberley, and the unusual high spirits she had shown in his presence. "Let us not be too hasty to make a decision. Love can sometimes be found in the most unexpected ways."

Darcy looked at her questioningly. "Do you think so, Elizabeth? Is it your opinion that we should allow my cousin to court my sister?"

"I think she should be told of his interest in her, when the time is right. She should have *all* the information she needs in order to make an informed decision, and then she can decide for herself."

"Very well." Darcy pressed her hand as it lay in his. "Richard, if your feelings are in a year what they are now, I will allow you to speak to Georgiana. But she ought to have her season first. Allow her to be exposed to all that society has to offer. After that, if your affections are unchanged, you may make your case to her."

"My affections will not change. They have already withstood several months' suspense."

"Then a year should not pose a problem." Darcy's voice was firm but courteous, and the colonel nodded reluctantly.

"I will wait, then, for her to have her season. Thank you for hearing me out. I had not expected such a favorable response to such an unexpected question, but it is clear that marriage has changed you, Darcy."

"It is my hope, Richard, that you will one day experience all the joys of marriage for yourself."

The colonel smiled, and then bowed. "If you will excuse me, I will go see if Georgiana needs assistance with the children. I will see you at dinner."

They both nodded and watched as the colonel went ahead of them into the house, following the same path taken by Georgiana and the younger Gardiners just before.

"I am not entirely sure that I like this turn of events," Darcy said, frowning slightly as they continued to walk together. "Did you have any idea of this happening, Elizabeth?"

"I did not. This is as much a surprise to me as to you. But I think it could be a good match for both of them, despite its unlikely beginning. As I said before, love can sometimes come in the most unexpected ways."

Darcy's troubled brow relaxed as he looked down at her, and he and Elizabeth, along with the Bingleys, made their way into the house together.

∞

That evening the three families sat together at dinner, with the Bingleys on one side of the table, the Gardiners on the other, and Darcy and Elizabeth at the head and foot. The colonel and Georgiana took the remaining seats, one on each side of the table, and together they all made a merry party. When they had finished the meal and were about to rise from the table, Bingley asked for everyone to remain seated for a moment. "I am delighted to announce," he said proudly, keeping his eyes on Jane the whole time, "that the new year will see the arrival of the newest member of the Bingley family!"

Jane smiled and blushed as congratulations rose all around. Elizabeth reached out and grasped her sister's hand fondly across the table while Mrs. Gardiner smiled beatifically from her seat. Even Georgiana offered shy congratulations from her end of the table. Darcy came around the table to shake Bingley's hand enthusiastically. "A toast!" called Mr. Gardiner, and was strongly seconded by the colonel.

"Yes indeed, a toast!" All eyes turned expectantly to Darcy, who returned to stand behind his chair and lifted his glass, taking a moment to look around the table.

"To our families and friends," he said. "May those near to our hearts be ever in our homes, and may those we love continue to increase in number!" Glasses were emptied, chairs were pushed back and the ladies prepared to separate from the gentlemen. Elizabeth drew Darcy a little aside as the others left the room.

"I would like to wait just a moment before going in, William."

"Are you well, dearest?" Darcy asked her. "You have seemed unusually fatigued today."

"The Bingleys are not the only family who will be increasing in size next year," she told him, her eyes dancing. "I was waiting for the right time to tell you, and this seems to be it."

"Elizabeth!" Darcy held her by the shoulders, gazing into her eyes. "You are with child?"

"I am indeed."

"When? When will the child be born?"

"Sometime in June, probably."

Darcy continued to stare, his face a study in competing emotions. Elizabeth wondered what he was thinking.

"Are you pleased, William?"

"I am blessed beyond words. *We* are blessed, that we will have a child born of both duty and desire." He pulled her close, and they sealed the moment with a kiss before going, hand in hand, to share the news with those they loved most in the world.

THE END

About the author

Elaine Owen is the pen name of a married mother of two who found her own Mr. Darcy years ago, but who never tires of reading and writing about the fictional one. She is an active member of Austen Authors (www.austenauthors.net) and also participates regularly on www.DarcyandLizzy.com . In her spare time she participates in church activities, especially those involving children with special needs, and actively pursues training in martial arts.

Elaine's previous works include Mr. Darcy's Persistent Pursuit; Love's Fool: The Taming of Lydia Bennet; One False Step, and Common Ground. All of her works are available on Amazon. Her next work, An Unexpected Turn of Events, will be released sometime in 2017.

You can catch up with Elaine at www.elaineowenauthor.com or write to her at elaineowen@writeme.com. She also has a steady presence on her Facebook page, ElaineOwenAuthor, and on Twitter under the name OwenElaineowen1.

Preview from *An Unexpected Turn of Events*, the sequel to *Mr. Darcy's Persistent Pursuit* and *Love's Fool: The Taming of Lydia Bennet.*

Chapter One

The very thing Mrs. Bennet had spent most of her adult years avoiding finally came true, but in an unexpected form. Mr. Bennet had the great good fortune of outliving his wife.

In the end, her nerves, which had long been Mr. Bennet's good friends, became her downfall as she succumbed to an apoplectic fit.

None of her children were at home to see the sad event. Jane was with her Mr. Bingley at Vinings and came rushing to his side with appropriate speed, accompanied by her husband, and Elizabeth came with Darcy at the same time. Mrs. Bennet had certainly chosen a convenient time to die from their standpoint, since the Darcys had been visiting the Bingleys at the time, and so the sad announcement could be made with great expediency in their case.

It was nearly as convenient for Kitty and her Mr. Masterson, at their small estate, Hazelton. Mary was with Kitty when the special messenger made his announcement, and for a full minute even Mary could think of no comforting platitudes to offer. They stood together in shock, and then Kitty began wailing, Mr. Masterson began directing the servants to pack at once, and Mary resumed her seat at the tea table, determined that it would be a waste to lose perfectly good scones even at a time like this. She did, however, pause for a moment to offer a private prayer for the repose of her mother's soul. Afterwards, she packed.

Lydia, influenced by her military husband, had the most practical approach. The messenger had not long been at Godfrey House when he was dispatched back to Longbourn with a business-like missive. Did Mr. Bennet want them to come at once? If he did, how did he plan to house his five daughters, their four husbands, the various children, and all their servants? Would it be best if they planned on taking rooms at the inn in Meryton, or did Aunt Phillips perhaps have accommodations for some of them? Had he had time yet to arrange for poor Mrs. Bennet's services? Please reply at once, she said, so that they could make the necessary arrangements.

No children, Mr. Bennet said by quick reply. He wanted none of the grandchildren present to aggravate his own nerves at such a time. Arrangements had already been made and the services would be carried out as soon as all of Mrs. Bennet's five daughters could be present. As for accommodations, he really did not care where they stayed so long as they stayed out of his way. He told them to make whatever arrangements pleased themselves. The said daughters made their way to Longbourn with all appropriate speed, accompanied by their appropriately supportive husbands, and services were carried out in due course.

Mr. and Mrs. Collins were present at the services. Mr. Collins would lose no opportunity to comfort where comfort was not wanted or needed, and he prevailed on his newly bereaved cousin tediously, until Mrs. Fret threatened him with bodily harm if he said another word. Collins was, to be honest, slightly disappointed. It was the duty of Mr. Bennet to predecease his wife, was it not? Had history followed its divine order, Mr. Bennet would have died first and he himself would now be in de facto possession of Longbourn. Instead it looked like he would have to keep on waiting for what should have rightfully been his already. He would return to Hunsford with ideas for multiple sermons on the vengeance of a divine being.

Mr. and Mrs. Phillips were present, along with Mrs. Gardiner, who was now a widow herself. She comforted her nieces as best she could and was comforted by them in return. Mrs. Phillips comforted herself by looking at the well to do husbands of her nieces and imagining the pin money they all enjoyed, and wondering how generously they shared their wealth.

It was a successful funeral, if such functions can be measured as successful or not. The minister spoke with touching eloquence on the life of Fanny Bennet and afterwards, her friends and relatives spoke movingly of how much they would miss her. She had been, they all said, a most devoted and attentive neighbor, eager to participate in the life of the community, concerned for the good marriages of her daughters (in which she had succeeded marvelously in four out of five cases), and a steady and loyal companion to her husband to the end. In other words, the usual kinds of falsehoods were told and accepted without question at Fanny Bennet's funeral.

Afterwards, all the Bennet daughters and their matching husbands sat around the dining room table at Longbourn with their newly widowed father and made plans. It was not long, just a few weeks, before those plans were carried out, and a messenger of a very different sort was sent to the Collinses. Mr. Collins repaired speedily to Longbourn, gratified that divine providence had chosen to smile on him after all, though perhaps not as kindly as he had first hoped.

Longbourn would be let to Mr. Collins, the house and surrounding properties together, for a very small fee each year. The small fee was so small that Mr. Bennet wondered why he bothered charging Collins anything at all. He certainly did not need the money. He and Mary would be well supported by his married daughters and he would spend a portion of his time in each of their households by turn in the upcoming years. But it was the principle of the thing---Collins should not receive for free what could not be truly his for, hopefully, a number of years yet. Accordingly, the contract was drawn up and signed, and Mr. Collins prepared to take possession of Longbourn in just under a month's time, which made him smile with happy anticipation. The parsonage was beginning to be a bit cramped for him, Mrs. Collins, and their three children, and even he had begun to tire of constantly dancing attendance on the ever imperious Lady Catherine. It was time for a change.

And so Mr. Bennet stood in the graveyard at Longbourn church one dreary November day. In the distance he could see the carts and carriages hired by Mr. Collins, transporting his family's possessions to Longbourn's back door. He himself had left through the front door not half an hour previous, his own few possessions having preceded him only a short while before.

He stood with hat in hand for a few minutes, contemplating the grave of one Fanny Bennet. His contemplations were not all pleasant. He had held little affection for Fanny, but he had held some, and there was a part of himself that felt he had let her down by being the one to outlive the other. It was not the natural order of things, or so he felt. He ought to have been a better husband to her when she was alive, he thought, so that she might have been a better mother to their children. He ought at least to have passed before she did, so that she could have enjoyed the life he would now have with his various children, a life she would no doubt have enjoyed more thoroughly than he would.

But what was done was done, and could not well be undone. He said a quick prayer, replaced his hat on his head, and began to turn away from the grave that was already beginning to fill in with grass and leaves. But before he left, he placed his hand on the new placed gravestone and caressed it briefly, remembering the first days of his marriage with Fanny. Then he strode away, mounted the stairs that had been placed before the carriage with an ornate D engraved on the side, and rode away from Longbourn forever.

41968146R00133

Made in the USA
San Bernardino, CA
25 November 2016